A Reason to
See You
Again

Also by Jami Attenberg

A Reason to See You Again

A Novel

Jami Attenberg

An Imprint of HarperCollins*Publishers*

HarperCollins books may be purchased for educational, business, or
sales promotional use. For information, please email the Special Markets
Department at SPsales@harpercollins.com.

Ecco® and HarperCollins® are trademarks of HarperCollins Publishers.

FIRST EDITION

Designed by Jennifer Chung

Library of Congress Cataloging-in-Publication Data
Names: Attenberg, Jami, author.
Title: A reason to see you again: a novel / Jami Attenberg.
Identifiers: LCCN 2023052332 (print) | LCCN 2023052333 (ebook) |
    ISBN 9780063039841 (hardcover) | ISBN 9780063039858 (trade paperback)
    | ISBN 9780063039865 (e-book)
Subjects: LCGFT: Domestic fiction. | Novels.
Classification: LCC PS3601.T784 R43 2024 (print) | LCC PS3601.T784 (ebook)
    | DDC 813/.6—dc23/eng/20231120
LC record available at https://lccn.loc.gov/2023052332
LC ebook record available at https://lccn.loc.gov/2023052333

24 25 26 27 28 LBC 5 4 3 2 1

PART I

MOVES

CHAPTER 1

1971

O h, the games families play with each other.

In the Cohen household, it was Scrabble, and they played it every Saturday night. This was one of Frieda's rules. Telephone unplugged, the whole family together. The girls were still young enough that they had nowhere urgent to be but right there. Nancy, fifteen; Shelly, twelve. Idling in the living room with their father, Rudy, while Frieda made popcorn in the kitchen. Tonight Lawrence Welk led some orchestral tribute to America on the television set, Rudy nodding his head along to the music. Rudy: frail, angular, fading, but loving and present. A real bon vivant when he had the energy. I want him alive, thought Frieda. I must feed him. A frantic feeling. *Him*, she must take care of him. She salted and buttered the popcorn in good, thick, fatty layers. Humming as she delivered it in a Tupperware bowl to the family, who sat, sunken in a green velvet conversation pit. A Lucite table at the center, set up with the game board. A family waiting. Press play.

Shelly clapped for the popcorn. "It smells divine," she said. "What a delicious and satisfying treat." Shelly always trying on words for size. She popped one piece after another into her mouth; she liked to have something to do with her hands. A place to direct her nervous energy, thought Frieda. This whole family was nervous. Everyone was worried about Rudy, who had been sick and then not sick and then sick again. It had been this way for years. Malnutrition in his youth, in the camps, and all the stress, then and always. Now he had a bad heart. He was forty-one and looked sixty. A little worse this year, but then again, what did worse mean when things had been bad for so long? So it was good for them all to be together, thought Frieda, every Saturday. A regular moment for the family, private, after the crowds at shul the night before. But also: she wanted to win at Scrabble.

The girls were good at the game. Competitive enough to keep things interesting. Frieda had taught them some tricks. All the two-letter words, the most potent available ways to use Q and X. Their little sponge minds preparing for their next moves.

There was Nancy, organizing her tiles to be just so. She liked it when ideas clicked together easily and was sharp enough to find a few five- or six-letter words here and there. A tidy girl. Demure, pretty. Mildly interested in lots of things but not one thing especially. She'd do all right, thought Frieda. At this game. In life.

Shelly was the real challenger in the family: strategic, focused, unflappable. Dark-haired, dark-eyed, healthy, peach-toned skin, a generally intense presence, even for a child. She left no loose ends behind, blocked every exit and entry point if she could help it. Our little winner, thought Frieda. Smarter than everyone in the room, perhaps. But she better not beat me, thought Frieda. Not yet.

Rudy was a useless competitor, just there to have fun with his family. English was his second language and though he spoke it well, he didn't have the same competitive spirit attached to the game. "Now if this were in German, I would defeat you all," he said. "Lawrence Welk is who I should be playing." He was daydreamy and faint and beautiful; their thin, pale Papa, who had been released from the camps barely a teenager, starved, starving, and made his way to America to exist as a hero in their eyes. The girls could not ever imagine being as hungry as he had been. All of them wondered, marveled at his presence. He knew how to hold a room—even if it was simply by being alive.

For a while, when he was younger, he had given speeches to temples across America about his journey. What was it like in the camps? The American Jews really wanted to know. Most survivors didn't want to talk about it, but Rudy thought it was important they hear the truth. When Frieda had met him, he had seemed so sophisticated even in his frailty. An elegant speaker, and funny, too. That silk scarf he had tied around his neck. What a story. He told it well. People warmed to him quickly. He had needed a secretary, he said, and she traveled with him, until it was just easier to be married. Frieda was only nineteen. Attached, already, to a man. She thought he'd be the breadwinner forever. He should be paid for what he went through; she firmly believed that.

Once, Hollywood had even been interested in what had happened to him. Rudy and Frieda as newlyweds, poolside, sunburned, giddy. A cabana boy dipping to serve them. A producer who had rushed in, ordering a drink from no one in particular as he moved along the patio, then shaking Frieda's hand and holding it for a moment with both of his.

And then: nothing happened. Letters still arrived on occasion, typed, formal, offering a travel stipend and maybe a small speaker's fee. They saved them up and placed a down payment on this house that Rudy, with all his stylish desires, had wanted. This modern home. But then there had been new wars. And then fewer speeches to give, and, after a while, less of everything else in their lives. Bookkeeping work for him, shifts in a nursing home for her. Popcorn at home cost less than popcorn in the movie theater. No one knew how to budget quite like Frieda. Scrabble—Frieda's favorite—was entirely free, of course. And tonight, Shelly was winning. By a lot.

"Does anyone want some more popcorn?" Frieda didn't wait for an answer. In the kitchen, she stole sips of slivovitz from a handle of it hidden in the cupboard behind the teakettle. A fresh bottle, purchased last week, after she had started work in a new home. She was an aide like her mother, Goldie, had been before her in her way, always tending, tending to people. One husband for Goldie, and then another, until there was no one left, and certainly no one to take care of her, Frieda already long gone. She, too, had liked her sips of slivovitz to pass the time, sometimes sharing it with young Frieda to keep her quiet.

Frieda didn't even like the taste of it, hadn't then, still didn't now, but the general effect of it was soothing and familiar. Someday she would develop a new favorite drink. Someday she would drink whatever was around, no matter what, just to be drunk. Thoughtlessly. In between caring for others. Care was what she was good at. The care of strangers. Strangers and husbands. Not children. Whose children were these? she sometimes thought. Now they were people. Who beat her at Scrabble. They would leave her someday and not look back for a long time. But she didn't know that yet.

When she returned to the living room with the popcorn, she snuck a glance at Shelly's tiles from behind. Maybe she had a chance yet. She rubbed her hands together as she sat, a little less steady now from the slivovitz. But buoyant for the moment.

•

THIS GAME THEY PLAYED ON SATURDAY NIGHTS DID NOT BRING Rudy the same kind of pleasure it did his wife. He watched now as she taunted Nancy, who had put down *BOY* and missed a nearby double-word score. "That's all you have to show me?" said Frieda. A tart, sharp laugh.

"Frieda, my dear," he said, but did not continue. He did not have the energy tonight to either start or finish a fight.

"Is there something you need to say?" she said. A curdled flirtatiousness.

"We're just having fun," he said gently. More and more lately he'd had to step in between her and the children. She seemed angry at them. He couldn't bring himself to discuss it with her, not in a real way. Her competitive energy wasted, he thought. Stuck with all of us. Here in the suburbs. With the wrong man, he thought. The wrong house, the wrong life. (Or was he thinking of himself?) But the girls were sane and healthy and smart. He had wanted children desperately, to bring more Jews back into the world. A kind of compensation. Sometimes he had nightmares that he couldn't protect them. Last year he had given them both matching gold necklaces with paper-thin gold *chai* pendants, and oh, how they had hugged him. They loved him, even though he hid from them. On Thursday nights. That was the night just for him, in the silk robes.

What if things had gone differently? He thought about California all the time, though it had been years since he had been there, the sun imbuing his flesh and bones with possibility. Alive, I could be alive there, he thought. What that producer had wanted, he had wanted, too. The three of them in a cabana, the curtain closed. An old, hairy, horny, powerful man, with a stiff grin on his face. Loosened Rudy's robe for him. Took him in his warm hands. It had confused Frieda. She didn't understand that kind of decadence. She wasn't built that way. I married this young girl, he thought. Still, I thought maybe she knew. My fault. That day, she had asked the two men to stop, and he couldn't argue. They never heard from the producer again. California sun, so far away now. At least he had his Thursdays.

And now they had Shelly to manage, their champion. Another shot at the sun. Her test scores were off the charts, her school had reported. She'd skipped a grade already. The school wanted her to start competing on the math team. She would be bored soon enough with what they could do for her. Last week, she'd asked if she could study Latin. Just to try it. He looked up at his youngest daughter. Casually chewing on popcorn. This wasn't even a game to her. Just a problem to solve. She had put down *PETRIFY*.

"Excellent work, darling," he said.

"Sure, sure," mumbled Frieda, who was frantically reordering her tiles. Auburn, frizzy hair, tall, strong, handsome, with mountainous tits he fondled helplessly upon her request once a month. "Why do I always have to follow Shelly?" she said.

But this was the order they played in—every time. Shelly before Frieda, Frieda before Nancy, Nancy before Rudy, and Rudy before Shelly. They had tried it in other formations over the years, but it never worked. Frieda wanted to follow Rudy, who scattered letters on the board carelessly until some sort of shape formed. Shelly had no feelings about anyone else, one way or the other, who she wanted to beat: she was simply a machine, looking for the best path.

Nancy would spark when challenged but was also happy to coast. This wasn't her game and never would be.

•

WHAT WAS NANCY'S GAME? IN THIS HOUSE, SHE EXISTED IN THE context of others, specifically Shelly. Nancy, aware that there was a specialness to her younger sister, or at least that Shelly was more special than she was, more obviously bright, quantifiably brilliant, real brains that could be measured, tested. Perfect math scores. The Golden Ticket, her brain, like Charlie had sung in *Willy Wonka & the Chocolate Factory*, a movie Frieda had let them sit through two Saturday matinees back-to-back because they had loved it. Nancy, mixed with jealousy and admiration for Shelly, who already knew so much. But also, maybe Shelly was too eccentric. A disqualification, in Nancy's eyes.

Outside the house, Nancy moved easily through the world. Hair, already curled; clothes, just so, pristine. Impeccable makeup. Boys liked her. She got invited to all the parties first, bar mitzvahs, and birthdays, and then the dances. Shelly obviously thought her older sister's concerns were ridiculous. "Parties and boys, who cares?" said Shelly. "I'm going to rule the world someday." But nevertheless, Nancy sensed Shelly envied and was curious about Nancy's life. Catching Shelly alone in their room, fingering a blouse laid out on the bed. "Poor jealous girl," said Nancy. Did they snap at each other sometimes? Yes. Never like their mother did at them though.

But Nancy would always tell her the truth, and Shelly would do the same for her. Even as they challenged each other, moved in and out of each other's lives over the years, disappearing entirely at times, it was a thing they thought they could count on when they needed it. The truth. Even if other people lied to them, they knew where to go for answers. If not each other, then who? Truth or dare, and they always chose truth. Until it turned into another kind of game: How close could they come to saying something to each other that they'd regret forever? Chicken.

•

THEY WOULD PLAY THREE GAMES EVERY SATURDAY, THIS FAMILY. That's how long they could tolerate it, the game, each other. The first game was fun and loose; the second game the girls were warmed up, absorbed by it all, prodded by Frieda to pay attention; and the third game, Frieda was tense, and a little mean. Maybe even the girls were scared to win.

Rudy didn't care about any of that. He just liked to move things along. His wife claimed he wasn't fun to play with, but the girls would have been desperate without him there. He didn't care if he won or lost. Saturdays weren't about him. They were about the family. He had his own day, when he could dress as he pleased in those garments made of silk, sashes at the waist, sometimes alone and sometimes in the company of others like him, or who admired people like him. A small club on River North, a private lounge. Rich and luxurious perfume scents, musky, sexy, mingled with cigarette and cigar and hash smoke. He was an elder there, but at last no one saw him as a survivor. He was simply beautiful.

He had caught the girls playing in his trunk a few times and had let them try on some of his clothes. "But don't tell your mother—I'll get in trouble." "Why?" "It is just the way it is. We are doing nothing wrong, but still we must not discuss, OK, *liebchen*?" Nancy twirling around, Shelly sniffing the sweet, scented material. Why couldn't he tell her? Wouldn't it make their lives easier? He didn't have the answers though.

What he did know was that he felt better and more like himself on Thursday nights. He could shut off the noise of his past that made him toss and turn every other night of the week. On Thursdays he entered his house quietly, late, showered, and then slept soundly, completely, through till the morning.

But on Saturdays he was meant to sit in the middle, between his sharp and ferocious wife and their children. Frieda complained about where they sat, but it *was* the best order for them to play the game. He was supposed to shield them from who she was, at least the way she was on Saturday nights, after a long week of work, tending to the sick and dying, sneaking sips of slivovitz—oh, he knew about that, and he did that, too, could you blame him?

Parents, children, secrets. These rules that other people wrote for them before they were even born. Give the man a drink already.

When Rudy dies a year later, the Scrabble box will gather dust for a while, and then the three remaining Cohens will try and play it again, and it will not end well: Frieda, now entirely incapable of playing nice, taking big, blatant swipes at her daughters, Shelly grimly staring at the board, and finally, Nancy bawling, and stomping out of the room. (Why am I always the baby here, thought Nancy that night, wistful, alone, in her room, when I'm the oldest? How did it end up like this?) They needed Rudy to balance things out. But Rudy was gone.

·

IT WAS SHELLY'S TURN AGAIN. *QUEER*, A TRIPLE-WORD SCORE. Frieda threw her hands in the air. "You set her up, Rudy! Don't you care at all about winning?"

"No," he said, and his daughters chimed in with him, a loud, laughing, united, "No!" "You're the only one who cares," he said. "I care, too," said Shelly. "OK, Shelly cares, too," said Rudy. "I care about having a nice time with my family."

Shelly patted the bag of Scrabble letters before she picked her next round, feeling for how many tiles were left. She glanced at her score on the pad in front of her mother. She counted what letters had been used, and what remained. She could hold all that information in her head. She looked at the faces of her family members. She knew what they had to give, how much they cared, what their stakes were in the game, what they were capable of. She did all the math. There were actual numbers and then the people were numbers in their way, too. She calculated, and then she realized she'd won. And she could do it again. She'd figured out a way to beat her mother.

Then she saw the look on her mother's face. Was there even an ounce of pride or just pure annoyance? She looked to Rudy instead. Smiling at his smart little girl. There, now, was the love she needed.

Her mother bumped the board with her arm and the girls gasped as the tiles suddenly shifted, and the words scattered. The game was ruined. "Whoops," she said. "No, we can fix it," said Shelly. "I think I remember all the words." And she did, she could have. She had the entire board frozen picture-perfect in her head.

But it was enough already, for everyone. "I think that's it for now," said Rudy. "Bedtime for this family."

•

SHE'S CLEVER, THOUGHT FRIEDA OF SHELLY. IN ALL WAYS. NOT just at this game. "She'll be a successful person," she tells her husband later in bed. "Of course she will," said Rudy. "She comes from us." But was that even true? Was there anything they had succeeded at? A tiny house in a tiny town, outside of Chicago, admittedly a good city, but the rest of this part of the country, *feh*. A little money left from Goldie, sitting in a savings account. It would disappear soon enough.

"She knows how to read all of us," said Frieda.

"Well, that she gets from me," said Rudy.

Frieda rolled over, away from her husband, and thought more about her daughter. Her big vocabulary. That ironclad memory. Shelly could do numbers in her head, and she could project into the future, see holes and crises and mistakes, and how to solve them. Frieda should feel better about this realization, that her daughter might be a big deal someday. Like she could have been (maybe) before she took a roll in the hay with some Holocaust survivor. But all she could think in the moment was that winning in Scrabble was all she had left. She started to sob.

"No, no, it's fine," said Rudy. "Shh."

"It's not fine," she said. "It's our lives. It's everything." Everyone got to be special but her. Nancy was pretty and feminine like Rudy was, with his glacial cheekbones and doll-like eyes. Shelly was smart like Frieda's father had been. Frieda was somewhere in the middle of everyone else.

"Our lives are beautiful," he said. He pulled her close to him and pressed his body up against hers, two cold slivers of flesh warming each other for the moment. "I promise you it's beautiful." And he told her one more time about where he had come from, how hard it had been, the death and destruction he had seen, and how he had barely escaped with his life, only to find his way to America. "This is how I know; this is how I can be sure that what we have is good," he said. Their fucked-up bedtime story, they both knew it. And in this story of tragedy he had witnessed and escaped she took comfort, but also she berated herself. How could she be anything less than grateful to be alive? He held her a little bit longer and then she would pull him closer and then he would pull back and return to his side of the bed and she would be stuck spinning, wondering, what life was supposed to be like, what marriage was supposed to be like, if she were too ugly or too heavy or too weird to be loved by him, really loved in the way she wanted to be, and she would live with that feeling for the rest of her life, even when it was only the faintest strain of a feeling left, the remembrance of heartbreak, the sense of missing love.

But then, a moment later, he would squeeze her hand. And they would settle in, him on his side, her on her side, and, for as long as he was alive, she always felt lucky not to be alone.

CHAPTER 2

1976

The school year was nearly over, but the math team wasn't finished with their season. There were still regionals. Maybe state, if they won, but who was anyone kidding? It all rested on Shelly's shoulders. Frieda dropped Shelly off at 6:00 A.M. in the high school parking lot and said, "Your father would have been proud of you," which she already knew. She only wondered if her mother was proud, too, but Frieda just stared straight ahead, dead-eyed, waiting for Shelly to get out of the car and join her teammates so she could go back home and go to sleep.

The team was loading into their school van. Everyone was gritty and hyperactive. A trip away from home, and the chance to compete one last time before summer. Shelly had fought for them to be here, carrying the entire team on her back all year, but it was important that it happened, that they got here. An away trip instead of a day trip.

She was nearly seventeen then, lean, boyish, with short hair, a streamlined punky look, efficient and serious. Big lips, thus-far-small-chested, a denim jacket, tight jeans. She was a good teammate, fair, supportive, never rubbed it in their faces that she was miles ahead of them.

Her traveling companions were boys, six of them: unshowered, greasy, pimply, but still pink-cheeked in their youth, with Jack Klein-schmidt as their leader by default, because of his height. Tall and steady. The boys did drills, and gossiped about which questions they thought they would be asked during the competition. A small wager emerged as to whether they would be asked about the quadratic formula.

Supervising all of this was Ms. Luther, the advisor: pink drugstore lipstick, blond hair dried straight, a tan London Fog overcoat stinking of cigarette smoke. A few broken capillaries on her cheeks. No one's business what she did in her off-hours; she was good at her job, an excellent advisor, brisk, professional, yet supportive. Not overly motherly or indulgent, but decidedly female, which the boys liked. She was also the guidance counselor, and one of the few people to know that Shelly was graduating early from high school and going to college out west in the fall. How would Shelly tell her math bowl comrades they'd have to play without her next year? She was their highest scorer.

"I can't do it," she told Ms. Luther in her office a few weeks before, after she had gotten the acceptance letter. "I can't tell them."

"It's your news to give," said Ms. Luther. "Although I don't advise keeping secrets for too long. It can eat you up inside."

"And you can't tell them either," said Shelly. "Please!"

"Don't be so dramatic," said Ms. Luther. She tapped her cigarette in the ashtray. "You're not the first kid to run away from home."

Shelly liked Ms. Luther and her no-nonsense ways. She was what newly divorced looked like to Shelly: too skinny, pristine angora sweaters, always a little on edge, but sharp and funny, so it was worth it, worth hanging out on the edge with her. Ms. Luther and Shelly's mother, Frieda, had even tried to be friends, two ladies on their own in the same town, but it had turned out the devastation of being a divorcée was different from the devastation of being a widow. Although they both agreed they missed their husbands—or at least having a husband.

"That woman is so negative," Frieda had huffed one night, sipping a can of beer at the cracked Formica kitchen table, home after a dinner with Ms. Luther. You're no ray of sunshine in the morning, thought Shelly. Frieda tossed the beer can in the trash and flipped on the television set, to watch trim, smiling Bonnie Franklin suffer through single parenthood on *One Day at a Time*. "Look at what this poor woman has to go through," said her mother wryly. "With her ungrateful children."

Her guidance counselor had only ever been encouraging and supportive of Shelly's dreams, so Shelly didn't see what her mother was even talking about with the negative comment. She and Ms. Luther had plotted together for the past two years, adding an extra class during both semesters and another at summer, giving her enough credits to move on to the next phase of her life, far away from here, this town. The town was fine: it had served its purpose, provided her safety and shelter and a reasonable education. But Shelly wanted to move away from Frieda, who was angry all the time for no reason, had been for years, criticizing her, starting squabbles like little brushfires. Always picking on both her daughters, only more over time, after her father's death. Frieda had sold their family home and moved all three of them into this small complex with mansard roofs, occupied otherwise by what seemed to be dozens of rootless single people, just working, sleeping, passing through on their way to whatever happened next. It was a tight fit, that house.

Last year her sister—her only other real ally in the world besides Ms. Luther—had gone off to college. When Frieda and Shelly dropped Nancy off in Wisconsin, the two girls held each other for a long time as they said goodbye. When Shelly started to sob, Frieda wandered off. Who knew what she was thinking about? Who knew what went on in that woman's head? "I'll miss you so much," said Shelly. "And I'm so jealous." "Your turn next," said Nancy. "I'm two steps ahead of you," said Shelly. They had so little in common in a way—except for the source of their pain. Within the year, Nancy had found a boyfriend, a Winnetka boy, a business major with big white cheeks like two dollops of whipped cream. She lived with him now in a grubby apartment building off campus and almost never came home. I see how it works, thought Shelly. Anyone can just leave and start fresh. Why can't I start now, too? When she presented her plan to graduate early, she waited for her mother to disagree.

But there was no disagreement from her mother, collapsed in her pink aide's uniform in front of a TV dinner. "Fine, go," she said. At last, no new arguments. As if her mother were acknowledging: the game was over. Things had been bad between them, and now they were just neutral, or perhaps numb. Once Nancy left, their lives had leveled out. Not gotten better—just not gotten worse. Frieda used to scream at Shelly and Nancy, but mostly Nancy. Once she called her a "cunt," a word none of them had even heard her say before. Two nights it got so loud the neighbors called the police. Frieda at the front door, trying not to slur her words. "You know how teenage girls are." Nancy nodding, taking the blame, though no crime had been committed. "I stirred her up, that's all." Everyone mortified.

It was quieter now. A residue of pain, maybe, yes. But never mind, just leave it behind. On to her future, studying math at Berkeley, where she had received a scholarship, not a full ride, but enough matched with an award from an organization who sponsored bright young descendants of Holocaust survivors. What was sad about her life had made it possible to move onto a happier place. Don't think about that either. Deal with it all later. When? Who knew. She had to keep her head down and get the hell out of there. Discussing her feelings or that she was leaving at all was not a great idea. She didn't want anything to get in her way. She would not alert the math team, now groaning as they fit their limbs into the van, of her departure.

She hadn't even told Jack, or maybe especially not Jack. His head leaning on the van window, which he had cracked open for some air. He had dark hair and a wave of fuzz on his upper lip, and he wore stiff blue dungarees he got at the feed store and white T-shirts he had newly outgrown, which he did not seem able to acknowledge. His hair was long, his mother occasionally forcing him to sit for a trim at the kitchen table. Entirely thoughtless about his appearance, and despite that, he was still handsome.

Jack: awkward and too tall, but also strong. Those new muscles of his. Hefting the luggage into the van. Shelly was silent and happy, watching him be capable and healthy and alive. With those big arms. She didn't care about regionals or state. She already knew she knew all the answers. The winning was secondary. Because here was Big Jack.

•

PAST CURFEW, IN THE HOTEL, JACK AND SHELLY WERE IN THE hallway, by the vending machines, their teammates high on soda and candy, racing each other up and down the stairwell. Shelly was proposing they make out with each other, maybe do more than that.

"I thought you were a lesbo," he said.

"Who said I'm not?" she said, even though she wasn't even totally sure what that meant, to be that, or to be one thing or another 100 percent. She just knew that she felt this constant thrumming of sex in her, like a marching band ceaselessly playing its instruments in a parade, and the path was in her pants. Sex, sex, sex.

He apologized. "I don't know why I said that." But he did. Because he had heard other boys say it. "But if you don't want to . . ."

"I do," she said.

Jack, who would love her at least a little bit for the rest of his life. These past few semesters, staring at the soft hair on the back of her neck during their advanced math classes. Through college, grad school, a few career changes, two divorces, even, he never forgot about her. Adding her as a friend on Facebook late one night thirty-one years later, just casually saying hello, only to find out her mother had just passed away. Bad timing, Jack, once again, he thought. But in their youth, now, she knew every answer. She knew everything. And now here she was, wanting him. The smartest girl in the world.

They snuck into the indoor pool area, closed for the night, through an open locker room, plastic bathing loungers lit in the faint lozenge-green light beaming from the water. The walls were made of glass, and the front lobby was visible in the distance, and beyond that a bar. They nestled themselves in the corner by the hot tub. The water was still warm, and they took off their socks and folded up their jeans cuffs. They kissed, a direct smack on the mouth, like stupid hungry little animals, and then they slowed down and connected easily, tenderly, and made swirls with their tongues, and moved their mouths up and down on each other's necks, too. He put his hands on her breasts but barely fondled them. She moved one of his hands down to between her legs, and again he just rested his hand there, but even the heat of his hand alone felt fantastic. The not moving was sexier than the moving, she thought. The pressure of it all. The sustained pressure. "Oh my god, Shelly, this feels so good," he said. "Why didn't we do this before now?" She noticed a pimple on his nose. Had it been there all day? She leaned into his neck, again smelled him. Old Spice. His mother had bought it for him. It was so basic and satisfying, thought Shelly, who had never smelled the neck of a boy before. Citrus, the woods. She would be horny forever for Old Spice. She wanted to eat him alive. She put her hand on him, too. Together, they held, and then they pressed. And then what was left? They both came through their pants.

•

WHEN THEY PARTED WAYS AT THE ELEVATOR BANK, SHELLY TOLD
him she needed some fresh air. She made it as far as the lobby, where
Ms. Luther sat with a glass filled with brown-colored alcohol, cigarette in hand.

"Shhh," she said to Shelly. "Don't tell."

"I would never tell on you, Ms. Luther," she said. "You saved my
life." She sat across from her at the table. A chessboard built into the
wood. A queen knocked over, defeated, left behind. "You're getting
me out of my house." She added, "Away from that woman." Both surprised and not that she had said it. But it couldn't just be about that.
She was running toward something, too. The future.

"You got yourself out of your house. You did all the work," said
Ms. Luther. She cheersed Shelly with her glass and took a steady sip
from it.

"You stayed late with me so many times," said Shelly.

"I can only help those who want to be helped," said Ms. Luther.
To think she had done something right for once in her life. "Well, let
me save your life one more time." She felt bold. "Whatever you think
you're doing with that boy, don't screw up your plans." She pointed
at Shelly's stomach. "You don't want a baby in there."

"I won't mess up my future, don't worry. I'll make it to Berkeley.
They'll have to try and catch me on my way out of town, that's how
fast I'm gonna fly."

"Also . . . ah, never mind." Sipping, still sipping.

"No, tell me."

What did she want for Shelly? Freedom.

"Tell me."

"I don't know if you'd be a good mother."

Motherhood, an idea that had never occurred to Shelly, except as a recipient of its benefits. She was barely out of childhood herself. "Why do you think that?"

"I mean I don't think you'd be a bad mother. You'll never be bad at anything. I just don't think you'd be happy there. I don't think that's your natural inclination. You wouldn't screw it up, but it would screw you up." She sighed. "I'm not being very good at my job right now, am I?" She was just trying to be a truth teller. These kids needed the truth. This was her job, the truth. She had insisted this to Frieda the last time they had seen each other. "I wish they'd had a little less hard reality in their lives. I regret that," said Frieda. The two of them knee-deep in a box of wine. "They need to know what life is going to be like for them," insisted Ms. Luther. Frieda had looked shocked. "You're not their parent," she said. "You don't even have a child."

"You're doing a great job," said Shelly to Ms. Luther. She was accustomed to negativity. It didn't even occur to her that what Ms. Luther had said to her was maybe a fucked-up thing to say to someone. She was just happy for the attention. She smiled, stared out at the lobby of the hotel. A stack of local newspapers waiting to be picked up and swapped for the next morning's batch, last-call lights flickering in the bar behind it, where there were only two patrons left, businessmen, swollen in their suits, their ties loosened, their conversation jangling like loose change. What business did they have in this town? Maybe they were just passing through. Maybe someday I will just be passing through, she thought. No children to worry about, just tending to her brain, that's it. She'd be in a nicer hotel than this one, though. She knew that much already.

•

THE NEXT MORNING SHELLY WORE A BLUE SHIRTDRESS TO THE competition and Jack told her she looked pretty, and she acted like she didn't care, but she held on to that blue shirtdress well into her twenties, tossing it only when she was forced to admit it just didn't fit anymore and never would. Their team took third. Shelly knew all the answers, but let her teammates fend for themselves. Maybe I don't want to go to state after all, she thought. Maybe I'm already gone. Maybe I'm in California. State will just slow me down. I'm such a smart girl. I won't even say goodbye when I leave.

CHAPTER 3
1976

I t was Nancy's birthday. She was turning twenty-one.

Tonight, she was working a dinner shift at the inn because she needed the money, but later she'd go home and celebrate with her boyfriend, Robby, in their dim, smoky apartment they had rented because it was near his favorite bar. There would be a cake and a joint and some cans of Old Style and some food, probably takeout. Nothing too complicated, but that was supposed to be the thing she loved about Robby, that he was smooth and funny and easygoing. She had spoken to her sister out in California and her mother, who still lived in their hometown. No one saw each other in person much anymore, but she could always count on a call on her birthday. Her mother said, "Time flies, I guess." And it was true: she felt solidly on the precipice of adulthood. She was not old beyond her years, like her sister. She was not an aged wretch like her mother, who lost her youth and vitality the minute her father died. She was exactly the age she should be right now. Time was moving at the appropriate pace. Happy birthday to Nancy: she felt just right.

Twenty-one. At family meal, the inn's owner, Stiv Henderson, served her a cupcake with the age written on it in frosting. He handed her an envelope, too, with five ten-dollar bills in it, which she knew for a fact was twice as much as what he gave Candy Lorimer on her birthday, but Candy didn't let him pat her ass in the kitchen. It wasn't some competition, of course; but if it had been, she had won. What did it matter if Stiv cupped her behind on occasion? It was their little secret. Nancy found secrets sexy, even if Stiv was way too old for her, with his white-blond hair and deep smile lines and corny impressions of Jimmy Carter and Georgia twang.

Nancy, not old at all: sandy long-bobbed hair and the pleasant blue eyes and the trim waist, nearly sculptural in its conciseness. Her nose, a little big for her face, a little Jewish, her only tell. Otherwise, she could have come from anywhere, been anyone. She blow-dried her hair diligently every day, set curlers in it on the weekends. She didn't dress sexy, even if she was sexy: she was cute, and she knew it. That was her best approach in the world, like a small animal who knows how to curl up and hide in plain sight. She had a plump behind, and that's why Stiv liked to grab it. Fifty bucks, that was nearly her share of the rent.

This was her current identity: the cutest waitress at Stiv Henderson's inn. Cute and convincing. Good at getting people to order appetizers they hadn't been interested in before she suggested them, and making people feel confident about their choices after the fact. The more expensive bottle of wine, a bottle of champagne on their anniversary. Good at selling goods. Not dumb, like her mother had always said she was. No genius like her sister at Berkeley, but Nancy had a B+ average and she was getting a degree in mass comm, which meant she understood the history of how people talked to each other. She thought she'd like to work in advertising or public relations someday. She had a general idea of what that would entail. An office job, a nice suit, heels she would carry in her purse and change into at her desk. Hold my calls, I'm in a meeting. File folders full of important documents. A hand salute to her boss. "On it, chief." It meant safety to her, that's what the whole system meant to her: safety. A thing she was desperate for, even paranoid about, when she remembered where she came from, where her father had come from, and how easily it all had fallen apart. The system would protect her, she hoped. Give her health insurance, Social Security, a retirement fund. She didn't understand the stock market, but she believed in it. She believed in the future. Having a future. She could have it all, or at least some of it, and Robby would fill in the rest.

For now, it was waiting tables at the inn. High wooden ceiling beams, a wall of windows facing a beautiful sunrise in the morning, and antiquities passed down through the Henderson family or plucked from garage sales around the Midwest. A half-dozen rooms, with quilt-covered beds and phonograph record players and creaking rocking chairs. Everything was for sale in the inn. Everything could be purchased. But the real moneymaker was the dining room.

The inn's specialty was duck, roasted and served with wild rice and one of three sauces: à l'orange, mushroom, or cherries jubilee. Stiv's nephews were hunters, and every fall they bagged hundreds of ducks, which they stored in two enormous freezers on the land behind the inn. When Nancy first trained at the restaurant, Stiv had served her the entire duck entrée (she chose à l'orange, their most popular preparation) so she could speak confidently about it to the customers. At the time, he had joked, "They flew all the way in from Canada just to feed you." Was that funny? Did she even like duck? The skin was crisp, certainly, the meat plump, but the sauce was a sugary mess, a candy-store version of fine dining. Did she laugh at his joke? Yes. Did she say it was delicious? Yes. She was doing the thing she knew how to do. The customers seemed to like the duck anyway: it was the thing you were supposed to order.

She slipped the envelope from Stiv into her purse in the employee lounge before dinner service began. The inn mostly catered to the parents of visiting students, but also to guest lecturers the university brought in every few months. It wasn't just Stiv groping her. Candy

Lorimer, appalled, at the end of the shift, every single time. Acting surprised, but why was it news that these men were this way? Men were terrible, and you accepted it, rolling your eyes, was what Nancy had always thought. "Did they leave a big tip at least?" was the question Nancy asked. "You're missing the point," snapped Candy, three years away from dentistry school, five years away from a bad marriage, seven years away from a divorce, ten years away from a second marriage, a move to Cincinnati, a baby, a daughter, training for and running a 5K race, then a 10K, and then eventually, the New York City marathon, which she ran at forty, and did not flinch once, because you'll never stop Candy, just try.

The night went fast. A couple, giddy and nervous, leaving the baby at home, their first night out in months. A quiet fiftieth anniversary party, the husband with thick, gray muttonchop sideburns, drinking more than the wife, who was dressed for church rather than for a party. Short ribs, duck à l'orange, duck à l'orange, duck à l'orange, steak, the pasta special (salmon and peas in a cream sauce), duck à l'orange, duck à l'orange. She scanned the people, looking for her future self. Twenty years from now would she be like them, happily eating duck?

Then it was nearly the end of her shift. She paused as she prepared the dessert course setup. Alternate opinion: Would she actually ever want to eat duck again in her entire goddamn life? Was duck disgusting? Was all food disgusting? Suddenly she was begging Candy to take her place at the bananas flambé cart, running to the workers' restroom, efficiently hurling out the remains of the birthday cupcake, wiping off her face, washing her hands, and reapplying her lipstick. It was the third time she had vomited that day. She skimmed through calendar pages in her mind. She might not be a math whiz like her sister, but she could still fucking count.

•

AFTER HER SHIFT, SHE TOOK THE BACK ROAD TO HER APART-
ment: behind the inn, past the deep freezers humming in the quiet, all
those ducks inside, waiting to be eaten; down a starlit path, around
a huddle of willow trees until she reached a small frozen pond. She
stopped and stood at the edge of it for a while. Utter silence. Moonlight on the glassy surface of the pond. Happy birthday to me, she
thought, and she screamed. A gaggle of birds scattered in the dark
and then up toward the sky. Then a crack formed on the surface of
the pond, and she watched it spread a foot, and then another few
feet, and then it maneuvered away across the icy exterior. Screaming
under the moonlight on her birthday, watching a frozen pond split in
two. Twenty-one.

•

SHE CARRIED ON DOWN THE ROAD HOME. THE WOODS DUMPED
her out on a small cul-de-sac, which turned into a bigger byway of
houses, a small city hall building, until it became the university's territory, the student union in the distance, and then a side street filled
with bars, kids still out, even in this cold. A messy-haired redheaded
girl being carried home by two of her friends, singing "Let the Sunshine In" to them. They were all laughing; she'd be hungover in the
morning, but she'd be all right.

Nancy stopped at a pay phone on the corner, a half block from
her apartment. What will Robby think? Who knew? But Shelly was
the smartest person she knew. That's who she wanted to talk to
first. She pulled out from her backpack the roll of quarters she used
for her laundry and deposited enough change in the phone for a

long-distance call to Berkeley, the faraway city where Shelly lived. Not in a million years would she call her mother. She'd just love to see me fail, wouldn't she, thought Nancy. Tell me what a fool I am. Shelly would never tell her she was stupid though. Even though Shelly was much smarter than Nancy. Shelly would only tell her the truth.

Her sister had it so easy, knowing what she wanted from life right away. Computer science, it didn't even sound real. Nancy had only known that she had to get out of their house, away from their mother, and once she found Robby, she had felt safe. Had she ever liked to do anything? She had thrown in with Robby: that was what she had done with her time in college. His family had money—or more money than the Cohens did anyway. He would get a good job automatically, just by being himself. His family would help him. Maybe he would even go to work with his father, although he didn't like him, with all his girlfriends on the side, his cavalier treatment of Robby's mother. She was not a catch, she knew it, except that she was willing to work hard, and she had her looks. She clung to Robby. Wrapped her small hand firmly around his dick. Kept it close. On their second date they had walked past a man so drunk he was swerving, and Robby had pulled her close, possessive, protective. His. Robby and the man had exchanged nods. They were having a conversation that excluded her, but that was fine. She only needed Robby to speak for her. But right now, she needed to speak for herself.

Shelly answered. Dry, droll, a little buzzed. "Didn't we talk already today? Do you need me to tell you how pretty you are again?" she said. "You're a pretty, pretty girl."

"I needed to talk to you alone, without Robby in the room."

"Uh-oh," said Shelly.

"Think of what the worst thing it could be, and it's that," said

Nancy. They'd already had the worst thing in the world, actually: their father's death. This was second. "I was so careful," said Nancy. But was she? "And it still happened." She leaned her head against the glass wall of the phone booth, her classmates streaming past her on the sidewalk. Was it her fault? Don't cry, she thought. Everyone will see you.

"Don't say another word," said Shelly. "Don't question it, don't rationalize it, don't see both sides of it, don't feel anything. Just get rid of it."

"But why can't I keep it?" She didn't want to. She wanted high heels and an office and a paycheck. But what if she did keep it? A thing to love. A future with Robby. All the puzzle pieces already laid out on the table, slotting into place. Would that be so bad?

"Because then it's the rest of your life already, Nancy," said Shelly. "Then the rest of your life starts now."

Nancy, with her eyes closed, breathing deeply, listening. When she opened her eyes again the glass of the phone booth was fogged up around her.

"Please listen to me," said Shelly. "Are you really ready for everything to start now?"

Twenty-one. Only twenty-one.

•

HOME TO THEIR DINGY, SLOPPY APARTMENT, CIGARETTE BUTTS in ashtrays everywhere, the burnt-up nubs of joints, too. A baby-faced man on the couch, a little belly sneaking out from under his T-shirt. Headset plugged into the stereo, to keep the neighbors at bay. Spoiled Robby, who was taking the semester off, and his father said he had to work, but his mother still slipped him cash. She loved him, but she couldn't say why he was necessarily any more special than anyone else. He was easy. He liked to drink and carouse. A good talker, too. Sure, he had some secrets—she thought maybe he played around. She had hers though, too. She had Stiv.

But she and Robby had fun together, and that felt right, that she should finally be having fun in her life. He knew everyone around town. He worked at the bar on the corner, a no-name bar; that was his job this semester. He was a big and friendly guy, not mean or intimidating. A good guy, that's who they wanted in charge of the door. She liked a man in charge.

She liked their sex life, too, the regular, horny, sweaty things they did to each other. She could count on it, the end-of-the-day sex, the morning sex, the after-class sex, the before-study-group sex. She liked to ride him; get on top of him and ride him steadily and intensely and feel him up so far inside of her. It was wild to her how much she cared about sex, how important it was to her value and self-worth. Her house when she was growing up had not been one full of any kind of sexuality. Her mother wasn't sexy, her father didn't flirt with her mother: their love was so specific and bonded and nearly platonic. But sex made Nancy feel valuable, not just to Robby but also to herself. She could give pleasure, she could feel good, she had a skill, a power: that must be worth something. She must be worth something.

To this stoned man sprawled out on this gross couch. The couch had been there when they moved in. Burnt orange, velvet, stained. I'll get rid of it, she thought. I'll get rid of everything.

"Robby." She snapped her fingers in front of his face.

He pulled the headset off. "Hey, birthday girl." They kissed for a long time, and he reached up to her breast. She pushed his hand away.

"Am I in trouble? I meant to clean up, I'm sorry. And I'm sorry I didn't get you a cake. The bakery was closed by the time I got there and I was messing around over at Byron's pad playing records—he just got the new Iggy Pop."

"No, it's not that."

"But look, I got you a pizza, extra cheese, sausage, and there's a case of beer in the fridge and . . ."

She let him rattle on for a while. *Was* she mad about this lackluster celebration? "I should have gotten you flowers." It was so hard for him to just be sometimes, she thought. Jesus, I shouldn't even tell him. He won't be able to handle it.

"I'll get you flowers tomorrow, first thing."

If she told him, would he even know the right thing to say to her? (What was the right thing to say?) However she was feeling, he would surely make it worse. Except that he was the one who was supposed to be of comfort to her. That was the choice she had made by being with him, both of them, moving in together, when their parents didn't agree with it. Catholic on his side, Jewish on hers. Money versus no money. Too young. Both sides of parents thinking the others were trash, she could tell. "The Irish like to drink," her mother had murmured, even though her mother liked to drink herself. Robby's parents had told him she was the kind of girl you dated in the summertime. But they had thrown in with each other at nineteen anyway. They were each other's people now. He was the one she was supposed to tell.

She felt a gigantic pause in herself, and then a thumping sensation, like a bassline from a rock song, a pressing desire to go somewhere else for a while, and then she was gone, hovering above, in the sky and near the stars, and he was still talking, smoking, sipping from his beer, making excuses, but not really looking sorry.

"Baby, I'll get you everything you want tomorrow if you just come sit on my lap and kiss me today."

What if everything just stayed like this forever? she thought.

Then he said, "Where did you go? Look at me," scared that she wasn't giving him her attention. He needed her to see him. The on switch flipped in her, and she was back in this room, with the wallpaper torn at the edges and the smoke-stained curtains, the rusted-out barbecue they dragged to tailgate parties, gathering dust in the corner, the stacks of used textbooks, this work-in-progress life of theirs. Theirs! Shared.

And then she was telling him what she thought to be true, that it was a possibility, she wasn't sure yet, but what did he think if it were true? She knew what *she* thought, but what did *he* think? She found herself apologizing, and crying, then wishing she hadn't apologized to him—what did she have to be sorry for?—but that's how it came out; she was just sorry in general, because her body had failed her, or succeeded, depending on how you looked at it, so she was just overwhelmingly sorry. But anyway, just tell her already, what did he think about it? Because Shelly would tell her the truth, but Robby was all she had. And that's what mattered in the end to her. To not be alone. To be with him. To be safe.

But, of course, she knew what he thought all along. Catholic, mama's boy. The way he always buried himself in her breasts. "It's the nicest place on earth," he'd told her. He traveled the path he knew. He wanted to be connected, united. Why was she even surprised? And wasn't it a relief to have someone else to make decisions with now? Even if they were possibly the wrong ones? He would get his act together, he told her. His uncle would get him a job in sales. "I'll take care of this baby," he said. And he did. He always paid the bills. For the rest of his life, he was good to their daughter.

•

WHEN SHE QUITS THE INN TWO MONTHS LATER, SHE SHYLY TELLS Stiv the reason why, a small diamond ring cocked on her finger. Stiv looks her up and down, unabashed, emotional, already sentimental for her youth and her flesh as it exists in that moment. He sighs, and says, "Well, that's a shame." He smiles at her, takes her hand in his, kisses it. "Oh, honey, don't look sad. I'm sure you'll bounce back." When he hugs her, he holds her so close it's as if he's trying to keep her youth with him at the inn forever. Why do they grow old? he thinks. Why do they leave me? Why do they always fly away?

CHAPTER 4

1980

Frieda abided by a strict schedule, for fear she would fall apart without it.

Monday through Thursday she worked at the nursing home during the day, tending to residents who had lost their recent memories but spun tales about long-ago events, which she would listen to when she had a moment, pausing as she wiped their mouth or gathered their linens. On Wednesdays, after her day shift, she would sup at a small Italian restaurant named Milo's in Oak Park, where she would drink imported Chianti served in straw-wrapped fiasco baskets. On Thursdays, in the evening, she cleaned an office building in a business park off the expressway, a job she worked specifically as a kind of penance for past misbehaviors. On Fridays she went to shul, dressed in a blouse, skirt, heels and hose, lipstick, and perfume, tidying her wild auburn hair, now with thin strands of gray in it. On the weekends she rested.

It was Wednesday.

Sometimes she dined alone at Milo's, eating spaghetti and meatballs, twirling the pasta, always searching for the perfect forkful. Lately she'd been joined by a coworker, Carolina, a widow like her, although Carolina didn't miss her husband like Frieda did. Carolina was thick-thighed and chubby-armed, and had a warm laugh and big, blue-black hair, bangs blow-dried straight, and she wore slick lacquered lipstick and had a terrible complexion, made worse, she claimed, by these Midwest winters. Carolina's husband had been a Chicago police officer and had died young but no big loss, according to her: he had been abusive, little slaps and punches for the entirety of their marriage. "He kept things interesting, I'll give him that," she said. He died on the job five years ago—Carolina never said what happened, just wiped away the memory with her hand—but she refused to touch his pension, just let it sit earning interest. The bank account of a ghost.

Their husbands had died, oddly, within a few days of each other. Frieda liked to think of them as widow twins. And both women were the same height, the same age, had the same job. And they were the same size, too, though not quite the same shape, although they were both busty. But Carolina wore her clothes differently, as if she were proud of her heft and curves, whereas Frieda was indifferent now to her flesh. For the moment, she had lost interest in the idea of making herself appealing to men or finding a new husband. Once had been enough for her. "What I need is a friend," she told Carolina.

Tonight, Carolina was telling her a story about a chaotic moment in the game room that day. Two men playing Monopoly. "Mr. Schnapps and Mr. Chase, you know them. Thick as thieves usually." Mr. Schnapps was winning by a lot, a landslide. Mr. Chase was more of a card shark. The two were buddies, sure, but competitors, too. "I mean who really cares, Schnapps has a bad liver and Chase needs to lose forty pounds and he's had two strokes that we know of in the last three years. What are they even really fighting about here?" said Carolina.

But Frieda got it. Sometimes you wanted to win.

"So then Chase just threw the game up in the air," said Carolina. "All the pieces, the board, everything, just saying, 'F this' and 'F that' and 'You always cheat.' I don't even know how you cheat at

Monopoly. Chase wheeled himself away and Schnapps was just sitting there by himself. He looked so sad." Carolina was thoughtful for a moment. "Do you think they're boyfriend-boyfriend?" she said. "With all that passion, I mean."

"I don't see it," said Frieda. "But love comes in all forms, of course." Something on the tip of her tongue. She took a sip of her wine instead.

"Anyway, do you know how hard it is to pick up all those little pieces? That tiny little top hat? Impossible! I just felt like if this is my life, if this is what I'm going to do, I want to be somewhere warm." Carolina was always cold. She was wearing fake fur–covered winter boots, thick tights, a wool dress, a turtleneck under that, a cardigan over that. A mauve puffy winter coat was hanging by the front door of the restaurant on a wooden hook. Carolina had had enough of these layers. She had been weighing a move back to Miami for months, where she had lived for a few years as a child. She had some family there, an aunt who also worked in nursing homes, an uncle who managed a movie theater, programming Spanish-language films for the Cuban expats.

"It's probably so hot there in the summer," said Frieda. "Too hot."

"I'd get used to it again quick," said Carolina. She was taking business administration classes at a community college. She would not be picking up Monopoly pieces forever. She wanted Frieda to come with her to Miami. They could be roommates. They could get into management.

"They just need bodies down there. We're still young. There's still time. What are you doing here? Why are you staying here? For these ungrateful girls you gave so much to? They're never coming back here. They have to live their own lives now." She had told Frieda a dozen times that the way she had treated her daughters was no big deal. "It's not like you slapped them around." The way that woman lingered in the guilt. "What are you gonna do, grow old here, thinking maybe you'll see them again sometime? They'll come home and take care of you in your old age? I know you love them, but those girls are selfish. They miss birthdays, holidays, everything. When was the last time they came back? Don't even answer it." She dismissed Frieda's far-off daughters with a deadly shake of her head. "You and me, we're working-class ladies. No one's looking out for us. So we have to look out for ourselves."

Frieda missed her husband intensely, that was the biggest difference between the two women. She had liked living in service of his needs. It had given her a real purpose. The wife of a survivor. She had survived nothing, but she was with him. Now she had survived his death. Left alone with two daughters who had always preferred him to her. They had been stuck with the lesser parent. She agreed. He was more fun, a better time. She had done all the hard stuff, the heavy lifting. But she had a less obvious love to give.

"I have this routine here, it makes me feel comfortable and safe," said Frieda. She couldn't imagine gathering the strength to leave Chicago. It would be like leaving him. When she stayed in Chicago, she honored him, she felt. She could not explain this to Carolina though.

"Routines are made to be broken," said Carolina. "I'm saying, set your life on fire."

Frieda, staring at her, unable to make the connections Carolina was presenting to her.

"Sit with it," said Carolina. "See what happens."

•

THURSDAY NIGHT AT THE BUSINESS PARK, THE LONELIEST NIGHT of the week. A temp job she had gotten when both girls were undergraduates and she was still paying for their schooling as best she could, but she kept working even after they were done, Shelly now in a fully paid PhD program. She still sent them money once a month, and the checks were always cashed.

The office was an accounting firm. It was empty while she worked, and she had grown fond of the people she never saw. The framed photos on their desk, the tchotchkes they kept as distractions, sweaters tossed on the backs of chairs. Corkboards and thumbtacks. Their file folders, color coded and neat. Adding machines, rotary phones. Someone forgot to take home their banana, and it sat rotting on the kitchen counter. She tossed it. She vacuumed, pulling out loose change when it gummed up the machine; dragged the trash to the stairwell for the morning crew to pick up and deposit in the rear of the building; ran a duster along the tops of cubicles. She saved the bathrooms for last. There, she wore plastic gloves. The pink soap scum pooled in the sink from an errant drip signaling the end of the evening.

But first, a stop in the supply closet. A bottle of turpentine. A paper bag. Her bonus prize. She huffed it in the bathroom because sometimes she vomited. Not as much lately though. Now she was so used to it all. The feeling of not feeling anything, she was used to that, too. The blazing neutrality of the mind. To not think for a while, what was that worth?

She had been so awful to them when they were kids. That year after his death she had fully snapped. She had just felt so devastated he was gone, he who had been the light of her life, and the girls were no comfort. The things that were left, the objects they could not afford, they were no comfort either. And maybe had she wasted her life, too? All that time she had spent with a man who didn't desire her. She had nothing to show for it. Nothing but these girls. Who didn't seem to like her. And she had been drinking more than usual, more than she could handle, and she picked at them all the time. She never hit them. That was not her way. Carolina said as long as she didn't hit them, she didn't do anything wrong. But she smacked them around with her words. The smart one and the pretty one became the weird one and the dumb one. In that era of their lives together, she could not see their value, only that they were sucking her dry. Where was her pleasure? Where was her joy? Her husband was gone, what was left? They could just be young and free and walk down the street and see a future ahead of them. It was just a year she was like this. This angry. Maybe two years. Hanging it over their heads. Everything can be taken away from you in a second. She would have them clean the house when she was done yelling at them. Make their beds, mop the floors, fold the laundry. Scrub the bathroom. Again. You didn't do it right the first time. No complaints. No one likes a kvetcher. These are the skills you need to have, she said. If you ever want a man to marry you. Marriage was the end goal, she insisted, especially to Nancy, even if she didn't believe it, even if she was living evidence that you could survive without it, although she wouldn't call it much of a life.

She didn't remember exactly when she stopped being so cruel. Only that there was a détente once Shelly was in high school, too. She could see their escape plans in their eyes. Why bother fighting with them then? They were already on the way to who they were going to be. One foot out the door. She had left like that, too. Once she met him.

She huffed until she saw white. She laid her head down on the cool tile of the bathroom floor. Freshly mopped. Frieda, not yet fifty. Frieda who was once a good student. Frieda holding hands with a boyfriend. Then her husband. Frieda at a funeral, feeling decadent in her grief. These girls, they don't love her anymore. That first Thanksgiving when neither daughter came home. No repercussions for their

38

disappearance. What could she say to them to make them love her again? Frieda, still here, waiting. For a daughter to show off at shul.

She fell asleep on the cold floor. She dreamed of her dead husband, dreamed he was on fire, and she had set the fire herself. Set the house on fire, set him on fire. When she woke, she was terrified, shivering, and alone in the office building.

It occurred to her she should have been home by now.

•

FRIDAY-NIGHT SERVICES: FRIEDA FELT EXHAUSTED, WITHOUT faith. The men off together in the corner, talking about sports scores and mortgage rates, hustling business deals. The women in their blue eye shadow, carrying pristine Coach purses. Kids running around the undeveloped field behind the synagogue. Someday there would be an outbuilding there for separate studies, if they could just raise the money. The women were talking about their children though, not fundraising. Friday nights were for bragging.

Doris Hoffman, on and on about her daughter, Sylvia, who had married a doctor, lived in the city. Doris with her new Oldsmobile Cutlass with the license plate PRNCSS. The audacity of a woman who work a mink coat to shul, thought Frieda. Doris who was always inviting Frieda to the Weight Watchers meetings she ran, even though Frieda obviously showed no interest each time. "Just come and try it," said Doris. "I'll think about it," said Frieda. She wasn't invested in her appearance like the rest of these women. They were so worried about being fit and young, keeping their husbands happy. We all end up dead, Doris, thought Frieda. We either die gracefully or we die with someone wiping our ass, but we're all headed to the same place.

Sylvia, though, the way Doris talked, was immortal, a goddess.

Frieda had known Doris's daughter for years and, in fact, did think she was lovely. Doris had done a nice job with her. Well groomed, bright, quiet, pliant, even-tempered. Neat bangs, pale, soft-looking skin. Sure, she lived in the city but came back regularly on Friday nights, dragging her husband with the Coke-bottle glasses with her sometimes when he wasn't working late. The real brag about Sylvia was not that she had married well—although that was nothing to sneeze at. Money, Frieda didn't care about one way or another. She hadn't come from it, never expected it. The brag was that her daughter came home to visit—in rush-hour traffic on a Friday night, no less. "Oh, we're best girlfriends," Doris always said.

"Sylvia's under the weather, that's why she's not here tonight," said Doris. I didn't ask, thought Frieda. She imagined that Sylvia had finally realized what a pill her mother was, that was the real truth. "She's a little sick in the tummy," said Doris. "You know." She gave Frieda a wink. "We're not announcing anything yet though. It's bad luck."

"And when will we see your girls?"

Everyone in this temple knew her daughter Shelly was the smartest out of all the children, but she hadn't shown her face in town since she left but a few times. The other one, Nancy, had gotten married, had a child, and then bounced all over the West with her salesman husband. Frieda had a granddaughter she had met only once. She wanted to scream when she thought about it.

"They're so busy with school and their families," said Frieda.

"Still, there's always time to come home," said Doris.

"Excuse me, Doris, I need to go," she said. Before she left she took a pause at Rudy's yahrzeit plaque on the wall. Allowing herself to miss him one more time. It seemed like the best way to remember him, here, with this object, on this wall, in this building. But also, she would like to stop remembering him all the time.

In the parking lot, she paused with her key in the ignition. I can't win, she thought. I can never win. She drove around the lot looking, searching, until she saw that PRNCSS license plate. Just a little swipe, it was all she wanted. Just to take the edge off her feelings. It was nothing, a dent, and then she kept driving. But people saw it. She heard gasps, a "Hey—" Saw fingers pointing. Keep driving, Frieda. Was it an accident? She would need to explain it next week, maybe. If not before then.

It occurred to her that maybe she needed a new shul, one where people didn't ask so many questions.

•

SUNDAY EVENING: A COFFEE MUG FULL OF MARTINI (NONE OF her glasses were clean) and a bowl of popcorn, dosed heavily with salt, for dinner. Her husband's clothes boxed in the closet. Framed photos of him everywhere. His notebooks he used to read from when he spoke about his time in Germany. Books he had collected over the years; he was a real intellectual. The playwrights, the poets. She had never read them. The albums of all the Broadway shows. All of this was his, not hers. These objects kept him alive in her mind, held her feelings in place. These things were glue.

She stretched out on the couch for the beginning of *60 Minutes*. She loved all those men so much. Reliable, safe, constant, even when they were bearing bad news. Harry Reasoner, droning on in his staccato voice about solar power. How America was building homes—two million homes a year!—but not building for the future, draining the same energy resources over and over again. How we are repeating the same problem. How we are not thinking ahead.

Frieda nearly passed out now. Why doesn't everyone want solar power? It's the money, stupid. Reasoner ending his grim report by indicting politicians and businessmen. Everyone is always looking for who to blame. Then the ticking clock of the show's outro to commercial. Reasoner had talked about what the world would be like in the year 2000. Where would she be then? Would she still be on this couch? With the pile of dirty dishes in the sink? Tidying up the lives of others while her own was a mess?

In the morning she woke, early, hungover, and the television set was still on, a game show, *Family Feud*. Boozy-sounding Richard Dawson interrogating someone's mother, someone's father, chit-chatting with them about their lives, his hands on their shoulders, leaning in too close, nearly leering. Frieda watched through one eye as he asked them the first question of the game: "Name a reason for a family reunion." A hand on the buzzer: "A birthday!" The number one response. The Bloomberg family decided to take the question. "Funeral," said Frieda from her couch. That's the only way I'll ever see my kids again, she thought. When I'm dead. "Wedding," said a Bloomberg daughter. A ding. "Funeral," said Frieda again, a little louder. "A graduation," said a Bloomberg son. Another ding. Wild applause from the family. Only one more to go and they would win this round. "Funeral," yelled Frieda. "A sporting event," said Great-uncle Joe. One big *X*. "Funeral," said Frieda, quieting down. "Why does no one listen to me?" "Fourth of July," said Mrs. Bloomberg. "Show us 'Fourth of July,'" said Richard Dawson. Another *X*. Back to the beginning of the line, back to the father, Mr. Bloomberg. "A bris," he said, and Frieda started laughing. Leave it to the Jews to think anyone cares about our little rituals besides us. The third and final *X* buzzed. "A funeral, you morons," said Frieda. A moment later, she watched the other team steal it handily. They knew, these people knew. Death comes for us all.

It occurred to her that maybe what felt like home was actually a trap, and that if death were coming anyway, maybe she should squeeze a little more out of this life already?

•

THEN IT WAS SUMMER, AND IN A NEW HOUSING DEVELOPMENT outside Fresno, air conditioner blasting, Nancy Cohen Beck opened her front door to a knock from a moving man. A delivery of a half-dozen boxes. "I didn't order these," she said. "It's your address on the boxes," said the man. She pointed him to the garage. He stacked them in a corner. She dug in her pocket for a tip. When he left, she ran a razor across the top of a box, and before she even peered inside she knew it was from her mother. That stale scent, that frozen-in-time, dusty, musty odor of her mother's home. She pursed her lips and threw her hands up. "Well, I don't want it," she said. She taped the box back up again.

Later her husband, Robby, would ask her about the boxes when he got home from work, and she said, "Ignore them," and he did, and so, mostly, did she, and they carried them from house to house for the next decade, the six boxes becoming part of their possessions that had to be lifted and moved and then lifted and moved again, until they parted ways, the two of them, Robby and Nancy, and finally, at last, someone had to deal with the boxes.

PART II

VACATIONS

CHAPTER 5

1981

Shelly at the airport bar, communing with a Bloody Mary, lemony, heavy on the horseradish, one lonely celery stick. The departures were always better than the arrivals. She liked the state of limbo, the moment when she was still on her way somewhere instead of already there, *there* always being at least a little disappointing. She pulled out a small spiral-bound notebook from her front shirt pocket, flipped it open to a page where a business card fell out. A casual regard of the card, the name. She had already thought about it enough to bring it on this trip. She took the pen from her front pocket, wrote "Pros" on one side of the page and "Cons" on the other, then drew a line down the middle. Then she remembered: I should bring something for my niece. I'll never hear the end of it if I don't.

At the gift shop, she was stopped by the magazine rack: Gaddafi was on the cover of *Time*. A whole row of last week's issue still on the stands, one face after another. Gaddafi, Gaddafi, Gaddafi. His pitted, gloomy, angry face beneath his military cap. Doom for the holidays, she thought. Her sister made her take this trip. "When was the last time you took some time off?" she said. But Christmas meant nothing to her, a Jew. Life outside of work meant nothing to her, too. Holidays without the families meant she never had to place herself in history, or on a calendar or anyone else's timeline. Nancy picked another strategy: guilt. "And you don't even know your own niece. Come on, you're my only family," she said. "What about Mom?" "That old drunk? No thanks." Shelly bought a ticket. Now she was on her way to Arizona for some weird holiday moment. She lingered in front of the magazine. The headline read: THE SPECTER OF TERRORISM. You know who the real terrorists are? Your family.

•

IN PHOENIX, NANCY AWAITED HER AT THE GATE. AN OPEN, SIS-terly examination of each other occurred as they moved through the airport. Changes were clocked. Shelly looked the same, but two years older, still lean and punky except, now, for her hips. She had cut a few inches off her hair since the last time Nancy had seen her, not short, like she had it in high school, but still shorter, a little less feminine than it had been before. "Ah, I don't want to deal with it," said Shelly. Black sweater, black jeans, and she wore the gold *chai* around her neck, the same one Nancy had sitting in her dresser drawer, ones that their father had given them as a reminder of who they were and where they came from. Of him, and of a people. All they needed to do was wear it and *remember*. But Nancy, married to this Catholic man, was pretending for the moment to be something else.

Nancy had cut her hair shorter, too, but hers was in a style—it was a saucy look, a fun bob just below her chin. She was a little chunkier, a little sexier, and more obviously made-up than usual: she wore denim jeans and turquoise rings and blue eye shadow. "It's just a phase," said Nancy, as if she were talking about someone else other than herself. As if she hadn't picked these clothes out that morning, smeared the eye shadow on in the mirror, determined to transform herself into what, she did not know.

She hurled Shelly's bag in the trunk of her car and slammed the door shut.

As they drove, Nancy pointed out places where she had worked. A strip mall, another strip mall, and then a big, brand-new mall. Nancy was working retail for the moment, a waste of her brain, they could all agree on that. The Cohen girls were smarties, but Nancy had had the baby—and then what happened? Nothing. Now she was selling bras to dried-out retirees.

"We're going to move to Chicago soon, where there's more opportunities," Nancy insisted. Trying to beat Shelly to the punch before she said what was on her mind. No lies between them. Nancy needed her to know: this life was not permanent. The husband was, the child was, but life in Arizona was not. But did Shelly see their new car phone? "Robby got it as a bonus," said Nancy. That thing won't exist in a few years, thought Shelly. It was already outdated. Start with the fact that it was stuck in a car and attached to a cord. Someday they'll be better, more functional, more integrated. She could go on. But she kept her mouth shut.

Forty-five minutes later they were at the front gate, and Nancy punched in a code, and the gate swung open. For a second, this impressed Shelly. Stabilized her. This felt real and authentic and grown-up, and the code, the numbers, made it feel orderly and secure. But beyond the gate it was empty of structures except for a house about a quarter of a mile away. The rest of the land was under construction, plots in varying stages of progression, deposits of lumber, bricks, hand trucks, bags of concrete mix. Only the one house stood proud in all of it, and it was blinking and glowing even in the sunlight. Holiday lights.

"What are all those lights?" said Shelly as they emptied the car of her luggage. "It's Christmas," said Nancy. "Aren't they great?" "But we're Jewish," said Shelly.

Inside the house it was even brighter. Shelly left her suitcase in the foyer and walked, mouth agape, into the living room. The tree, the tree, the garish tree, twenty feet tall, stinking of pine scent but somehow not made of pine, or anything of nature, a small fortune in string lights wrapped around it, red and green and silver and gold tinsel dripping from its limbs, a hundred ornaments—more, hundreds? Shelly wanted to stand there and count them—on top of all that, sparkling. Around the room was an array of stuffed animals dressed in Christmas attire, some of them battery-operated and turning and moving in time to their own internal rhythm, maybe twenty of them, so there was just a constant sway of motion accompanied by creaking, squeaking sounds. Holiday music playing from a speaker system. It all felt nearly amorous, orgiastic, as if all of Christmas were screwing wildly in this room.

The house was otherwise mostly empty: a couch in the living room, a plastic-covered easy chair next to it; a small circular café table near the kitchen with four chairs; and in one guest room, a flattened air mattress, waiting to be inflated. The room was missing a door. The walls were painted a soothing avocado color, but it bore no signs of actual lived-in-ness or emotional investment. Was it . . . a model home?

"There's no privacy in this house," said Nancy. "There's just the phone out here and the one in the den and that's it. You make a call and everyone hears it. Just a heads-up."

"Maybe if you put some furniture in this house, it would absorb some sound," said Shelly.

"We're not staying," said Nancy. "There's no point to it." They had been there a year by then.

Sitting placidly in the middle of the room, drawing on a sketch pad with crayons, was a four-year-old girl, dark-eyed, petite, a little glum. Hair down past her shoulders, soft ringlets, careless, even complicated, perhaps, to carry around with her. Pretty though. She was a pretty little girl, thought Shelly. My niece. Jessica, Jess. Last time she saw her, she had looked entirely different. She watched as Jess pushed her hair out of her face, away from the notepad. It was in the way, thought Shelly. I get it.

"Where's your father?" said Nancy. "What are you doing in here all by yourself?"

"He told me he'd give me some Christmas candy if I sat here and played quiet."

Shelly stared up at the tree again. "Couldn't you do even something a little Jewish?" she said.

"What? I get a deal on the decorations because I work at the mall. And they were going to throw most of them away. I'm friends with the manager. They were basically free." She gestured at a small menorah on a coffee table. "We lit candles," said Nancy. "OK. Whatever. Jessica, come hug your aunt."

Jess hopped off the couch and made her way Shelly, who leaned down and embraced her. "Hi kid," she said. This unfamiliar child. Hers to love though. She felt this instantly.

Shelly pulled the stuffed monkey from her bag. "I got you something," she said, and handed it to Jess. She felt guilty, still, that she hadn't even known what the kid liked. Family, an afterthought. She had just moved too far away—a child herself when she moved! Only sixteen—and hadn't seen her niece enough to remember she had existed in the first place. Her head was in her work, the place she loved most. A year left on her PhD. She could stay in that life forever, if she wanted. Just quietly solving problems.

"Isn't that special," said Nancy. "What do we say?"

"Thank you," said Jess. She hopped back on the couch, seated the monkey next to her, and turned her attention back to her sketch pad. Fair, thought Shelly. Why should she be expected to give a shit about a stranger?

Nancy began arranging liquor bottles in the kitchen. "Should we start with something fancy?" said Nancy. "How about a Manhattan?" She shook her shaker in time with the sound of "Jingle Bell Rock." "With cherries?" She poured, they toasted, they drank, and they waited. How long would it take for Robby to show up? One cocktail, halfway through another. And then there he was. "At last," said Nancy. "Here's Daddy."

Robby with his full cheeks and husky, aggressively masculine build, the big arms, the big belly, but tender-lashed eyes, and childish haircut. A giant man-baby. He made his way to his daughter first, and discreetly dropped a candy cane in her hand while examining her artwork. Jess had drawn a row of sunflowers, and they were building up to the sun, and each petal was outlined in black and painted a blazing yellow. It was an optimistic painting in a lot of ways, it was hard not to look at it and smile. The sky was a watery, appealing blue, and everything on the paper was composed in an orderly and organized fashion, except for one thing: a thin, lightly jagged stroke of red from one corner to another, slicing the image in two. Robby paused at that, traced it with his finger, and asked what it was, and Jess said, "That's the scream."

"Who's screaming?" he said.

Jess shrugged. "I don't know—the flowers, maybe." She had only sensed a scream was necessary, and that it should be red, and a line. That's what she felt at that moment, what she saw: not just sunflowers and blue skies. If the red line went there, it wouldn't be in her anymore.

"A scream. I like it. It's top-notch, Jessica. You're already so talented. You're probably going to be a famous artist someday."

The kid leaned her head back on her father, smiling, less interested in the prospect of fame, more interested in the attention. The two women in the room beamed at him—they couldn't help themselves—and he smiled back, patted his daughter's head. A task done for the day, and he hadn't even had to try that hard. Shiiit. Parenting was easy.

"Shell, what's shaking?" he said, and gave her arm a squeeze.

"This enormous tree has obscured all of my thinking," she said. "I cannot see beyond that to respond."

"Wild, isn't it?" he said, his voice even. "I've tripped on that power strip like ten times already. For sure it's a fire hazard, but I don't have the energy to deal with it."

"Robby," said Shelly. "It's so much."

He still held Shelly's arm in his grip, leaned in close. He said, "Shelly, baby. You can't fight Christmas," and then he kissed her forehead. The scent of booze covered him like early morning dew. Two battery-operated squirrels turned and creaked and squawked. "I'll catch you gals later," he said, and wandered out again, back to his den, to his records and whiskey, the new Talking Heads album. Every time "Once in a Lifetime" came on he'd shake his head. David Byrne singing about having beautiful houses and beautiful wives and driving big cars . . . if he only *knew*. But he was just a cool dude in a weird, big suit. He didn't have to know anything of Robby's life. David Byrne did not have to suffer the basic, boring, normal people. David Byrne sang of family from a distance.

And now here he was, himself, hiding in his own house, even from his own daughter, who he loved more than anything else. But to be in the same room as Nancy right now. He just couldn't.

•

LATER, THE TWO WOMEN WANDERED OUT TO LOOK AT THE sunset. Drinks in hand, blankets wrapped around their shoulders.

The mountains in the distance, carving out their place in the land-scape like they were trying to secure themselves in history. The sky was absurdly pink, hot, hot pink, birds swerving and soaring above. Maybe it wasn't so bad here in the middle of nowhere, thought Shelly. A hike, she would have liked a hike, but sensed arranging that scenario would have been complicated, what with a child being involved.

"What kind of birds are those?" said Shelly.

"I think they're hawks," said Nancy. "But sometimes we see eagles, too."

"It's gorgeous here, I'll say that much," said Shelly.

"Yes, at least there's that," said Nancy, but she didn't sound ex-cited about it.

"You should learn to enjoy yourself a little more," said Shelly.

"It's always the same mountains," said Nancy. "It's always the same sky, it's always the same sunset, more or less."

Shelly noticed just then that her arms had begun to itch, dry from the desert air. Her skin was bright red. "Is this normal?" She showed an arm to Nancy.

"You'll get used to it," said Nancy. "Mom was always allergic to everything, too."

"Allergic to *us*," said Shelly. "Should we talk about Mom?"

"What, that it's cuckoo that she moved to Miami? Do you know how much of her shit I have in my garage right now?"

"Maybe she'll find some rich widower to take care of her," said Shelly. "And then we can have a new daddy."

"We'll probably get stuck with her in the end," said Nancy.

"Not I," said Shelly.

"Me neither," said Nancy, although they both knew it would prob-ably be her. She was more capable of looking out for people other than herself.

"Should we call her though?" said Shelly.

"If we call her then she knows we didn't invite her," said Nancy. All those missed holidays. "Let's eat first and then think about it."

●

A SPREAD OF FOOD HAD APPEARED ON THE KITCHEN COUN-ter; the presentation of it the handiwork of Robby, who had risen hungrily from the den. An unexpected skill of his: feeding the masses. A seven-layer salad. A hollowed-out bread round filled with onion dip. Potato chips, cheese slices, pumpernickel bread. A roasted ham. Shrimp cocktail covered in plastic wrap, which Nancy removed and balled up. Robby was licking his fingers as he left the kitchen. "We're casual around here," said Nancy. "Just help yourself." She made a plate for Jess, now wearing flannel pajamas, Robby somehow miraculously tending to his parental duties once again. Then the two women just stood there and ate directly from the trays. Hungry, ravenous whores. "This is good," said Shelly. "Nice work." Everyone felt a little more sober.

Jess was on the couch, gnawing at some shrimp. "Why don't you go talk to her," said Nancy. "She's your niece." Shelly hesitated. Jess had been small and then less small and then walking and talking and here she was. By now, Shelly was terrified she'd fuck it up, especially because she'd been drinking. And she couldn't watch what was going on between Robby and Nancy anymore. The presence and absence of it all.

"I'm going to bed," said Shelly.

"What? It's so early," said Nancy.

"I have some work to do," said Shelly. "I'm going to read and go to sleep."

"Sure, sure," said Nancy. "Run to your books and hide."

"Look, I traveled all day, we've been drinking, I'm tired."

"I haven't seen you in three years, and now you're checking out as soon as you got here."

"Nancy it's just . . . that I don't understand what's going on here. What are you doing exactly?" Shelly a little too sharp for her own good these days. Living the life of the mind, not quite sure how to come back down to earth. Sometimes she felt out-of-body. When she broke out of it, she felt wild and delicious, drinks with the other grad students, sometimes they went dancing, and there was even a hiking buddy from her cohort whose arms and thighs she had admired, and told him so, but he had turned down her pass, telling her someday they might work together, and then that would always be between the two of them, one indulgent moment. She had shut off her body for a while. Anyway, it was hard to find something that gave her the same pleasure as her brain did, and her brain was telling her that nothing was making sense to her at Nancy's house. Nancy had married this man—why hadn't Nancy listened to her about everything? Why didn't everyone everywhere just listen to her about everything?—and now, to Shelly, she seemed stuck. "This seems stupid," said Shelly.

"What seems stupid?" said Nancy.

She was about to say *Your life* but she didn't. She paused. Shelly sounded familiar to both of them. She sounded like Frieda. How deep her voice had become. No one wanted to sound like Frieda.

"Did you fly all the way out here to judge me?" said Nancy. "To tell me how I took all the wrong turns and made all the bad choices?" She lowered her voice. "Now I have this life in fucking Phoenix and you think I'm an idiot."

"I said no such thing," said Shelly. Now she was in the bathroom, digging through her toiletries bag.

"I'm right here," Nancy said at the doorway, but then she walked away.

Shelly started brushing off the Bloody Marys and the Manhattans and the shrimp cocktail and the taste of family. Voices coming through the air vent. Shelly heard Nancy and Robby talking—in the living room? In the den? Upstairs? "She has spent three seconds talking to her niece. It's like I don't even know her anymore." "You two just need time to catch up," he said. His voice was taut, nearly bored. Was he bored with his wife? This life? "And did you see that monkey she gave her?" said Nancy. "Jesus Christ, what a joke. It's Christmas!"

Shelly in bed, with her notebook, click-clicking her pen. Money, she wrote down. Agency in the world.

●

ROBBY PUT JESS TO BED, THE TWO OF THEM MOVING AROUND Nancy as if she were an object rather than a person, and then eventually Nancy was all alone at the café table in the uncomfortable chair. All the lights were out except for the ones on the tree.

Nancy continued to drink until it was a bad idea, and then she drank a little more past that. Then she collapsed on the couch, a place she ended up on a lot lately, never making it up those long circular stairs to the bedroom; so mostly it was out of laziness, but she supposed also a lack of *desire* on her part. A strange thing to admit. It wasn't that she had lost desire entirely, but there was a certain lack in their marriage in general, of many things, because there was a lack in her life. She needed something to stimulate her, a place to put her brain, and the mall wasn't it.

It wasn't much different from what Robby did; his job was to

convince people that whatever piece of plastic garbage he was selling was valuable, in fact more valuable than the price on it. No matter what he was selling it was a deal, and the customer was lucky
to get it. Everything was an opportunity for him. Somehow she had
run out of them. She nearly had a degree, was just a few credits
short, and they had talked about her going back to school, but they
never stayed anywhere long enough for her to enroll. She felt dried
up inside because of it. Sleeping next to someone who had all the
opportunities in the world made her miserable. Once she had asked
him if there was any work available through his company and he
had said that it was best they keep their lives separate. She could
feel the wall between them every night in bed. Better to sleep alone.

Yet somewhere along the way she had convinced herself that it
would be nice to have company. This is why she had insisted Shelly
come for the holidays. But here it was, same as always, Robby in one
room and Nancy in the other. And Shelly doing whatever she liked.

She thought about the idea of having company for a while, giving
it, receiving it. Joe Urquhart, the manager of the Christmas shop, giving her a little spank on her rear, after filling up the trunk of her car in
the loading dock of the mall with all those Christmas decorations. It
was the first time he'd noticed her after months of her trying to get
his attention, for no other reason than sport, she supposed. "Looking real cute, little lady," he'd said. Nancy halfheartedly stuck her
hand down her pants, thinking of Joe, but then, even in the midst of
all the blinking lights and creaking noises from the Christmas decorations, she passed out.

•

IN THE MORNING, THEY OPENED GIFTS. NANCY HAD SHOWERED
and washed off her makeup, and was snuggled in a quilted robe. All

the adults had put Baileys in their coffee. Jess wordlessly opened the presents, one after another, as if it were a formal duty.

Robby had done the Christmas shopping. It was a gesture both he and Nancy had agreed upon. That he would show up for this family with presents. He had wandered through that same mall where his wife worked, specifically on a day she wasn't there so she could be surprised by whatever he bought. The mall had been in business for less than a year when they arrived in town. All the stores were clean and well organized. New cash registers that flung open with ease. Teenage girls cracking gum and folding T-shirts. A hulking man in a green polo greeting people in front of the Christmas store, a cowboy hat on his head, a name tag that read, YOUR BUDDY JOE. He was eyeing the teenage girls, thought Robby. If I spent enough time here, I'd probably be doing the same.

Then he stumbled upon the lingerie store where his wife worked. It was dim in there—no one wanted to contemplate their tits in bright lighting—and it was empty except for a salesclerk and a heavy-chested woman poking at a sale rack, a child in a carriage at her side. Robby thought about that woman trying on a bra, and then he felt tight in his pants, and he whistled nervously and kept walking. His wife claimed it was depressing to work there, and he believed her, but also, wow, what a great job. He cooled off at the Toys "R" Us, pushing a shopping cart and just dumped toy after toy in the basket, commanding himself to stop thinking about the breasts of strangers, and it took a half-dozen store aisles until finally the image had disappeared. I'm just a man, he thought. It's not my fault—I'm just your average American man.

And now here were the results of that long, sexy, guilt-ridden stroll through capitalism: a Rubik's Cube, a Magic 8 Ball, and a Lite-Brite. Three Barbie dolls, so they could have some friends, throw a party, plus a pink plastic sports car. A stuffed Smurf with a jaunty white cap. LEGOs, at which Shelly brightened. "I spent hours with LEGOs when I was a kid," she said. "Our little nerd," said Nancy. And then a big pile of board games, too, some of which Jess already owned, but Robby couldn't recall what was stacked in the toy closet. The more gifts the kid opened, the smaller she seemed to be getting, as if she would soon be buried under the weight of packaging. Her legs dangling over the edge of the couch. She would not remember these toys. They would be left behind when they moved. She would barely even remember that year they lived in Arizona.

"Oh look . . . Candy Land," said Jess cheerlessly.

"This is so over-the-top, Robby," said Nancy. She rested her hands on her daughter's shoulders, stroked her hair, so silky and still baby-ish. This hair will be helpful to her someday: Nancy had told her that before. People will admire it, admire her because of it. "Who knows if your hair will stay this way forever?" Nancy had told her. "But men will love it." Nancy's hair could only grow so long before the ends got ragged—this was a post-pregnancy problem, and she'd tried every-thing, vitamins, treatments, but nothing worked.

"It'll take a year to get through all these games," said Nancy.

"Well then it'll be just in time for next Christmas," said Robby. "And a whole new round of games, huh, Jess?" Jess was motionless, buried in paper. "You told me to go shopping!" he snapped at Nancy.

"It's just too much stuff," said Nancy.

Robby motioned to the tree behind him, the bunnies dressed as Santa's elves, the three giraffes attired as old wise men. "Too much! This is too much. You want to burn us all down?" "It's just nothing, nothing, nothing, and then all these things at once," said Nancy. "Well, here's another thing," said Robby, and he lobbed a small velvet box at her.

Nancy continued to rant while opening the box, though he

thought he saw her smiling. "I'm filling in the blanks for months here, and then you just show up and think if you—"

It was an emerald ring. Shelly leaned in from the plastic-covered easy chair and assessed it. A gift from a man who loves you.

"I picked it out for you myself, sweetheart," said Robby. "Because you are my wife and the mother of my child and I adore you." And he was smiling, and he was saying this sweetly, but he was thinking: My god, this is all wrong. I have chosen the wrong path. I did it all wrong. I want a do-over. Someone give me a do-over. "If you don't want it, I can take it back, it's fine. I just want everyone to have fun. I got a Christmas bonus, and I wanted to spend it on my wife and child. Yeah, yeah, I've been on the road a lot. Earning this money. Apparently to keep this house lit on fire with the spirit of freaking Christmas."

Nancy got up from the couch and strode behind the tree, and with a growl detached the power strip from an outlet. All the lights went out, the music stopped, it was just dark and quiet in the room except for a few creaking noises from battery-operated squirrels dressed as elves. It was then that Jess started to sob. She had liked all those lights. This was the part she would remember later. The moment when her mother pulled the plug on Christmas. Robby pulled his daughter close to him on the couch.

"I just wanted something shiny," said Nancy, bitterly.

"Just calm down, sit down," said Robby.

Nancy sat back down on the couch, grabbed the jewelry box from Shelly, who was examining it. "It looks real to me," said Shelly, then covered her face with her hand. "I mean, sorry, of course it's real," she said. Inside her, a surge of sympathy.

Nancy put the ring on her finger. It was two sizes too big.

"Do you even know me at all?" said Nancy.

Shelly leaned toward Nancy, spilling a little coffee on the blanket wrapped around her lap. "It's really nice, I think," said Shelly. "High quality. Don't you think so, Jess?" Smoothing it over. Filling in the blanks. The excuses women made for men.

"You love green," said Shelly. She stroked her sister's arm.

"You do, Mommy," said Jess, between sobs. Something shifted in Nancy's face. The two of them telling her it was going to be OK, so it would be.

"Well. I can get it resized," said Nancy.

"There you go," said Robby. Relief. In fact, it had been a haphazard pick, that ring. Last minute in the basket. I'm going to need to get better at this, he thought.

Then they all shushed Jess until she was calm again.

•

THEY HAD OPENED A BOTTLE OF CHAMPAGNE AND THEN AN-other bottle and had attacked the carcass of the roast ham and now there was a frying pan full of scrambled eggs, Robby cheerily dishing it out to his family.

Perched on the kitchen counter, Shelly watched her sister teach Jess how to make origami birds out of leftover wrapping paper. Goddammit, I should have tried with LEGOs, I love LEGOs, thought Shelly. But LEGOs were for playing by yourself in a corner when no one else was around, she thought. Someday I'll be the right person for you though, kid. Just because I don't know how to play doesn't mean I don't know how to have fun. Someday I'll be your friend.

For now, she watched. Shelly, removed. Her hair a mess in the morning. She was two years away from discovering mousse and going big with her hair. Real big. Currently, she was efficient in her looks. Sleeveless silky tops or Hanes men's T-shirts, dark jeans, running shoes or boots with short heels, a dusting of hair on her upper lip, olive skin, thick eyebrows she trimmed with scissors, good jaw, good cheekbones. She photographed well, especially when she was being serious, one of those people where the photos capture her perfectly, on her university identification, her driver's license, her passport, and later her corporate IDs; office parties when she wasn't paying attention and looked up, surprised at the camera; a photo at city hall, once, embarrassed in the moment, but also happy just like everyone else; a few times in newspapers, when she would have preferred to be left alone; and, of course, her obituary, for which her niece, Jess, dragged up a shot from an old digital camera that was somehow still operational. That picture was taken of her in London, that year she met her there in the 1990s—god, what year was it again? What a weird time they'd had together. Jess, Shelly, and Margaret. Oh, Margaret.

Shelly ate another piece of meat, rolling a slice of Swiss in the center. Just some Jewish girls eating ham beneath a Christmas tree, she thought. Thank god their father was dead so he didn't have to see it.

"I'm sorry I'm not good at playing," said Shelly, eventually, to Nancy. Thinking of their father. Missing him still.

•

AFTER THE REMAINS OF THE HAM HAD BEEN PLUCKED AND picked thin and the bottles of booze had been emptied, an impromptu dance party was held in the den, Robby playing disc jockey, happy at last, operating with a real purpose. Lots of Aretha Franklin and James Brown and Donna Summer. "Screw Christmas, let's dance," he said. Spinning his daughter around, stealing a smooch from his wife, who had wedged a damp piece of paper towel between the ring and her finger so she could wear it without it falling off. This was fun, right? Look at them, in love again. Shelly ended the night doing a little shimmy with her sister. A reconfigured family, all of them together, thought Nancy. Jess went to bed, wondering who all these people were in her home after so many months of what felt like no one at all. Nancy and Robby grudgingly held each other in their room, kissing each other slowly, until finally easing into a naked, quiet, hot embrace, all the parts fitting together like usual. Nothing broken permanently yet. Everything still functioning as it should.

CHAPTER 6

1985

Four years ago, Shelly had dropped out of her graduate program, packed up all her things in her car, said goodbye to her cohort, lied when she said she'd keep in touch, drove up I-5 for thirteen hours, then gasped as she saw the Puget Sound, the Olympics behind it, a clear-skied sunset lighting the whole thing up, signaling to her she had made the right choice.

An hour after she arrived at the hotel, her new boss, Monroe, called up from the lobby for her to come down. They sat in the hotel bar, near a fireplace with a mosaic of an Italian landscape, sea green, promising of a world far away where life was simple and easy. He wore a tan three-piece suit and looked like a million bucks. A circular skylight dimmed with hazy drops of rain. Things felt faded but still beautiful. Knee nearly to knee. Was it her knee that was so close or his? She moved it. Then he had her sign some paperwork at which she barely glanced. "Keeps us both safe," he said.

He was more handsome than she had remembered, a lean, tall, blond man with a thick jawline. Masculine and convincing. She asked him about his life for a moment. A wife, a new house. "Here, I have a picture of her," he said. He pulled out his wallet. "She gave it to me," he said. "If I didn't carry it around, I'd be in trouble." Clips in her hair, blond waves, a shirtdress. A nice jawline of her own. "We met in college," he said. "What does she do?" said Shelly. "Nothing," he said fondly. "Keeps house, I mean. She would be so mad if she had heard me say that!" He laughed. "She's a good little homemaker." Shelly didn't know what was so funny, so she asked him. He said, "Well, she's only OK at it. That's the funny part."

His wife didn't like being a homemaker, only because she wasn't happy on her own. "My mother loved fussing around the house," he said. "You know how some women are like that. Not you, of course." His wife wanted to know what he did all day. "And how do we explain what we do?" he said. "It's boring to most people." "But not to us," said Shelly. "She's ready for a family," he said. "Maybe she'll leave me alone then." He laughed again. Still not funny, thought Shelly.

"You're not going to go and have kids on me, are you?" he asked. "No way," she said. "Good girl," he said. He told her to find a place to live; he needed her at work. "Take as long as you want but also don't dillydally," he said. "Do I strike you as the kind of person who wastes time?" she said.

Later Shelly called her sister, so she would know she'd arrived. Told her about the sunset. "Ooh, Seattle," said Nancy. "I've always wanted to visit."

"Don't come right away," said Shelly. "Let me get settled in." That was the last thing she needed, her family showing up, when she was trying to work.

•

IN A WEEK, SHE FOUND A GARDEN APARTMENT IN A VICTORIAN house on Capitol Hill. The owner, Vickie, lived on the top two floors. An old hippie. Long salt-and-pepper hair, which she split between two braids. Tai chi every morning at dawn. She had three dead ex-husbands, each one fluidly mentioned at any moment, as if her conversation partner had met them before. Vickie threw mushroom parties during the summer and was exceptionally high all the time, but the house was well maintained. When she was at home, Shelly appreciated living beneath all those Buddhist prayer flags lining the front porch, hoped they would protect her. Mostly she was at work.

Six days a week she went to the office and stayed late. She loved her project: building a chip to improve the sound quality in mobile phones. Digital signal processing. Turning real-world sounds into math and then back into sound again. Their chip would be better than all the other chips out there. More battery efficient, and with a crisper sound. She did not run the team (yet) (although basically she did) (if you asked her), but her opinion was crucial to every decision they made. She was obsessed with her job, but she found nothing unhealthy about being obsessed. She also wanted to make money, because she never for a second forgot about her father, and his life, and that it could all be taken away from her in a moment.

Nevertheless, she was unhappy. Her coworkers handled her with kid gloves. There were thirty-four other employees. All men. There was always an awareness in the conference room, in the hallways. No one would make eye contact. They looked around her, beyond her, at the man next to her. In graduate school she'd had plenty of male friends. Now, no one would have lunch with her. By then she'd been there a year already, and she knew practically no one in Seattle.

Her birthday came and passed without note except for a call from Nancy, now back in Chicago with her family. "When can we come visit?" said Nancy. Shelly demurred. Work, always work. Nancy talked about a self-help book she was reading and recommended it to her, but Shelly said, "I don't need any help." Nancy passed the phone to Jess, who sang a sweet, off-key "Happy Birthday to You." Then, just before midnight, her mother called from Miami, with the sound of street life behind her. "They shut off my phone," said Frieda. "I just forgot to pay it, it's no big deal. How's work?" *No one likes me,* Shelly wanted to say. *No one will sit with me at lunch.* Instead, she told her mother she'd wire her money the next day. She resolved to talk to Monroe.

•

ALONE IN THE OFFICE AFTER DINNER AT HER DESK, A WEEK later. A noisy Chinese takeout dinner; she could hear herself chewing. Where were the men? Gone home to families or at drinks, chain-smoking. She knocked on Monroe's door. She boldly pulled up a chair. "I see how hard you're working," said Monroe to Shelly, and god, that made her feel good and warm, nearly hot inside. To be seen in that way. To be seen at all. Don't let him distract you, she thought. You're here for a reason—to ask him a question.

"Why am I the only woman working in this office?" she said.

They went back and forth for a while. Kathy at the front desk didn't count, she said. He was hiring as fast as he could, he said, and not enough women out there were trained in this way. Not everyone wanted to move to Seattle. He could not be honest either, which was: he had liked it being just her. One was all he could handle. He had what he thought of as "wandering dick disease." If he filled the office with women, he was just going to want to fuck them. He could keep himself under control with Shelly (wry, quirky, pointed, direct, Jewish Shelly, *not* his type), but sooner or later he was going to mess up. "I promise, soon," he said. "I know it's lonely for you." He told her the other thing he'd been thinking. He couldn't tell if it would hurt her or help her. It was only a problem he could see that he thought needed to be solved, or could be solved anyway. Sometimes we solve problems incorrectly.

"Maybe soften yourself up a bit," he said, motioning to her body, up and down the length of it.

"Hey," she said. "Not cool."

"You want to get along better with the gentlemen in the office, this is my suggestion, and it's merely that."

How had this turned on her? But he had done it. It stuck in her side like a poison dart. She sat with it overnight. The poison sunk in. It couldn't hurt, she thought. To try something new.

She studied the appearance of other women, learned how to shop, to dress, read fashion magazines, quietly contemplating cuts and colors and price tags in boutiques. She wished she could dress more like Stevie Nicks with her big suede hats and vests and swirling skirts and high-heeled boots. But now was not the time for it. She needed to be professional but with flair. She wore blazers and silk shirts with puffy sleeves. She grew her hair out big and luscious. She bought lipstick in a dozen shades. She spent thirty more minutes a morning on her appearance, blow-drying her hair. Thirty minutes she would not get back, she mused, when she had so many other things she could be doing with her day. She calculated all the hours, days, weeks, she would lose in her life to her hair. Her least favorite kind of math.

But it worked, in a way. She still had no friends, but at least there was a promotion. Praised for her ability to predict and solve problems before they happened. *Impressive* and *straightforward*, sure, but suddenly also *charming* and *energetic*. Now she was in the room with investors on occasion. She was brought into meetings to explain, to sell, and to be a woman. She had practiced her handshake on herself. The grip of a leader.

•

A DINNER RESERVATION THE NIGHT OF THE PROMOTION. SHE would celebrate on her own, fine. A bistro downtown, with picture windows at the front of the restaurant, and the Sound beyond it. She sat at the bar, by herself. And, a few minutes later, at the other end of the bar, there he was by himself. A good-looking man, looking at her. Two people alone on a weeknight, grabbing a bite after work. She was wearing a pink silk blazer with shoulder pads and a bolo at her throat. They toasted each other from afar, and soon he was by her side.

His name was Asher. He was handsome in his suit, navy blue, shirt open at the collar, hair slicked back, a little gray at the temples. Early thirties. A five-o'clock shadow at nine o'clock. He was dark, maybe Middle Eastern, but a little European-looking, too, in the upturn of his nose. Hair poking out of his shirt collar and a gold chain. She reached out—"May I?"—and examined it. He had a gold *chai*, too. She pulled out hers and showed it to him. "Our mothers would love this," he said. She felt for a second a kind of desire she had not known before. For his Jewishness, yes, because it was not just her mother who would have liked it—Rudy would have wanted it, too. But also for a permanency. All this moving, all this hustling, all this work she'd been doing for the last seven years, since she was sixteen years old. Running away from home. What if she just fell into this man right now? What if nothing held her back? Nothing from the past in her head.

He worked in money, a curious idea to her, a weird way to phrase it. Banking adjacent. He worked with banks but not *at* banks. It was complicated, he assured her.

I'm smart, she wanted to say. Try me. But something stopped her. It was annoying, but she wanted him, and she felt that he needed to run the conversation if he was going to want her back.

"You smell good, what is that scent?" He liked to know what a woman wore, so he could buy it for her. In case he ever needed to apologize for something someday.

"It's just me," she said.

"Well, you're delicious."

"You smell good, too," she said. Like leather, overwhelmingly masculine, but like something of the earth, too. Lavender and rosemary. He told her the name of it. Drenched in Drakkar Noir.

They kept it light. He didn't need to know too much about her fucked-up family and she didn't need to know too much about his terrible ex-wife. They existed. There was a past. Some other time, maybe. Should we get the cannoli?

Asher drove her home, and Stevie was on the radio, Fleetwood Mac still intact that year, and it was warm, a warm spring night, and she had the window open, and Stevie was singing about players only loving you when they're playing, and Shelly didn't care if anyone was playing here, she was enjoying herself, finally. They passed the grocery store, the Safeway on Fifteenth, and he commented on the butcher there, how he cut a nice piece of meat, and this made her like him, that he had feelings about the way things were prepared, that he could appreciate someone being good at a job different from his own. He parked in front of her house, and they looked at each other goofily, drowsily, and then suddenly with a great and embarrassing hunger, and he kissed her hard, and she kissed back the same way, not a fight, not an argument, just an enthusiastic expression of desire. They made out in the front seat of his car for a while, Asher kissing at her breast, sucking on it, the windows fogged up slightly, until a neighbor walking his dog stopped and gave a whistle and Shelly popped her tit back into her bra and Asher adjusted his crotch and groaned and then laughed, and she laughed, too, both of them briefly humiliated again by their desire. "Oh god," she said. "We should slow it down." "Yes," he said. He pushed up her skirt and pulled down her underpants and put a finger in her and finished her off. She was surprised at how good it had felt, how quickly her body bloomed and came, and his absolute utter confidence in his actions. "Now you finish me off," he said. He put his hand behind her head. He's going to push my head down there, she thought. This she did not want, not then. She wanted to sit there and feel the warmth, tell him how good he was at making her come. "Your turn," he said, in a singsongy voice. Another car pulled up and parked in front of them. Then it was Vickie, waving at the two of them, thinking, *At last that girl's found a man.* "That's my landlord," said Shelly. She kissed him goodbye.

The next week Asher was in Los Angeles on business and decided to stay a few extra days to see some friends. The weekend after that he was also out of town, location unnamed. Answering machine messages left in a curt voice. At the office, Monroe hired five more men, and handed them off to Shelly to direct. Midweek, they solved the last remaining problem of a battery-life issue. The team met in the conference room and popped cheap champagne and looked at each other dazed, for a moment, with no work to do. No problem to solve. The weekend after that Asher was back.

This time, she dressed a little more like Stevie and a little less like herself, the long swirly skirt, the caramel leather vest, but she instantly regretted it when she arrived. He lived in a corporate apartment building, and she felt overdressed and flashy. There was nothing on the walls of his apartment. It was just spare and white.

"This is only temporary," he said, acknowledging the bareness. "How long have you lived here?" she said. "Two years this summer," he said. "Since the separation." "Doesn't seem very temporary," she said. "It's not bad," he said. "A cleaning service comes once a week whether I'm here or not and changes the sheets. Everything is just so, and I like that." "I can appreciate that," she said. "But you still don't care that it's not much of a home?"

He sighed and then sketched out quickly a childhood for her of constant motion. His mother, the immigrant French-Algerian Jew, who had struggled with poverty in her childhood. It haunted her, and so it haunted him, too. A father in the military who had moved them from base to base, all over the world. Four years in private school, which he had fought his family for the right to attend. They wanted to keep him close, but the idea of home to him was negotiable. What he wanted was money, piles of it, but what to do with it, he didn't know. The focus was on earning it. The making of a home was in someone else's skill set, for which he would happily pay. Brazen in his efficiency. He knew himself, she thought. I'll give him that much.

He handed her a glass of wine and led her to a small balcony, which overlooked a pool. They sat on two uncomfortable plastic chairs and faced each other. She took a hearty sip of the wine.

They talked about work for a second, her work. A small crisis in the office. She had nearly lost her temper.

"When the situation gets hot, keep it cool," he said. "Don't get emotional. You've got a good brain. You know that. You don't need me to tell you that. You're . . ." He was looking for the right word, and she flinched for a second, thinking he was going to insult her, find a way to turn this positive thing of hers into something a little negative, or at least softer, or more controllable (as people had been doing to her entire life, she would say miserably to her therapist years later, the one she went to as her mother lay dying, only realizing it then, a little late), but he merely said, "Astute." Winning her love. He had no reason to feel competitive with her. He was not her coworker. He *could* have been though.

"Enough business," he said. He took the wineglass from her hand and put her hand on his crotch. "I've been thinking about you," he said.

"Oh yeah? What have you been thinking?"

"I was thinking we have a little unfinished business." He re-arranged her hand. "Yes, right there," he said. "Now you finish me."

"That was a month ago," she said. "You want me to finish what we started a month ago?" She wanted her wine back.

"But I've been waiting all this time for it to happen," he said. "I had so much work to do. And then I had to visit my mother in New York— she had a fall a month ago, and I wanted to check on her. My father is truly fucking useless at those kinds of things. I had to arrange for a nurse to visit her. Oh, I know this isn't too sexy, sorry." He moved his hand on top of hers so the two of them were stroking him together. "And then last weekend some bullshit with the lawyers. This divorce. Never get married. The paperwork alone. The headaches." He kissed her and sighed. "And the whole time I'm thinking there's this hot chick named Shelly, and when I get to see her again, she's going to finish me off and then we're going to start touching each other all over again. This is my fantasy—I've just been fantasizing about it for weeks. Starts like this." He rubbed their hands together harder on his crotch. "Then keeps going. Please. I've been thinking about it."

He wasn't lying, she thought. He wanted her so badly. It made her want him. And she was curious to see it, his cock. She rubbed her hand on it now without him. She wanted to know how big it was. She felt like he led by his cock, walked his body as if he were carrying it, interacted with it on his mind. It was just so present in him, on him. She was both offended and aroused. She squeezed gently. It felt tight and thick and nice.

•

FOUR MONTHS, SIX MONTHS, ASHER WAS IN AND OUT OF HER life. It didn't matter, she was busy: a company in Chicago wanted the chip, but Monroe wanted the company in Chicago. It was all anyone talked about.

One day Monroe took her to lunch. Damp sandwiches at a picnic table, on a sidewalk outside a strip mall. "I found you someone," he said. "A gift from me to you. A woman to join the company." "Hiring another person is not a present," she said. "You know what I mean," he said. Her name was Margaret, and she would be arriving after she finished her degree in Pittsburgh. It had been dragging on for a while, this woman's education, but she was worth the wait. "She's weird, you'll like her." What does that even *mean*? thought Shelly. On the side, Margaret made music, on computers. Had studied at Juilliard, too. "She'll give you a run for your money," said Monroe.

So: a few months yet till Shelly met Margaret. For now, it's just Shelly and Asher having a sea of meals in his apartment. Naked, he made her steaks. She was conning herself into believing they were growing closer, or that she was developing feelings for him; there *was* an affection there, an intimacy. Now she knew his ex-wife was from Portugal, and was dramatic and crazy; now he knew Shelly's father had died thirteen years ago, and her mother had been cruel to her as a child. But their relationship was flatlining. They were never in the outside world. They didn't know how the other interacted with strangers. They didn't know how they would walk down the street together. She had a faint memory of him guiding her by her elbow from the car to the restaurant the one time they'd had dinner. He'd had excellent manners in the restaurant. He knew what a good bottle of wine was. But that had been months ago. She longed to know how he behaved out in the atmosphere. She asked if they could go out to dinner, go to a movie, go for a hike, anything. Always, he was too busy.

Only once did she see him in public, and it was an accident.

At the Safeway, the one near her house. She followed him from a distance for a while, daydreamed about crashing her cart into his. She pictured his surprise, his delight, their flirtation, maybe they would even pretend like they were meeting for the first time, and he would ask her to the bar down the block for a drink, and then she would invite him over to her house. But first she was curious to watch him, to see how he behaved, treated everyone else when no one was watching. She knew how he treated her. How he tossed her around in bed. Did two hundred push-ups to make her laugh and also to impress her and turn her on a little bit. Listened to her talk about work. Respected her brain and took her seriously. At some point he had figured out that she was good at her job, and when she would tell him about her crises or successes or conflicts or triumphs, he would listen and applaud her when she needed it or deserved it. But also, he was good counsel, he helped her strategize, he knew how to operate as a man in a man's world, but he also knew what men were looking for, too, from a woman, in that world. "Don't just be good at one thing," he said. "Be good at *everything*." A crisis she had more lately in her heart: she was a woman, this was her world, her brain was her universe, too, and she was giving Monroe and her coworkers and this company access to all of it, the benefits of it, the fruits of her mind and labor, and yet still, somehow she was in *their* world, but they were not in *hers*.

He wandered on toward the direction of the meat counter. The butcher, she thought. That's why he's here. He likes the way he cuts his meat. They greeted each other with familiarity. A raised hand, a head nod, Asher pausing and squinting in the case and the butcher motioning at one cut in particular, more head nodding, an agreement arriving. He would travel for a quality product, she thought, loving him a little more. But this was strange for a moment: the butcher was handing him wrapped package after wrapped package. That's a lot of steak, she thought.

She followed him after that a little farther, when he bought the packages of hot dogs and buns, all the paper plates and the napkins and the condiments, and then the cases of beer, one, two, three. He was having a party, she thought. That he hadn't invited her to.

She burned, blushed, turned, and escaped. This is what I get, she thought. This is what I deserve. For looking for these kinds of answers.

•

THEN IT WAS SUMMER, AND HERE, AT LAST, WAS MARGARET. Standing at her office door, Monroe next to her, grinning like he had invented her. Shelly could barely control herself when she met her. "I've been waiting for you for so long," she said as she shook her hand with vigor.

Margaret with the neat red hair and the button-down shirts with threads of silver running through them and the comfortable shoes and the dungarees and cool, soothing voice and the intense need for organization and structure. The two of them side by side, working, clicking, making things happen. Margaret, late at night, in the conference room, talking about how technology made her feel liberated but also how she was afraid to stop working for a second because it all might disappear. "Yes," said Shelly. And Margaret, at the rock-and-roll clubs, and dive bars, and at dinner, and, hallelujah, at lunch. Margaret wearing a skinny black tie. Straight baby bangs. Shelly watching her perform in the basement of a house on Capitol Hill. Margaret stressed-out and intense before the show, and Shelly soothing her. All these moody men smoking cigarettes, admiring Margaret from afar as she twisted all the knobs on her synth. See, you had nothing to worry

about. Patting her shoulder. Margaret heading to London for a music
festival, how cool was that? Margaret had requested the time off, and
Shelly had to approve it, sealing an envelope shut and sending it off
through interoffice mail. Margaret was the coolest person she had
ever met.

Shelly tried to teach Margaret everything she knew at work, and
the two of them were becoming a united front. Two of us, then one
more, then another. If it's only men, we're in trouble, said Shelly. Not
just at this company but in this industry, in this world. They both
talked about how they could blow things up, but maybe it was just
Shelly who felt that way when Margaret was around. Spinning around
in conversation. All those late nights at the office.

"We need some fresh air," said Margaret, one night, the two of
them eating cold sesame noodles with chopsticks in Shelly's office.
"No work talk."

·

MARGARET, PICKING HER UP ON A SUNDAY IN HER MINI COO-
per, for a day trip, a hike. The car was beautiful. It had been her
father's, shipped over from England to New Mexico to remind him
of his homeland, and then put in storage and never touched again.
He had no wildness in him. Just a need for control. Like he did with
her mother. Kept her close when things went wrong.

"A car like this wants to be driven," said Margaret. She pointed
at the pockets in the front doors. Designed to perfectly fit a bottle of
gin and a bottle of tonic, she told Shelly. Margaret stopped herself
then. She was being too enthusiastic, she felt. Too gushy. Margaret
could hear herself talking more than usual, and it was overwhelming
her. It wasn't right to love anything too much. It was just an object.
But it was in such good condition, and it was a real smooth ride.

Thinking about how well it functioned stabilized her heart. Margaret
pulled out onto the road.

They were going to the woods to record some sounds for Margaret's weird music project. Field recordings. Margaret said it wasn't
just the sounds themselves, it was how they got them that was important, too. "It's not just the sounds, it's me listening to the sounds.
So when people hear a song, it's the listening to the listening, that's
what I do, that's what I make."

Margaret told her about growing up in New Mexico. All the noises
of the desert, the wind rustle in the shrubs, the skittering from liz-
ards, bugs chirping, the whistling hoots of the screech owls. Learning how to listen. How hot it was in the daytime, sometimes, and
how she waited out the heat in the arroyo with other kids, and then
it could be freezing cold just a few hours later. How fresh the air was
no matter what. That was a long time ago though. Now she was supposed to be finishing her PhD, *and* she was supposed to be making
music, maybe writing an album. She had trouble finishing anything
that felt big and important.

It was partially not her fault. The world didn't make it easy. She
had given up on classical music after a year at Juilliard. She had seen
the limitations of being a female composer. How much work she
had to do just to make the space for herself, so she could actually
have her music performed. Had shifted into electronic music, so she
could make things, play things whenever she liked, be heard. Her
notes. The devices were so sensitive, their output easily expansive.
She had found herself facile with technology, and then stumbled into
the program at Carnegie Mellon. An accident, to study computer science. She just happened to have a good brain, was that her fault?
Sometimes she felt like it was a bad brain though.

"Ridiculous," said Shelly. "It's a perfect brain."

As she got older, it kept changing—but how to explain this? She felt like she heard *everything* at times. At any given moment, she could be either boundlessly growing or completely overwhelmed. Often it felt like both things were happening simultaneously. When Monroe had offered her the job, she took it just to get out of her life for a minute. So that she could just work on something not her own and not have to think about finishing these things that everyone said she should finish. No, don't tell Shelly that part. Shelly liked it when things got finished.

Ninety minutes more and then Margaret parked the Mini at a trail-head. It had started to rain, a light rain, so they both pulled up the hoods on their jackets. From the trunk, Margaret removed a bulky leather carrying case, which she arranged across her chest, secur-ing it with a canvas strap. Then she heaved her backpack onto her back. There was lunch in there for the two of them. Shelly stood there watching her struggle.

"Can I help?" said Shelly. "No," said Margaret stiffly. "I got it." "Seriously, I can—" "Shelly, I got it!" said Margaret, and Shelly pulled back. Margaret had had an explicit and detailed vision of what this day would be like, where they would drive, hike, eat, and in this vi-sion *she* would be the one carrying the backpack.

They walked for a while, taking the switchbacks. There were no dramatic vistas on this hike. But it was a good place to come if you wanted to see no one at all. Margaret was listening for the moment where there was no sound from the road anymore and they were fully ensconced in the woods. That noise would eventually end—it always did—and new ones would emerge. Then, she told Shelly, she could pay attention, at last, to everything that was going on around her.

People versus no people. City noise versus natural noise. The one thing that felt uncongested was light, and here it was now, for the rain had stopped. They arrived at a clearing in the woods and the sun was pouring down everywhere, on them, on the trees, and the grass, and the air felt fresh and silky and sexy on their skin and the pine needles sparkled and the clouds in the sky were enormous and plush and seemed holy.

"This is the place," said Margaret.

"You think?" said Shelly. "We could keep walking, I don't mind."

"Yes, here," said Margaret. She unpacked her recording equipment from the leather case. A microphone and her beloved Nagra tape recorder, which Shelly admired. "I got it at a yard sale in Pittsburgh from a guy who used to tape Grateful Dead shows," said Margaret. "It was a good deal. I promised him I would use it with care." She paused and fondled it, then cocked her head at the trees. "There are so many sounds," she said. Big eyes, big smile. It was the loveliest Shelly had ever seen her.

"OK, stand here," said Margaret. Out in the world, thought Shelly. "Stand still. Now listen to the birds." She described a particular chirp, fast-paced and high-pitched. They listened. "OK, now stand here. Listen to the rustle of the branches." She went on like this for a while, making Shelly pause for a bit, listen, stand still. "There's one more part to all this," said Margaret. Shy, suddenly. "Go on then," said Shelly. "Part of this is that we are doing it together. And whatever the final version becomes, you'll be imprinted in its memory, even if no one will ever know," said Margaret.

"It's like code." Shelly, unable to see anything in the world except through the lens of work. "OK, I get it," said Shelly. "Hey, are you hungry?"

They sat, cross-legged, on a sheet covered with a block-printed Indian design, dusty pink and green flowers, beneath a waning patch of sun. They ate ham and cheese sandwiches on wheat bread with a thin line of sharp deli mustard and sliced gherkins, some sprouts, too. They popped cherry tomatoes in their mouths. They munched on corn chips. Shelly nattered on about work, kept apologizing for slipping into it, she just couldn't help herself. "We forgot something sweet," said Shelly, and Margaret pulled out a bar of dark chocolate, and said, "Voilà." Shelly clapped.

They talked about their mothers, both absent from their lives, Margaret's mother long since passed. "Her brain took her out," said Margaret, elaborating no further. "I don't miss mine much," said Shelly. "It's just the idea of having a mother. That's what I miss."

And then Shelly suddenly grew drowsy. "It's all this fresh air," she said.

"We're stuck inside too much," said Margaret.

"We are. There goes our youth," said Shelly.

Shelly sat on the ground, arranged her backpack so she could rest her head. Margaret wandered away. Shelly looked up at the sky. God, she loved the sun on her face. Why did she live somewhere that rained all the time? She tried to hear what Margaret heard. She closed her eyes and listened. The whole of the woods was breathing, she felt. Then she thought about Asher, who she was supposed to see that night. Would she even tell him about this day? Would he even care? All he wants is to touch me. She grew grim and gloomy. Then she dozed for a while until she heard Margaret stomp back through the woods, eventually standing above her.

"Did you hear anything cool?" said Shelly. She shielded her eyes from the sun as she looked up.

"I heard an . . . odd bird."

"That's what you are," said Shelly affectionately. "An odd bird."

Margaret played with her loose camouflage jacket. Looked down at her and smiled.

Shelly checked her watch. "I forgot to tell you this. We need to leave sooner rather than later. I have a date tonight." The sun was moving already beyond the tree line.

"Anyone good?" said Margaret. The quiet intake of breath.

"No," said Shelly. "No one good at all." Certainly not better than you, thought Shelly, and then she pushed the thought away.

Outside Shelly's house, a hug goodbye in the car. Margaret held on for too long. They both smelled the same now, like the woods. She's feeling me, thought Shelly. Feeling my arms and my back and my heart through my chest. I hope this isn't going to be a problem. What kind of problem, she didn't know.

"Have fun on your date," said Margaret as she drove away.

"I won't," said Shelly.

•

IN THE SUMMER, NANCY PLANNED A VISIT, FINALLY JUST IN-sisted on it. "I will not take no for an answer," she said. "You can work, and we'll sightsee. Just eat dinner with us." Bought the tickets already, too bad, Shelly.

For their first night there, Nancy made a reservation at a pricey seafood restaurant downtown, near the market. "I can make it for five, if you want to bring a friend," said Nancy. Shelly thought about inviting Asher, but Asher didn't even invite her to his parties and only returned half her messages. "I'll bring Margaret," said Shelly. "Who's Margaret?" said Nancy. "She's my friend. We work together." "That's weird." "Why is that weird? You said I could invite a friend. Margaret's my best friend here. What, do you not have any friends?" "I just meant more like—" "A boyfriend? I don't have a boyfriend. I have Margaret. Should I not invite her?" "No, she can come." "You know what? I'm not going to invite her. Because you're being awful about this." "I am not coming all the way to Seattle to fight with you." "Well, then maybe you shouldn't come." "Oh, we're coming." "Fine." "And I want to see you. Don't not see us." "I said 'Fine,'" said Shelly. "But don't tell Mom, OK?" said Nancy.

A month later the four of them—Robby, Nancy, Jess, and Shelly—sat and ate milky clam chowder, the city one direction, the mountains the other. They seemed closer though, Nancy and Robby. He stretched his arm around her shoulders. "Isn't this great?" he said. Between courses, he took Jess's hand and escorted her down to the dock to look at the boats. I wish I knew her better, thought Shelly, as she watched Jess walk away. She seemed clever, and quiet for a child, which Shelly appreciated. "We're really trying," said Nancy. "We took some classes together. I've been reading some books." "You and your books," said Shelly. "Someday when you have a husband of your own you'll understand it's worth fighting for," said Nancy.

Shelly looked at her sister and wondered if she even liked Nancy as a person at all.

·

AFTER DINNER, SHE DROVE TO ASHER'S, BULLSHITTED HER WAY into his building, knocked on his door. "Hi, sexy," he said.

Soon enough they were half-clothed and fighting. "I don't know why I'm this way," he said. Shelly kept trying to get dressed and stopping. "I mean I guess it's the divorce," he said. "But it's been a few years now. I might be this way forever now but maybe I might change, who knows? You could stick around and find out. I could try to be nicer. I know how to be nice. You know that, right?" Shelly found herself nodding, and she turned away from him. I will not cry, she thought, but she did, a bit. "Who knows? I could turn out to be a hell of a guy. Everything you want." He stroked her hair. "Come on, Shelly. Don't be mad. Were we really trying to do something big here? Or were we just having some fun?"

She didn't sleep there. But she didn't storm out either. They had sex again first. She was curious about what having sex was like when she was feeling the way she was at that moment, messy and exhausted and sad and a little needy. How could she be doing so well at work and so terrible with this man? The softness had betrayed her. So how would it feel to have him in her when she was feeling low? The answer was this: she felt like she was an egg cracking. Breaking and then her insides spilling out.

"I don't want this to end," he said, and she believed that he believed that was true.

●

MONDAY MORNING IN AN OFFICE PARK. IT IS 1985. SOMEDAY they'll have ten times the space they have now, an entire campus in the woods. They'll gobble up a dozen other companies, and Shelly won't recognize this company that started on a singular passion: to help people talk to each other wherever they are, whenever they like. (A terrible idea, in a way, she thought sometimes, early in the mornings. Why can't we just be alone sometimes?) Still, she clung to that which she would make, could hold in her hand.

On her desk was an interoffice mail envelope. She unwound the tie. Inside was a tape cassette labeled DAY HIKE.

In the conference room Monroe brought up Chicago. He needed to send a team there to meet with their team in order to form a new team. What this team would do would be a great unknown. How powerful and important it would be, no idea. They just needed one to exist. "Shelly, can you leave your guys for a week? Are they on target right now?" Did she want to go to Chicago? Her hometown, of all places. Would she have to see Nancy? It would be nice to see Jess. She had liked having her around for those few days.

"I could go. It's just a week?"

Monroe said yes, but who knew how long anything would take? "This is new territory," he said. "But we told them a week." Send me for forever, was how she felt right then.

On the ride home from work, she played the tape in her car. It was a loop of chirping birds and fluttering wings and then a wiry electronic noise in the middle of it. And then it built so beautifully—all these layers of sound coming in so that it became a whole song—that she drove around her block a few times just to listen to it end. This is romance, she thought. And then she cast the thought aside. Who had room for romance right now? And not with Margaret. Never with her. She didn't have it in her to do that. It was enough just to be a woman alive and working. She had other things to worry about. And who she liked—and she liked all kinds of people—was not relevant to who she was in the office. Who needed to make life harder?

·

A FEW MONTHS LATER: IT HAD RAINED FOR DAYS. A DRY MOMENT now. Vickie was sweeping up some broken branches and errant leaves from the front porch. It might rain again tomorrow, more mess to arrive, but she loved her home, she liked to keep it immaculate, and she was trying to find a new renter. A BMW pulled up and parked in front of the house. It seemed familiar to her, although no one in this neighborhood would drive one of those fancy cars, even if they could afford it. A dark, short, stocky, masculine man in a suit, smelling of cologne. He headed to the downstairs apartment first, knocked and knocked, then looked up at her and smiled. He was looking for Shelly, he told her. "I must have missed her before she left town," he said. He was just looking for her new number, a forwarding address, anything. He was handsome and expensive-looking. A real catch. Each of her dead husbands had enriched her life in one way or another, even if it was just her bank account. Surely Shelly would want him to know how to get in touch. He looked like he had some money to spend on a gal.

CHAPTER 7

1986

When Frieda and Carolina first arrived in Miami, they moved fifteen minutes from the beach, as they had sworn they would do, into a sunny quiet home, and they adopted a cat, or rather, the cat adopted them. Showed up one day in the backyard, their first week there. They watched through the sliding glass door as he strutted through the yard beneath the palm and banana trees. Black, tiny, fussy, prissy, he was a prancer of a cat. Carolina said, "*Hola, gato*," and Frieda said, "That would be a nice name for a cat, *gato*," and Carolina said, "It means 'cat' in Spanish," and also, "If you're going to live in this city you better learn a little Spanish," and Frieda felt foolish, but regardless, the name stuck and evolved: Gato, Gatty, Kitty, Little Kitty Bang-Bang, Bing-Bang-Bong. A good cat.

Came when he was called, no matter the name. Happy to be with the two women in their new home. Watched as they decorated it with spider plants in macramé hangers, spritzing the green edges in the morning before the sun rose. Framed prints of beachy art, sunsets, and shells on the shoreline. In their private rooms, photos of dead and living relatives, and in their shared living space an altar of candles and incense burners and bunches of sage and sticks of palo santo. At a thrift store down the road, they found a matching set of wicker bookshelves, which they filled with romance novels

and a set of encyclopedias they found left behind by the last ten-
ants in the garage. For a few months they were always decorating
something new, dragging something home, making decisions about
what should go where. The cat napped on the daybed as they busied
themselves in their new life, ate kibble from their hands as treats in
the early evening when they came home from work.

They worked all the time. They turned the patients, they showered them, they moved them from their beds to the bathroom and
back again. They made sure they took their pills and ate their food,
especially their patients who couldn't remember that they were sick
or hungry. Picked them up when they fell to the ground. For a few
years did this. They worked harder than they had when they'd
lived in Chicago, they said to each other all the time when they got
home. This was a bigger institution, many more people, a sprawling
campus, and they were understaffed. The two women were happier
in the mornings than they were in the evenings. The cat slept with
the one who needed him most, usually Frieda, passed out from ex-
haustion and wine. Foot of the bed, a reliable companion.

·

OCCASIONALLY A DAUGHTER CALLED. ONE HATED HER JOB,
one loved her job. The one who hated called more often.

"I hate my job, too," said Frieda. "Do you think I like taking care of
sick people all day? So what? You go to work. You do your job. You
move on with your day. Your problem is not that you hate your job
but that you don't enjoy your life. You have so much more now than
you did when you were growing up and yet you were lighter and
easier then, even with all the problems in our house. I don't know.
Do you need a hobby or something? Maybe try going to temple."

Eventually they both sighed and hung up. Frieda wasn't even

sure either of them had said goodbye. No matter, she had the cat, and she had Carolina, and she had Miami, baby.

•

ON FRIDAYS THEY MADE MARGARITAS AND PUT ON MAKEUP AND cradled the cat like a baby and swayed to the music on the radio and then left, bustling, to go out into the night. Middle-aged, with hips and bellies and breasts and a weary optimism and the last burst of hormones driving their decisions, poorly, on occasion. "It's like we're always on vacation now," said Frieda. Florida. Sometimes they both came home, sometimes only one of them, sometimes neither, and on those days the cat went hungry until the afternoon, nibbling vindictively on the zinnias while he waited for their return. There were days and days when Frieda was gone. Living her life for the first time, she felt. The physicality of her encounters made her think something real was happening. Although she did not care so much about the sex as she did the touch. Because for so many years she went without touch, even when Rudy was still alive. And then after that, her girls were gone, never to return. And so when these men held her she felt their fingers on her and she felt alive or at least not dead. She thought about Rudy now more than ever, comparing the aggression of their touch to how he had gracefully, nearly wistfully, managed her flesh. He did not love me like that, she could see that now. All those years she had wondered what was wrong with her, and it had had nothing to do with her. But now, she felt a new kind of wrong. She sunk into the night.

When she would return after a disappearance, Carolina would yell at her. Carolina had been working hard, taking all her exams, getting all her certifications and licenses in order. She was serious as a heart attack about her upward mobility. She wanted more money, and she wanted a retirement fund, and she wanted a small office to call her own. (Somehow that office meant the most to her of all. A door she could close for even five minutes every day.) After a few years, Carolina was her boss at work. Don't show up at home, fine, who cares? But Frieda wasn't showing up at work either. The cat hid under the bed while the two women cursed at each other.

Then there was the time after Carolina loaned Frieda money, thousands of dollars accrued, and Frieda lied for a while, when and where she had spent it, when and how she would pay her back. Finally she admitted she couldn't even give her a date when it would be returned, stopped pretending that she knew when, and Carolina had screamed and slammed her bedroom door shut so the cat had no choice but to sleep with Frieda that night because it was the only room that was open, but also Frieda needed the cat, Frieda couldn't stand the loneliness, knowing Carolina was there, but so far away.

Work gave her no hope or comfort. No one ever asked her how she was doing. No one ever wondered about the people giving care to those who were sick or dying. She didn't even recognize the signs of burnout. She had been in a state of burnout for so long who even knew what it looked like to feel healthy? She only knew that she was chipping away at the sadness with booze. Or trying to anyway. The cat curled up at her feet. Little comfort, but some.

One day a truck pulled up, and all of Carolina's things were gone. A half-empty house. Before she left, Carolina begged her one last time to get help. She said, "You are my friend and I love you and there is still time to fix this." But Frieda only wanted to talk about the cat. Frieda wouldn't let her take the cat. "He's mine," she said. "He loves me best." Who could even argue! Goodbye, Carolina. A month later, they moved to a smaller apartment, farther from the beach, just Frieda and the cat. At night Frieda dangled a lazy toy at the cat to get a little attention, but it wasn't enough for her, not enough attention.

Then Frieda met one terrible man after another, all of them bad news, not a one of them gentlemen, and certainly none of them nice to the cat. By the time one of them hit Frieda, she felt it, felt that he was paying a kind of attention to her, too, but also at the same time she barely even noticed it, because she was drunk when it happened, and feeling nothing at all, except for missing Carolina. And also, her daughters, but they were a farther-off missing feeling, it had been so long since she'd seen them, the sensation of absence nearly being absorbed into her body. Don't even talk about her granddaughter. How could she have only met her but a few times? She realized she didn't have anyone's mailing addresses anymore, to even send them a birthday card. The shame. There was so much shame. All the feelings and not-feelings were swimming together in a giant river that ceaselessly rushed through her body. She worked, she went home, she disappeared into the river. She finally learned a little Spanish, so life wasn't a complete waste of time, but it was close. She practiced on the cat. *Lindo gato negro.* She wished Carolina would call. She knew the only way to make that happen was to pay her back, but that would require her asking someone for the money, one of her daughters, perhaps. But they had tired of giving her money a while ago, or she was too embarrassed to ask them anymore. She had run out of people to ask for help. "You're my only friend," she told the cat, but she didn't always remember to feed him every day.

She moved to an even cheaper apartment, and the cat hated it. It was an old motel that had been turned into apartments. At sunset everyone who lived there gathered around the emptied pool, legs dangling on cracked hot concrete, drinking beer or plastic cups full of boxed wine, and often there was more than that floating around, pills and powders, all kinds of substances. It felt like a community of sorts—sure, they all knew each other—but everyone came and went and no one was particularly kind, and whereas Frieda had looked ten years younger and glowing when she first hit Miami, that time had now passed, and she looked her age again and then some, after months of hanging out at the pool. Her daughters probably wouldn't even recognize her, she thought most nights. (They're searching for her by then, but they don't know how to locate her, no phones, no forwarding address.) Shelly would think she was a foolish drunk, and Nancy would think she was an ugly old hag. This is what she heard her two daughters calling her in her head before she went to bed at night. There was no ease left in her life. Even the cat couldn't help. She was just alone in the world. The sound of people laughing at an empty pool outside her front door.

For a while, the cat roamed around the complex, looking for food where he could find it. Until he wandered away entirely, to a new backyard, where there was a child and two parents, and he nearly forgot that woman he lived with for those years. Only when there was a sparkle of light that bounced off a toy, a crackle sound as he batted it with his paw, did he remember what it had been like to sleep at the foot of her bed and comfort her when she needed it.

PART III

AFFAIRS

CHAPTER 8

1989

Friday night, early fall, and no one was home but Jess. At the kitchen island, flipping through a stack of magazines she bought at the grocery store. No specific aesthetics or vision—yet—just every magazine she could get her hands on that didn't involve sports or politics. Jess, desperate for inspiration. A sharp pair of scissors on the counter. A stack of clippings atop a spiral-bound notebook. The edges in perfect straight lines. Above the magazines, a bowl of salt and vinegar potato chips. Jess took a chip, ate it with great delicacy, trying to make it last. Ten calories a chip, she had read mere pages ago—the first time counting calories had even occurred to her. A lifetime on the hips, it said. She felt, briefly, as if someone were trying to stab her with those scissors, but she processed the information anyway. This is what this many calories tastes like. I must remember that.

She was in junior high now, studying in a building that shared space with high school students. The loud hallways, the buzz of the lights overhead, the bathrooms that stunk of cheap pink industrial soap. She was overwhelmed every single day. Three hundred children in her class alone. And where were they all on this Friday night? Were they all somewhere, in the same place, at the same time? There was supposed to be a party; she had heard a scrap of information in study hall that afternoon. But here she was, alone. Her parents were out, away, though not together. Jess messed with her long hair, pushed it out of her face. A boy had tugged her ponytail in class. Her mother wouldn't let her cut it. Her mother was preoccupied with Jess's hair, had been forever. What this part of her physical self could do for her when Jess was entirely uninterested in the subject. "People pay good money for hair like that," she told Jess. "I always see women getting perms at the salon. You should treasure it forever." At night Jess dreamed of her hair wrapping itself around her neck and choking her. There she sat with her long hair and her ten-calorie chips. Waiting for something to happen. A curious girl in the kitchen.

Curious as in odd, but also interested in things. Whatever was put in front of her, she would read, she would consume. Or clip it and save it for later, to be pasted in the notebook, to be taped to her wall, to be scribbled upon, to be layered, collaged, not obsessively (not yet anyway), but as a form of relaxation. Her mind gathered the information and then transformed it into something new. The act of clipping meant she was claiming it for herself. It started one way and ended another.

She flipped to an advertisement for Nike. *Just do it*, a new phrase lately. Different from the potato chips information. More definitive of a command, though the information was more nuanced. A phrase her mother liked, with all her self-help books. Nancy had poked at another advertisement with the words once. "They're onto something here," she had told Jess. Now Jess paused on the page, wondering what the "it" was, what she was supposed to do, how would she know, would someone tell her? She sliced the paper neatly with the scissors, gratified by the sound. The sound of action.

She had taken so little action in her life yet. Kept her cards close, watched and waited. She wasn't emotionally immature, but there was a lack of experience. They'd moved a lot, she and her parents, but she'd done a lot of sitting. Still: she grew. She was tall. Her breasts were small, but they were present. She had gotten her period last summer. Squatting in the bathroom, pushing her hair back from her face, reading the back of the box of tampons. The idea of toxic shock as newly important as calories. Her hair, her hair, she tied it in a knot on top of her head. Thought again of her mother playing with it. "This is good hair. Boys will like this hair." She was lightly freckled, too, with clear skin otherwise, no blemishes. She had not made any mistakes yet. No scars, no broken bones. The last precipice of youthful perfection. Someday when I'm older . . . , she mused, often, never quite able to finish the thought.

But every day she *was* a little older. Tomorrow, inching toward a gray future. A cold snap would show up in the evening, and the week after that was Halloween. This was the last nice day until sometime next year. The down coats were still in the attic, last year's mittens stuck in the pockets. In January they'll go skiing in Wisconsin, the whole family, finally in the same place at the same time, and she'll get her period two days early, stuffing wads of toilet paper in her underpants, hoping the snow pants will hide the bulge. Her mother, lit in the lodge on hot toddies. Dad, somewhere else. Even when you're here, you're not *here*, her mother will say to him. Jess bleeding on the slopes. She was right there. Why wasn't anyone paying attention to her?

She glanced up at the television. The laugh track of *Full House* buzzing gently. Now, that house was never quiet. People walked into rooms all the time, looking for each other, trailing behind someone else.

"Am I supposed to feel bad that I'm all alone on a Friday night?" She said this out loud, just to hear the sound of a real voice. How am I supposed to feel about being alone? Is it like a sweater I put on, do I sink into the comfort of the feeling, the state of being by myself?

Or am I supposed to reach out to someone else? To achieve a different state? She just wanted to know, was this feeling she was having right?

And then in walked the aunt. The one who lived in the city. Silk shirts with pearl buttons and shoulder pads and tight jeans and high heels and big hair and big lacquered lips and blue-shadowed eyes and her strut, her chic strut. Her mother's sister. Arrived for a visit.

"Aunt Shelly," said the girl. "What are you doing here?"

If only you'd known the night Shelly had just had. "Listen, Jessica, let me tell you. I was supposed to have plans tonight," she said. Her hands went up to her ears, and she released her clip-on earrings. "But plans change." She drifted off for a second. "You know when you're just done with something? No, I suppose you don't. You're only just getting started." She put her earrings on the island counter. They both looked at them. They were a pink faux marble. They were cool, Jess thought.

"You like them?" said Shelly. "You can have them." Jess declined.

"I know what it's like to be sick of things," said Jess.

Shelly had been fighting with her ex, no longer her ex, years of this garbage, the back and forth. Seattle, Chicago, New York. He was trying to wear her down. Make her move to be with him. He had decided that if they were in the same place at the same time then everything would be easier for the two of them. *He* had decided. And then she would marry him, he had decided that, too. And she didn't even know if she wanted that in the first place. All right, she did. She wanted to get married and be with someone. She wanted that sense of permanency after so many years of running around. And she was nearly thirty. Her mother had had her by that age, and her sister had had Jess, too. But they could not agree on a place to live. Chicago was good for her. Where her town house was, in Lakeview, that she had bought on her own, a big deal. Where the work was. Her division had a new rollout coming up in a few months, and it was her show, she had run the whole thing. The market was expanding. Last time she went to New York to see him, she had watched, gaping, as suited man after suited man hustled down the street yelling into their phones. They weren't all her phones, but it didn't matter. They were out there. Why would she want to be anywhere but where the action was, especially when she was the one running it all?

"That's good, that you know that about yourself. What you get sick of. I mean, that's bad that you have to deal with the little annoyances of life already. But good that you start to know your boundaries. Took me a million years and then some to figure mine out," said Shelly. "And still, I don't abide by them sometimes." Her niece looked at her with only minor concern. "This whole family has terrible taste in men, you know that? No, your dad's all right. That look on your face right now."

"I don't care," said Jess, and she didn't. She liked her dad but didn't expect anyone else to, based on her mother's opinion about him. "It was more just thinking about men."

"Of course, you're too young to care about that nonsense."

Jess didn't bother to correct her. She had her period already. She cared about a lot of things.

"Anyway, after all of it, I just found myself driving here, thinking your mother might be home. Who goes out in the suburbs? And I thought we could stay up late together. I was looking for a little comfort and familiarity. But, of course, she's not here. Even your mother is having a better time than me. Where is she?"

"I don't know," said Jess.

"She didn't leave a note or anything?"

Jess shrugged. It hadn't even occurred to her to look for one.

"And where's your father?"

"Away on business. Denver? Houston? How am I supposed to know?" How *was* she supposed to know?

"OK, OK, he's away," said Shelly, her voice turned to soothing. Why freak out a kid? She thought her sister would be here, but she was nowhere. Weren't mothers supposed to be home on a Friday night? Why couldn't she find her? She had gotten used to being able to get in touch with whoever she wanted in her life—everyone in the office had a mobile phone now, they were all testing them out. Margaret, now in London, staying in some rich man's recording studio, didn't have one, but they wrote each other letters anyway, religiously, every two weeks. One showed up and then she would sit down immediately and write one upon return. (Once Margaret wrote, "I thought about you today in the park, it was such a nice sunny day, and I remembered our hike, and how you looked asleep in the sun." In her return letter, Shelly wrote, "I could give you money. So that you don't have to stay with him," but Margaret assured her she was fine, content, trapped with all those toys.) They both desired written objects. The post office was reliable, tangible, evincing an emotionality. It all felt intimate. *Asleep in the sun*. Who needed a phone?

But Nancy and Robby—they were in the suburbs. Everything was close. Everyone was supposed to be where they said they were going to be there. Who needed to find each other at every second? But Shelly would have liked them to be there, right then. She wanted to see what it was like when people were reliable to each other, when they were involved in something permanent and connected. How often had she looked for role models in her life only to find she had to be her own?

"Anyway, you and I can have a good time together." Shelly chucked her on the arm. "Come on! We'll have fun. Where's the wine? If you want a little, I won't tell."

"There's some in the fridge," said Jess.

Shelly rifled through the fridge. Pulled out a nearly empty bottle of white with a cork in the top. There were two more just like it, a half a glass in each. The forgotten bottles. "No thank you to the dregs," said Shelly.

"There's a new bottle on the counter, I think," said Jess.

"I already know that's not the good stuff," said Shelly. "Where's the good stuff?"

•

THE GOOD STUFF WAS IN THE CRAWL SPACE, WHICH JESS'S mother called "the wine cellar" and which Jess's father called "the junk shop." Jess didn't want to go in the crawl space. It was tight and airless in there, and the ceilings were low and made of concrete, and it felt like a trap. Her aunt was on a tear; her critical eye was on full blast. It reminded Jess of the laser light show they had gone to after the state fair last summer, Pink Floyd's *Dark Side of the Moon*. Her dad loved that album. They had stayed until Jess had gotten sick off the nearby pot smoke. But that laser light, probing the night sky. That was her aunt Shelly when she turned her gaze on someone. Like a laser shooting out of her forehead.

The night had turned strange. The hunt for wine, her missing parents, the awkwardness of the physical space. It was weird that her aunt was there.

"Where's the light?" said Shelly, who was reaching inside the crawl space, palming the wall. Jess crawled inside and, on her hands and knees, made her way to the light switch cord, dangling from the ceiling, and then tugged on it, and it made a satisfying noise, that lightbulb noise. "Hurrah," said Shelly.

The crawl space was shaped like a square, dusty, and dim, even with the lightbulb lit. There were boxes everywhere, some open, some taped shut, a set of broken skis, plastic tubs of toys, clothes, photo albums, files, paperwork. Finished and unfinished business.

"What a mess," said Shelly, crawling inside and then hunching over, her hands on her hips. "All that money your father made last year and he can't bother to fix this up?" Everyone talked about Jess's father's good year like it belonged to them. Some investments had paid off, he had sold his entire sales line to two new department store chains, an aunt had died and left him a house in Ann Arbor, which he now rented out to two professors at the university. The income stream was what they talked about. A good income stream, like it was a personality trait.

He owned a house in Mississippi, too, the family vacation home, where Jess always had allergy attacks, but that seemed like a money pit, and anyway Robby refused to rent it out, said it was for family alone. Somehow he had turned it into some kind of tax write-off.

"Where's the wine?" said Shelly. She didn't like how she sounded talking about Robby. What did she care what her sister's husband did with his money? She just liked busting his chops, but he wasn't even there to hear it. She kept bumping her head on the ceiling, so she dropped to her knees. "Guess these pants are going to the cleaners on Monday," she muttered.

"I think she got a case this week," said Jess, who dropped down to the ground, too. Now they were quiet, crawling, digging, opening. The two of them feeling like animals, and liking it. Shelly flapped open the top of one, looked inside, and then, briefly, a shadow fell across her face, and she closed it. "Not there!" she said. It was fake-sounding, and they both knew it, could hear that cracked quality. "What?" said Jess. Shelly rifled through the box and then pulled out a silk robe. "These were your grandfather's. He was a hero to us." She sighed, fingered the fabric. "Did your mother ever tell you he was a homosexual?" "No," said Jess. "She never mentioned anything to me." "Well, he was, and now you know." Shelly laughed. "It's so odd, but I actually never said that out loud before just now." Something about the conversation, the casual way her aunt reported the news, made Jess feel like she could say anything to her aunt and she would be safe. That whoever Jess was now, whoever she was going to become, her aunt would always accept her. And this made her feel like she could be anything she wanted in her life. "He had excellent taste," said Shelly. "I didn't even appreciate it then." Jess dug into the box and pulled out a robe for herself, lavender and silky. She smelled it: cigarettes. "Your mother and I have never even talked about it before, but she knew, we knew. That's just what he was." Shelly frowned. "Family secrets are such a waste of time," she said. "And anyway, he was just wonderful." She pulled out a green silk robe. "Look at this, look at this embroidery. It's gorgeous. Should we try some on? We should, right? They're so pretty and they're just locked away in this box. I think they want to be seen though." She wrapped the robe around her shoulders, fitted her arms through the sleeves. "Your grandparents, they were good companions to each other. But I don't know how much fun they had," she said. "But these robes, they're fun."

Shelly dragged the box with her, Jess inching along behind her. Just off the entrance to the crawl space, they spotted the case of wine. "Aha," said Shelly. "Jackpot." She pulled out a bottle, dusted it off with her hand, and read the label. "Is it good?" said Jess. "I don't know," said Shelly. "I just always want whatever isn't on the menu." She handed a bottle to Jess to carry. "I'm not really going to drink any," said Jess. "Oh, you never know what will happen," said Shelly.

•

THEY WERE ON THE PATIO NOW, ON THE PLASTIC LOUNGERS, A bottle between them, both dressed in Rudy's robes. Shelly was sipping from a goblet Jess had insisted her parents buy for her a few years ago at a Renaissance fair they went to in Kenosha. Her mom had dressed the two of them up like fairies, in dresses she had spent weeks sewing, made of a stretchy green material and covered with pastel-colored sequins. They had matching eye shadow and her mother wore fake lashes but told Jess she was still too young to wear them. Her hair in pigtails, her mother's in braids. Her father had worn the same dark cape he wore every year to Halloween and looked uncomfortable the whole time, finally taking it off in the peak sun of the afternoon. This was when he was working out of the house more, and in the summer they were spending every weekend trekking to outdoor events within the Wisconsin-Illinois-Indiana state lines. Her parents didn't want to sit still. They needed to keep busy, keep Jess occupied, keep themselves in motion; mostly it was him, he was the one who had needed to roam, this is what her mother claimed. "This was your idea in the first place," she'd counter whenever he complained about anything. That day had ended after her father had eaten a fried turkey leg that hadn't sat right with him. Jess made them purchase the goblet on the way out. Bejeweled with a purple tint. A memory of Ren Faire 1986.

Other things concerning Jess at the moment: How had she not known that those robes were there? That there were stories in her family that hadn't been shared with her? All she had heard was that her grandfather had survived the Holocaust and died too young (although not actually *young*, a nuance in the phrasing she never quite understood), a waste of the struggle. She had a grandmother distant and troubled in Miami—she had met her only a few times. Her parents squabbled about how much money to send her, her mother always triumphing with "Of course, she could always come live with us." But no one wanted that. A threat for both of them. Send some cash instead. But what if Jess wanted to know her grandmother? What if Jess wanted to know this secret about her grandfather? What if this secret had suddenly lit every cell in her body on fire?

Shelly was still upset about the unfinished crawl space, sipping the wine, ranting about all the things wrong. The dent on the car in the driveway, which had been there since last spring. And the paint chipping off all over the house. "They spend money on things and then they don't keep them up. Why bother buying them in the first place?" Jess felt like defending them for a second. "They're very busy people." "Doing what?" said Shelly. Jess had no answer.

"You really don't know where your parents are?" Shelly, draining her goblet.

"Dad's away on business. Mom went to services."

"Oh, she's back being a Jew again, is she?"

Jess's tumbler of wine had sat untouched until that moment, and she finally took a sip. She wondered if this was what fun felt like.

"It's really pleasant out, isn't it?" said Shelly. "We must remember this weather in a month when we're cold."

"I hate the cold," said Jess. And yet she would live in Chicago for most of her life. Sometimes people just stay put.

"It's not so bad if you don't ever leave the house," said Shelly. "But it's boring. So we should go for a walk now. While we still can."

"Where?" said Jess.

"I don't know—anywhere. Aren't you up for an adventure? Just a walk through the neighborhood to see what we can see."

"I'm fine," said Jess. It wouldn't have occurred to her in a million years to go for a walk, she thought. She wished her aunt would leave. She liked her, but also, she was exhausting.

"Oh, we're going," said Shelly. "Can't I have at least a little fun tonight?"

"I'm trying to establish boundaries," said Jess.

"Give me a break," said Shelly. "Let's go."

•

THEY WALKED SOUTH, TOWARD THE TOWNSHIP'S TENNIS courts, which stayed lit until midnight. They could see the blistering lights from a few blocks away, as the rest of the neighborhood wound down for the evening, save for the front porch lights, late-season moths flapping about them fruitlessly. Shelly had poured their wine into plastic cups. "What if we get into trouble?" said Jess. "Please, this is the suburbs," said Shelly. "No one gets into trouble here."

Shelly was wearing her sister's tennis shoes, which she had dug out of a box in the front closet. (She had noticed, also, a pair of red spiked heels jammed in the corner. What on earth does she need these for? thought Shelly. I don't even need these.) They took a nature trail behind a subdivision. They trampled off the path, closer to a narrow stream, for no real reason. Perhaps some sort of subtle indignance blooming in both of them. Mud on her sister's Tretorns. A vague rotting, earthy smell. Nearly the end of the bergamot and purple asters and black-eyed Susans. Fall leaves nearby, perched on tree limbs, ready to make their escape to the ground.

They walked in silence for a while, trying not to trip in the darkness. Shelly said, "I'm sorry I was bothering you so much about your parents." They stopped walking. "Is it bad?" said Jess. "Like are they being bad parents? I can't even tell. I don't even notice when they're gone until I do. There's always, like, food in the fridge, money on the counter. I'm not starving. I have everything I need. They're just . . . out somewhere."

Shelly had never thought of Nancy and Robby as bad parents before. She couldn't even process the idea. They had seemed loving, they sent out holiday cards with their photo and updates about their lives—although it had been a few years since she had gotten one, but she had changed addresses a few times in there, too. But they went on vacations! They owned this home, which was clean and functional. Jess was a healthy kid.

But no one was watching her, that was clear. Shelly recognized the aloneness. It wasn't so bad, being alone, if you had something to concentrate on. She had no idea if Jess had talent, but there was nothing wrong with focusing on something, putting your mind somewhere safe. She didn't want her to get into any trouble. She would encourage her, she decided. She would buy her anything she wanted. Someday she would pay for her to go to London for the year to study in an art program. She would buy a painting at her first show (a group show, but still), quietly, so that one precious sticker would go up in the gallery and get the ball rolling, and then later hang the piece in her office at work. And when Jess would feel like giving up on it all, Shelly would tell her she absolutely couldn't. She had come too far, Shelly would tell her then. They had come too far.

"What would you think about me getting married?" said Shelly as they wove their way through a patch of clover.

Jess looked up at her aunt. "I've only ever known you as just you, by yourself," she said. "I like you that way. Who would you marry?"

"Asher." Jess and her parents had never met him because he lived in Seattle and their time together was too precious to him to share her, he said, whenever he came to town. But now she supposed they would all meet. "He's been in my life for a while. We're very . . . connected. And he would like to marry me. And maybe we would move to New York together eventually."

"No," said Jess. "I think I like having you here."

"I didn't even know that you cared," teased Shelly. But she hadn't. "Well, I might do it, we'll see."

"Aunt Shelly, don't do it unless you feel like it's going to fulfill your vision for yourself." She sounded like her mother. She had heard those exact words coming from her mother's mouth, straight out of one of her self-help books. What did it even mean? "Unless it's going to make you happy," said Jess, correcting herself. She wasn't sure what that meant either. To be happy.

•

THEY CROSSED INTO A NEW SUBDIVISION, SPILLING OUT ONTO a cul-de-sac. A block away, there was a house party. This is where the party must be, thought Jess. This is where all the kids in school are, in one house. "Let's go check it out," said Shelly.

They rounded the corner. People spilled out from all the edges and corners of one home. The rest were silent, lights out, but this house was alive in this dead quiet town, thought Shelly. They got closer, and she could see that the party guests were adults, and even closer, they could see Nancy, in a short skirt, laughing, with a few men.

"Mom!" Jess yelled, but the din of the party was loud, and it seemed like maybe Nancy squinted at the distance for a second and maybe she saw them, but surely she didn't? Because she went inside.

Now Shelly was frozen. Did they go forward or back? Did she want her sister to know that they had seen her? Did she want to admire her? To say: "I get it. I get wanting this. I get life is tedious. I get wanting to make something happen. I understand. I want to feel important, too."

She looked at Jess looking at the front porch, now empty. "Just a bunch of boring adults," said Shelly. "I'm beat, how about you?" Jess kicked the street with her tennis shoe. "How about I spend the night?" said Shelly, hustling her niece toward home. "Who knows when your mom will get back, and I don't think I can drive anyway and I don't know if I want to be alone either. We can make pancakes in the morning. We can do whatever you want. I just think I should stay."

"OK, you can stay," said Jess. Not sure what she had seen for a second. Happy to forget it. Put it away in a box, hide it in the crawl space.

•

IN HOUSTON, ROBBY ROSE WEARILY FROM A COUCH. HE thought of the woman asleep in the master bedroom. He had just bought the couch that day, and they had argued afterward, and she had suggested he sleep on it. Furnishing a home from scratch had been more expensive than he remembered. She didn't have expensive tastes though, this other woman, or rather, she was practical. The money could be better spent elsewhere. So at least he saved on that.

I should call home, he thought, and then grew dizzy thinking about where home actually was. He dialed the Chicago number; he hoped no one would wake up and he could just leave a message on the machine. His sister-in-law answered.

"Shell?" What the hell was she doing there?

"Robby, Jesus Christ, at last an adult. Did you know your child was at home all alone?"

"Where's Nancy?"

"She's asleep." He heard the crackle of a bag, and then she began to chew. "Where are you?"

"Houston, on business. I've been catching up on work all night. I'm sorry I didn't check in sooner. I thought Nancy would be there."

"I'm the only one that's up."

"How's Jess?"

"I think she's wondering where her father is," she said.

"She knows where I am." And that he knew to be true. He had talked to her the day before. They'd had a long conversation about how her classes were, what she was reading, what she was thinking, if she needed any money for school, what she was watching on television, their plans to see a movie next weekend, likely *Dead Poets Society*, because it was PG and about high school and he had seen the commercial when all the schoolboys stood on the desk and he liked the look of that, young men taking a stand about something. "I know what's going on with my daughter, all right? And she knows I'm in Houston."

"Don't yell at me," said Shelly, but he kept going, and so she held the phone away from her head so all she could hear was a wah-wah-wah sound bouncing around the quiet of the living room.

Finally, she got back on the phone.

"Your house is not tended to," she said. "That is all I want to say." She started crunching again.

But what did she know of houses, he thought. Her life was so loose and easy. She was willy-nilly and single. All her choices led her back to herself, and all of his led him to other people. What did she know of mortgages and birthday parties and holding hands with someone you don't love anymore? She had freedom. She did as she pleased.

•

IN THE MORNING, SHELLY ROSE, DISORIENTED, FROM THE couch. The living room was empty and quiet. It was early, she realized. No one would be up in the house, in the town. It was the first day of what would become cold weather. The heat wasn't on in the house, that's what had woken her. She was freezing. This house had been warm and happy enough just last year. She had driven out for a barbecue. Robby at the grill, Nancy finishing up the potato salad in the kitchen, the vinegary kind that Shelly liked. "I made this for you, Shell," said Nancy. "It's just gotta sit for a bit in the fridge." They were planning a vacation. Jess was still young enough to be open to everything. She didn't know how to lie, thought Shelly at the time. An innocent kid. Nancy was older, had looked after Shelly, understood how to build things, make a life happen not just for herself but for other people. Families just didn't sprout out of nowhere; they required work. Shelly understood that. I'm glad someone cares enough to make this kind of life happen. Having a family was like having an extra spine. If it was strong. If it could hold together.

She dug out the box of her father's robes from the crawl space and put them in the trunk of her car. They'd be safe with her.

Then she went upstairs, to the master bedroom, looking for her sister, and the bed was untouched. A dozen bright lipsticks on the mirrored dresser top. A vibrator sat on the bedside table. It was about the size of Shelly's forearm. She wandered down the hall to Jess's room, opened the door, and Jess was wide awake, but curled up in a ball. Thinking, processing, chewing on the truth of the night, now lit by day.

"Let's go shopping today," said Shelly. "I'll buy you a dress."

Jess nodded. She was a size six. She needed bras, too. And new underpants. And fall sweaters. And a notebook for math class. And hair clips to hold back her bangs from her face so she could see the world for the first time.

CHAPTER 9

1992

Margaret hugged Ian goodbye at the front door, a sea of vines hanging on the trellis overhead, threatening to collapse. He stroked her red hair, which he admired in particular. He said, simply, "Come back to me," and she promised she would. He was a kind man, older, loving. Eccentric, but so was she. He loved her. He took care of her. He did not send her away when she got sick four years ago. He'd looked after her. "Of course I will," she said.

She hoisted her backpack onto her shoulders and walked the six blocks to the tube. She took it to Paddington Station, transferred to the train to Heathrow, found a seat, sat down, smoothed down the back of her hair, as if to check if it were all there, if she were all there. Then she adjusted her bag between her legs, rested her head behind her, stared blank, calm, empty. She had been practicing being neutral lately. In all aspects of her life. She had brought one book with her, the same John Cage book of essays she had been reading forever, and a notebook, and she thought she'd get some work done. But once she got on the plane she took a Valium and drank a glass of wine—why had she pretended she wasn't going to do this?—and slept nearly until they landed. Now it was her first time back in America in more than two years—Jesus, was it nearly three? The last time she'd visited, Reagan was still president.

In New York she took a taxi into Manhattan, to an address on

Forty-Sixth Street, in Hell's Kitchen. Already her backpack felt heavy, and she still had a week to go with it. No whining, she thought. You have a schedule to keep. She had been given keys by Ian—this was his home. It was a vast loft space, big windows on one wall, with a view of the building across the street, still plenty of sunlight though. Paint chipping from the ceiling. A girl could really have a think in here, she thought as she poked around. When she was younger and had lived in New York, still in school, hungry for fun, drugs, she used to feel through coat pockets strewn on beds at parties. Her father had cut her off quick. She lived in a room with no windows on Tompkins Square Park. Bought her clothes at thrift stores. That was how she thought of New York, through that lens: struggling, hungry, but she was free.

Now look at her. An apartment just sitting there empty! All the room you could want. No one had been there for six months at least though, and it smelled stale. Nothing rotting though. It was just that the apartment needed some tending to, she thought. She opened the window. Noise rose from the street below. *There is always something to see, always something to hear*, as Mr. Cage had written in his book. No such thing as silence. She found it quite gentle, the chirp of traffic. The loft started to feel better. She put fresh sheets on the bed, linen, colored a chalky blue. A little comfort. She took a shower. There was only a bottle of Head and Shoulders in the shower and a dry splinter of soap and she used them as best she could to clean herself. An unsatisfactory bathing. It would have to do. She was in motion now.

She dug into her backpack. A thin, clinging, silk black dress with crisscross straps in the back and a pair of small, walkable heels. She forwent any undergarments. It was too hot out; they'd just get soaked through anyway. There was no hair dryer to be found. She put on some lipstick. She removed a small square envelope from the backpack and put it in her purse. She walked, with wet hair, over to Broadway and then down to the East Village, just south of Union Square. She didn't want to mess with the subways. The crime these days. And she wanted to see the city, see the life of it. A crosstown walk on a summer evening.

On Thirteenth Street, at the corner of Third, she stopped at an Italian restaurant. Her cousin, Corrine, was working there and knew she would be coming. Their mothers had been sisters. But they had met only a few times, so this would be easy, not too emotional, not much past between them to consider. "We really do look alike," said Margaret. They both had red, straight hair, with a nice fringe, and good shoulders and pleasant faces, direct gazes. They embraced, and Corrine sat her in the corner and then brought her a plate of penne pasta with pesto and a warm, powdery roll and a side of asparagus and a glass of red wine. Margaret fell upon it, and while she ate, Corrine spoke.

Corrine had been waiting tables at the restaurant for two years while she tussled with finally finishing her undergraduate degree at Hunter. "What were you doing before?" Margaret asked her. "This and that, here and there," said Corrine. An ex-husband in Denver. She had been hoping the degree would give her more purpose in her life. "But each class just shows me there's always more to learn. It's endless." Margaret, nodding, just listening. Corrine thought she might just keep studying all different kinds of things. Hunter was cheap, and she liked this restaurant. Her apartment was an uncomfortable situation though: the landlord was unreliable, and the apartment was in the basement, the hot water pipes for the entire building running through it. "I keep burning myself on them. Here, look." She held out an arm. Three plump red scars. But on the other hand, she was barely home between work and school. It was just a place to sleep.

Margaret said, "I'm staying in this apartment that is almost always empty, it's really just a crash pad for people passing through that know the owner. He's . . . a friend of mine. Well, he's my person, I suppose." Difficult to explain. "There are two bedrooms. I could ask if he'd be interested in renting it to you." But Corrine didn't like the idea of roommates or unknown people passing through even briefly. "I prefer to deal with the devil I know," she said. "Well, if you change your mind," said Margaret. The idea of providing a home to someone seemed valuable to her. "I won't, but thanks," said Corrine. "I appreciate you looking out for me."

"Of course, we're family," said Margaret. "Speaking of which." She pulled the envelope from her purse. "A little surprise for you." She handed it to Corrine. "I've been dragging it around with me forever. I could have mailed it to you, I suppose. But I was afraid it would get lost, and it's the only copy. I thought it would be nice to see each other face-to-face, too," she said. Ian had suggested it, actually.

"It is nice," said Corrine, grasping Margaret's hand.

Oh well, now they were starting to feel things. Inside the envelope was a picture of their mothers as young women. Corrine's mother was graduating from high school in the photo, and Margaret's mother was a few years older and already engaged to Margaret's father, who would steal her away to New Mexico soon enough, where her mother's sickness would surface, and he would never tell her family how bad it was until it was too late, and she was nearly gone. Corrine's mother died a few years after Margaret's mother. There had been a car accident, broken bones, pain that followed and lingered forever. The sadness from a lost sister, too. And then she took her own life. Both their brains took them away from their daughters. "I've always felt like it was my job to live because she couldn't," said Corrine, wiping a boiling-hot tear from her face. It had turned out dramatic after all, thought Margaret. You never know with family.

"Does that make sense?" said Corrine. "I understand perfectly," said Margaret.

She tried to pay for dinner. Corrine refused her. "If you ever need anything, don't hesitate to ask," said Margaret. They hugged good-bye. Now they felt related. Now they felt connected. In a month a theme would appear in the composition she was working on, just show itself to her without her even realizing it was happening, and then she would think: Oh, this is what Corrine means to me.

She headed farther downtown, toward Ludlow Street, to a club, for an early show. A cool easy nighttime breeze was blowing. She felt in love with the city. She was jet-lagged but used to keeping late hours. She settled into the night. She slipped into her American self. She felt less apologetic here. Everyone just took what they wanted here. Why couldn't she do that, too?

The club's exterior looked like a grocery store, probably had been one once. There were some kids hanging out in front smoking, holding beer bottles and plastic cocktail cups, drained save for wedges of lime. White T-shirts and blue jeans and Chuck Taylors or combat boots, even in the heat. The uniforms of the boys and the girls. She was overdressed, had known it when she threw on the dress, but she wanted to tangle with the feeling of being older now. They noticed her, one or two of them recognized her maybe. She had been a student like them once, too. They were all the same anyway, she and the rest of them: they were all here to see their teacher perform.

She paid five dollars to get in. She would have paid a thousand dollars. Francisco didn't care where he played, just as long as he could keep playing. He played symphony halls and dirty downtown lofts and open fields in front of an array of folding chairs and in his brain all the time. Some shows were better than others. Some shows people talked all the way through, and he didn't even notice, he said. If it happened to her, Margaret would notice. She couldn't tell if he was telling the truth or not. How could he not notice?

This show everyone was paying attention. He was working on something new. The audience was mainly acolytes, she thought. What she liked about a lot of his work was that even though he had a specific, singular vision, it was all about collaboration. His compositions were written as deliberate instructions to the performers, maps, like to hidden treasure, and the treasure was a piece of music. The song did not exist without the input of those playing it. She didn't know how to do that, really. She didn't know how to work with other people anymore. She had become too inward.

Francisco started playing the same few notes over and over on a synthesizer and then occasionally a musician would walk onstage and play a different solo, guitar, saxophone, drums, whatever, she lost count, she stopped paying attention, she was bored, it was boring, like a run-on sentence, she thought, a string of questions contained within it, but she stood there anyway listening, because he knew she was there, he had spotted her, and she did not come all this way to be a bad audience member.

And then by the end of the show, just at the tip of it, all of the sounds began to make sense; some musicians got back onstage together, there were some new loops being played, more musicians, more layers, everything was thick now, and it became a gorgeous cacophony. Because that's what Francisco did with his music, he worked on a problem until he solved it. And in listening to all of this, Margaret solved a small problem she had in her own work. It was just one of many problems to solve, but it was a start.

Later they sat on the edge of the stage talking. People congratulated him or told him "nice show" or waved hello occasionally and then it died down and it was just the two of them. Francisco had punky jet-black hair; she was sure he was dyeing it by now. God, how old was he? Fifties? Sixties? His face was heavily lined. She wondered if things were bad or good for him, but she dared not ask. This was not the nature of their relationship. He kept his students at bay. She was sure she would always be his student.

He asked after Ian, had stayed with him before, sent him his regards. Then he asked about her work, her life. She did not mention the hard stuff. That there were some days when she was productive and happy and alive, and there were some days when she felt dead inside. And there were some days where she wasn't sure why she started making music in the first place, and there were some days where she was certain she'd die if she ever stopped. And there were some days when she had so many ideas she didn't know what to do with all of them, too many. On those days she had to sit still and stare at the wall. It was just up and down. Her brain had problems, she felt, she knew. Making music took a long time except it was going faster than anything else in the world. Everything was hard until it got easy. Everything was easy until it got hard.

Instead, she said, "I am making this album—I think it's about my family." "Ripe material," he said. "You can't outrun your family." He hung his head down for a second, nodding, then popped back up. "What else you got?" he said. "I'm trying to be more neutral in my mind now," said Margaret. "I still want to have a point of view, but I want to have fewer feelings about everything. I'm trying to be loveless."

A car squealed outside at the last part. Francisco leaned in. "Bloodless?" he said. "Loveless," she repeated. He closed his eyes and nodded for a second. "Well," he said. "That doesn't sound like you." "Maybe I'm changing," she said. He put his hand on her bare shoulder. "No one changes that much."

•

THE NEXT MORNING, SHE TOOK A CAB TO THE AIRPORT, SLEPT
again on the plane as it crossed the country, and woke just before
it arrived in Seattle. She took another car to a hotel on First Hill.
Quiet with a pristine glossy piano in the bar. Walking distance to
the waterfront. Margaret tossed her bag on her bed. Unzipped a
side pocket, dug around in it for a set of keys, made sure they were
still there. Took a shower. Took another nap. It was so quiet. She
listened to the quiet. What time was it? Her body had no idea. Alas,
she had to collapse again.

In the morning, she called Ian collect.

"I made it to Seattle," she said.

"Oh, thank god you called," he said. They hadn't been apart for
this long before. He trusted her, but he worried. He had been looking out for her so long he didn't know how to exist without knowing
where she was.

Years ago he had offered her studio space after seeing her perform in London. He did this kind of thing all the time. An inheritance
from his family made it possible. A studio in the back house. She
took the idea of work seriously, she told him. And she was happy to
leave Seattle. "There's nothing left for me here," she told him. She
was grateful for the chance. So she came to London and worked. All
hours of the day and night. This concerned him, but he was the one
who had invited her to make her music and so he could not argue
with it. He had met people like her before. He was like her. A person who liked to be left alone with their work. So he felt obligated
to respect it. Then she didn't sleep for a few days. He would wake
up in the middle of the night and see the light was still on, and he
could hear some tinkering, some crashing. He wanted to give her
privacy. He had his own matters to tend to. But he thought: maybe
I should check on her. Maybe I should give her a little of my attention. It costs me nothing but time. And he walked from the front

house to the back house, down a brick walkway lined with ivy, and past a small seating area where the ivy parted and there was a gap between buildings and the sun broke through all around him and he paused at the door, because once he knocked, he had knocked, and there was no taking it back. But he thought maybe she just might need some help. She did not answer, and he knocked again, and then finally she opened the door and she was pale and drawn and distressed and her eyes seemed like they might burst straight from her skull and her hair was sticky and he could smell her, smell this foul, unwashed, nervous scent, animalistic, like a dirty, lost dog. Some chunks of her hair pulled out, her scalp bleeding. Bits of red in the red. He said, "Dear, are you all right?" And she shook her head slowly no.

He took care of her then. He did not send her away. He had a doctor he knew come to her. Same as her mother, it came out somewhere along the way. This kind of obsession and anxiety. Anything could have triggered it. Being so far away from home, all alone in the back house. He would look after her, he promised. She could stay there until she got well, and if she wanted to work on her music then of course she could but it did not matter either way. Now she was in his home, and he was responsible for her.

Sometimes you just throw in with people. Sometimes you just have to trust them.

Soon enough he was buying her all the equipment she could ever want. Now she was making new kinds of toys to play with. Tinkering. It all took time. But he could wait.

•

IN SEATTLE, SHE SAID, "I NEED COFFEE, OR I'LL NEVER MAKE IT to where I'm supposed to be." They only spoke for a few minutes, but she could tell he was relieved, and she liked to make him feel good, feel safe, as he did for her.

She walked to Capitol Hill and down Broadway, all the telephone poles tattered with flyers—missing dogs, club nights, rock-and-roll shows. A few kids asleep on the street. Vivace was open, and nothing else. She had two espressos. Flirted with the barista, who had been working there for years. How had someone from Berlin ended up in Seattle? But he had. It was nice to see him. She admired his golden beard. He knew who she was. Had seen her play a few times. There was something about being recognized as that version of herself, just the musician, the artist, that thrilled her. She had a name, and he knew it.

He told her he had a show that night. "Ah, I'm hitting the road." "Next time," he said, and handed her a CD. "Look out for us." "I will," she said, and shoved some money in his tip jar.

At the hotel, she packed up her bag. Don't stop and think, she thought. Don't stop and feel. Be neutral. She took another cab. This time to a storage unit in the direction of the airport. She jangled the keys as she walked to the unit. Pushed up the garage door. There she was. Her car. Her little Mini.

·

SHE DROVE THROUGH IDAHO AND UTAH IN TWO DAYS. SHE DID nothing but drive. She spoke to no one. She just drove. When she hit Denver, she thought: if I turn off here, I can get on 25, I can drive to New Mexico, I can visit Dad. But she owed him money. And she owed him this car. That she had stolen in the night when she was twenty-two, on her way to Pittsburgh for a graduate school program she would never finish. She had asked him for it, and he had said no, and then she took it anyway. If she saw him now, she thought they would just fight, and that would be bad for her, bad for her feelings. Before she knew it, she had already missed the turnoff. It was the only chance she had to see him, but she didn't know that at the time. He would die in a year, and she would become an orphan—that was how she would feel, even though she was nearly thirty—and she would regret this experiment for the rest of her life, that time she tried to feel nothing. She would be marked by it. That time I could have seen him and didn't. It informed her work for years to come. She talked about it once in an interview and regretted revealing so much about herself. She was trying to talk about how she was interested in the noise between the noises. The weight of the emptiness. She veered off though. "In avoiding conflict, we sometimes create a new conflict," she said. Then she felt she had revealed too much. That time she missed the turnoff.

Now it was the weekend, and she arrived in New Orleans, at a hotel on the edge of the French Quarter, off Decatur Street. She could feel the heat outside before she even opened the door in the parking lot. It was going to be a sweaty couple of days. The lobby was small and moist and there were potted plants everywhere and a smattering of French-looking dusty porcelain lamps, with a small service setup in the back, a hand-carved wooden bar lit by a chandelier dripping with wrought iron flowers. She stopped first for a drink, and the front desk clerk left his duties and served her a gin and tonic with two slices of lime that he cut fresh. Lots of ice. He gave her a double without asking. It tasted so good that she decided it was the thing she would drink for the next two days. That and beer, but beer in cans, cold. She would strive for a sense of cool, a temperature of cool. Just here to drop off her car, and then return to London, where she would stay for the next dozen years. She was done with America for a while.

I am neutral, she thought. She ordered another drink. No one knew where she was right now, she liked that feeling. She hadn't told him about this part of the plan. Lately he was always checking in on her. He respected her space, still let her work in that back house, but now he wanted to know how her day was and what she had done with it. But he had no idea what she was doing now. She could be doing anything.

Then she heard her name and a wild laugh and then Shelly scooped her up in her arms, kissed her on her cheeks, rubbed her shoulders, an engagement ring occupying significant real estate on her hand. "Look at you, aren't you a sight," she said, and laughed some more. "When were you going to tell me when you got here? How dare you make me wait a second!" And then, at last, Margaret felt anything but neutral.

•

TWO DAYS LATER, SHELLY AND MARGARET WATCHED THE DAY break from a bench in Jackson Square. They were still in last night's clothes. Matching cinnamon-colored bodysuits, glitter all over them. Liquored up and rubbery with each other. The street vendors rolled in and began to claim their space beneath the St. Louis Cathedral, where the bells rang every fifteen minutes, to Margaret's great pleasure. At the doors of the church a couple stared up at the snowy white steeples overhead. Shelly squinted at the couple. A familiar face. "I swear to god that's my fucking brother-in-law," said Shelly.

Robby and his companion were dressed tidily, overdressed for the summer. She wore a linen dress with a blousy top and a swinging skirt, and he was in a summer suit and tie. He looked bloated and older, and the woman was younger, maybe thirty, if that. She was Black, and she wore her hair in a chignon, and was thin and elegant. Perhaps a little bony. Shelly realized she and Margaret were intertwined, sweaty, high, and still shimmering from the robustness of their night out, and she began to extricate herself from their embrace. Robby saw her, too—she saw him see her from afar. He took the woman by the arm and led her in another direction.

"Wild," said Shelly. "That's wild." She thought about how she had watched her sister flirt from a distance a few years before. Had never bothered to ask her about that, and she would never ask Robby about this. Who knew what went on in people's marriages? What they had agreed to in private.

"What do you think?" said Margaret. Shelly thought about all that she would have to explain to her sister about her being in New Orleans herself. The glint of her ring in the sting of the morning sun. "I didn't see nothing," she said.

CHAPTER 10

1995

They had a good time there for a few years, Frieda and Ray, a man she met in line at the grocery while they were both pie-eyed, their carts filled with snacks. "The most successful love affair of my life," he told her. "No muss, no fuss." They both liked vodka. One big bottle to share. The daytime hours were passed at his home, on the back patio, a sliding glass door to the kitchen behind them, where the bottles and the mixers and the ice sat, ten tall palm trees in front of them. Naked most days, shielded from his neighbor's eyes by the shrubbery, dousing themselves in bug spray, drinking vodka tonics, and letting it all hang out. He told her every morning she was beautiful and sexy, and she nearly believed him. After the stock market had closed for the day and he had made his last call, they went to the bar at sunset. There, he was a good-time guy and she was quiet, by his side. A beat-up middle-aged lady, funny if you got her talking, clever, even. Willing to put up with her man bragging about his financial success and world travel even though he always seemed to be in Florida and nowhere else. He tipped well, she nodded at his jokes. She was pliable and easy at that point in her life. The anger wrung out of her. How had she survived the past? But she had. He made sure she was taken care of. Drunks, but they functioned. They were both alive and dead at the same time. In this way they worked.

But he passed out earlier than her, leaving her alone to be manipulated by her demons. What kind of mother she had been. What had happened to her life? Would her daughters ever forgive her? How did she end up in this house? This was a home, but not hers. She could have used more company at times like that. Once in a while, she smacked him awake. "Frieda, what do you want? Woman, leave me be," he said. What good would it do if they both stayed up late? But what was the point of being with this person, going all in like this, if he wouldn't sit with her through the hard times? Still, in the mornings they held each other, laughing about their bad breath, sipping their Bloody Marys to start the day, and then they were close again.

She moved in with him after a few months. She needed a place to stay that was stable: that they could both agree upon. She had bad credit and had been fired from too many jobs. Now, when she worked, it was as a home aide for one of the worst agencies in South Florida, making a pittance, a temp for hire, often walking into desperate situations, clients who had been given up on by other aides. Sometimes it felt dangerous. Should she stay in his home for a while, just until she could get on her feet again? They both knew she would probably never leave.

Soon after she moved in, her daughter Nancy started leaving messages, looking for her, threatening to come down there. It had made Ray nervous, someone poking around in their life. "You should call her back every so often," he said. "I know she isn't so nice to you on the phone, but they like to know we're still alive." She hated calling her daughters because they never sounded happy to talk to her. But she listened to Ray—it was his home, after all—and started reaching out to her Nancy and Shelly, waiting for their voices to warm to her again someday. Now they were checking in on each other. Keeping tabs.

She found herself wanting to keep tabs on Ray, too. Not because she didn't trust him with other women, but because his mind wandered at times, and physically he did, too. Like he got in his goddamn car when she wasn't looking. Another DUI and he'd be in jail for a while. A narrow escape one night when the police had set up checkpoints on the Venetian Causeway. Luckily he had shaved that morning. He always looked a mess when he was unshaven. No handsome stubble for Ray, just a grizzled, uneven jaw, loose skin beneath the neck speckled with gray. He was a drunk who looked like a drunk. He made it home barely. She was too tired to yell. A little cat-and-mouse game, she thought, where he wanted to destroy his life and she wanted to stop him.

The morning after he had escaped the sobriety test, the invitation showed up in the mail. Shelly's wedding. Frieda asked him to come meet her family, and he agreed without pause. A party in Chicago? He was in. "We can't do it like this though," she said. "We can't go looking like this, being like this." A horror show of bottles, all over the house. She was too skinny, a tooth had fallen out, her skin was mottled. She had only known him one way, looking the way he had, so she couldn't say if he looked better or worse, but he reeked of booze. "We have to make a change," she said. He agreed to get sober with her for the wedding, knowing from past experience that he could do it easily but also that it would never stick. You never know though. Maybe this time it would.

The wedding was at the Drake. "Fancy, fancy," said Frieda. A small banquet room, immediate family members only: Shelly, with a tight smile and enormous hair; her new husband, Asher, a short, muscle-bound, Sephardic-as-hell man who had planned the entire wedding; her granddaughter, Jess, quiet, artsier now, a few piercings in each ear, who had taken the train in by herself from the suburbs to see her beloved aunt get married. Nancy didn't show because Nancy was mad at Shelly about something, but no one would tell her what, or maybe nobody knew. She thought: How hard is it to get my whole family in the room together? Impossible. Same with Asher's family: the only representative from his side was his wheelchair-bound mother, Mariam, her hair piled high, enormous diamonds in her ears, who was silent the entire night, whispering only a few times into Asher's ear. A small string quartet played. They were served chicken entrées and ice cream in silver dishes, but everyone barely touched their food, except for Ray. Shelly was drinking a lot, seemed dissatisfied with something, her hair, her dress, her skin, something. She seemed itchy. She snapped at Asher once. But then there was a sweet toast from Asher to Shelly. He told a story about first seeing Shelly sitting at a bar in a restaurant by herself through a window. He had been on his way to meet a friend at another restaurant down the block, but he rerouted himself to sit at her bar instead. "What the hell, I thought. Maybe this gorgeous girl will talk to me. And I never made it to that dinner." "I never heard that story before," said Shelly. "I figured I'd save it for our wedding night," said Asher. Everyone ahhed. He raised his glass and said he would follow her to the ends of the earth, and then he gave her a simple peck, his hand brushing her cheek. "This is really real," said Ray, and he started laughing and so did Frieda, and everyone smiled at the both of them because it was nice to see Frieda upright at last.

Frieda gazed on her child and grandchild, feeling like she might be allowed to love them again. Of the actual marriage she thought: Well, that's not going to last. They both wanted to be in charge, it was clear, and something would have to give. But she was happy to be invited. She was proud to have Ray with her. He wore a suit with a cravat. He was a businessman for all intents and purposes. She wore a pink silk dress with a drop waist she had purchased at Burdines with Ray's credit card and had dyed her hair bright red. Her skin was clearer. Her family told her how gorgeous she looked. They made promises to meet again. On the flight home Ray asked her if she wanted to get married, and she said yes.

They told no one. They married at a justice of the peace a month later. And that night, they drank champagne like idiots. A hundred and fifty days of sobriety gone. "Oh well," she said. "Oh well," he said. "It was worth it," he said, but was it? She was worried it would start all over again. She sat back and waited for them to start drinking like monsters and for everything to go to shit.

•

"BUT THEN GOD STEPPED IN," SHE TOLD THE AIDE AT HIS BEDSIDE. "God said enough already." Early-onset dementia. A series of small strokes. She could not believe she had been taking care of another dying man, more dying people, her whole life, but here they were. For a while, she hadn't even noticed what she had become to him. It had happened so slowly over the past year, that she was watching over him instead of living with him, partnering with him. They had known he would get sick, that there was a vague time frame, and he had started to forget more and more, sure, but he was still all there, all present. Maybe six months after the diagnosis, now there would be moments where he was clearly not present, frozen in his thoughts inside his head, and his face was pained, and he was somewhere else, not here, not now, even though his flesh was present, and these moments crushed her, watching the fear in his eyes as he searched through his mind for whatever the present tense looked like. "What can I get you," she would say to him, but then soon enough she stopped responding to those moments, would watch him for a while and then turn around and busy herself at the kitchen counter till whatever was happening had passed. His face wavering back and forth between lucidity and disorientation. His discomfort. All those older patients she had tended to over the years, but she had never spent days on end with them. Sometimes he would say her name over and over and sometimes that of his ex-wife, who he hadn't seen in a decade. He was looking for care. He was looking for help. She would wander into the room and ask him what he needed, but then he would shake his head. Nothing. He had already forgotten he had said her name. It was just a refrain perhaps. Frieda. She looked for patience then. She had never heard her name so many times in a day. Sometimes she held his hand, other times she ignored him entirely. How would she ever even know when he really needed her? She would find out when it was time.

They would talk about these moments afterward. He told her she could never leave him alone, and she agreed. They began to get their groceries delivered. They walked side by side around the neighborhood and down to the beach. They sat at matinees together. It wasn't a bad life they had. She fed him fruit salad. Once they went to Disney World but he stayed in the restroom for too long and she had to send someone in to find him. It was embarrassing for him, and she didn't want him to feel that way. She wanted grace and dignity for him. *Bikur cholim*. It was a mitzvah to take care of the sick and dying. When he grew less mobile, she sat in the living room while he napped and read whatever was around. She visited the library once or twice a week. Once a man knocked on the door offering magazine subscriptions for sale to benefit a local church and she said, "I'll take whatever you've got."

Her daughters checked in on her more now, fretted over her. Nancy more than Shelly. Do you need help? Do you need another you to help with Ray? But she felt like there could be only one her. She couldn't figure out what it would look like, what she would ask them to do, even though she had been an aide her entire adult life. How would she hand any of these tasks off to someone else? How could she let go of the one thing that was keeping her in control of her small but still important universe?

•

NANCY FLEW DOWN ONCE. RUDY WOULD HAVE WANTED HER to, Nancy felt. Rudy, everyone still thought about Rudy all the time. She shuddered at the dimness of the house and opened the curtains almost immediately. She noted her mother's physique: she was not fat, but she was slack, round and loose and fleshy. That woman needs some exercise, she thought. Not for the first time, Nancy thought about how she would end up taking care of her mother when she was old. She felt a ripple of resentment. Shelly and her high-flying ways, she thought.

They sat at the kitchen table and ate leftovers, grilled chicken from a Styrofoam container heated in a microwave and then dropped on two plates. "I meant to cook," said her mother faintly. "I didn't come for the food," said Nancy. "There's dessert anyway," said her mother. "I got a coffee cake." There was an open bottle of wine on the counter, but no one drank from it. They tried to remember the last time they had seen each other. "I thought I would have seen you at Shelly's wedding but no," said her mother. "Mother, I'm not discussing that with you," said Nancy. "I should have cooked," said her mother, again. Neither one of them finished their chicken.

After lunch, she told her mother to go for a walk while she sat with Ray. Her mother said she would be back in a half hour, tops. Ray slept for a while, and Nancy thought of her own father, how they had sat with him at the hospital, how he was awake and aware as he passed, clearly in pain until he was not. Rudy had loved them, and Nancy sat for a while, thinking of that love. In his eyes, she was perfect, pretty, well-mannered, a little sweetheart. Impossible to hold on to that feeling forever, but she allowed herself to linger in the sensation. Nancy wondered if she would ever love someone again. She was doing so well on her own now. What did she need a man for? Habitually, she wanted it. Her father's love, maybe.

Nancy had a notebook with her, and she wrote down her feelings, which she thought she might use somehow. Maybe they would help her understand what was going on in that moment. A funny idea, using your feelings. She thought maybe her mother was replaying her father's death, replaying all the people she had tended to in her life, by looking after this man. That her mother might be stuck in a loop.

She wrote down, "How do we break our patterns?"

Eventually Ray woke and smiled. They spoke of the weather, and of their garden, all the fruit trees, which astonished Nancy, now adrift in a small condo in downtown Chicago, a few potted plants on the balcony. It had been an hour, and then two, and then three, and Nancy noticed somewhere in there that her mother hadn't taken her phone with her, and she wondered for a moment if her mother might not come back, or if she had gone to a bar. But then she returned, apologizing. "I don't get a lot of time off, it felt luxurious," she said, and Nancy was glad she had come to visit. To offer this one piece of help.

•

FRIEDA TOOK CARE OF HIM FOR ANOTHER THREE YEARS. TIME compressed itself. She had a small life that she built. Financial stability at last, because of Ray. A friendship again with Carolina, after she sent her a check—double what she owed her—and a letter begging for her forgiveness. Carolina, now, at last, an administrator. With a companion named Tevan who aggressively opened doors for her. "A younger man knows what an older woman is worth," said Carolina, who made zero apologies for her choices in her life by then. A relief to know someone with that kind of confidence, thought Frieda.

Aides and physical therapists came and went. A new cat showed up in her life, a calico. She became invested in the garden, and the cat would sit and watch her as she worked, his orange tail wagging off the flies. The fruit trees she grew from scratch or the older ones that had offered mealy fruit, she fertilized them and nurtured them. Had solar panels installed on the house, why not? Got more thoughtful about what she ate and where it came from and what she was feeding this dying man. A few raised beds out back to grow her own food. A casual interest in the land. Not a job, but work. She thought about the difference between the two. She hired a business advisor to look through all Ray's dealings. He had lived humbly, but his accounts were full. Ray had made money off his money. Investments that would feed her bank account for years. Not a lot, but enough. A steady stream. It all seemed unfair because it was too easy. "Spend all my money," he told her. Still, she had no idea where she would turn after he died. She kept drinking, sometimes more, sometimes less, drank all the way through it, to the end.

When he passed, she was with him, holding his hand. I honor you, she thought. And I will not go through this again.

•

"THIS IS THE LAST DRINK I'LL HAVE," SHE SAID TO HER DAUGHter Shelly after his family funeral back east. Catholic, buried in a plot in Rochester. A space already waiting for him next to his ex-wife.

"Sounds good," said Shelly. "Whatever you say, Mom."

"I'm surprised you came," she said to Shelly, who had flown up from the city, taken a day off from work and everything. She had barely known Ray, let alone his family. "What? I can show up for you," said Shelly. "I care about you."

Now she was in her thirties, married, boring, bored, plucked chins from her hair on occasion, and had so much money in the bank. Frieda asked after her husband, and she observed her daughter's ambivalence. "Sometimes I wonder if I fight with him just to make it feel like something is really happening between us," said Shelly. She had come down to visit only twice when Ray was sick. Had offered to fly her mother anywhere she liked. A trip around the world. But Shelly could not deal with this dying man.

Frieda asked about her job, and Shelly lit up. "Can I tell you a story?" said Shelly.

The day before, Shelly had sat in on a meeting about battery life. The problem wasn't that the battery life wouldn't last forever. Everyone knew that. Not a single modern mechanical invention could exist without at least some kind of power source, even if that power source was natural, like the wind or the sun. The problem they were discussing was how much battery life people would be willing to pay for, or how much battery life they would be willing to tolerate having (or not having) attached to their phone.

"So then I said, 'Maybe we don't tell them it's not very long. Maybe we say that in fact what we're giving them is a long time. Maybe we tell them we're actually giving them exactly what they want. And then they just believe it.' They looked scared of me, Mom," said Shelly. "And that's how I knew I was right." She had spent all those years trying to make them like her as a person, be fond of her, friendly toward her, and then it turned out all she had to do was freak them out.

"Sounds like you're making a real impression," said Frieda. "A true success story."

Shelly didn't tell her about a phone call she had gotten that day from a coworker back in Seattle, one of the many women who had arrived after she had moved to Chicago. Tova, a Stanford grad who had served in the Israeli army. A decent and smart person, in Shelly's opinion. "He's back at it, again," said Tova. Monroe was fucking *everyone*.

Tova, the truth teller. With her brisk haircut and staccato accent and a dark, thick, but somehow still attractive or at least intriguing, mole above her lip. Tova in the dark suits and comfortable flats. Everyone just took her seriously. Shelly felt like she'd had to fight for it more. Maybe she'd made it easier for Tova somehow. She'd like to believe that was true, anyway.

This was not a story for Frieda though.

"Can you believe I started working there when I was barely an adult?" said Shelly to Frieda.

"You were never just a teenager anyway," said Frieda. "Being a teenager confused you. You went straight to adulthood." Shelly's eyes got bigger; her mother was right. "That's true, isn't it. I never realized it quite that way before."

"That's what mothers are good for, telling you who you once were so you know who you are now," said Frieda, and it suddenly occurred to her that she might have something these girls of hers would want after all, which was information about them. "A mother notices these things."

"When she's not drinking she notices these things," said Shelly.

"Even when she's drinking, but yes," said Frieda.

Was there an apology forthcoming, or would this acknowledgment suffice? They both waited to see what would happen next. But it would take years for an apology. At least it showed up when it did.

PART IV

EMERGENCIES

CHAPTER 11
1999

Three women walked through the park together: Shelly, her old friend Margaret, and her niece Jess, all in search of a cold pond. A sunny day in Hampstead Heath. Dogs ran off leash, and there were wildflowers everywhere and the air was a gentle embrace. The women swerved and converged and separated again on the dirt path, but there was forward motion. It was May.

They'd had drinks with lunch and then Margaret had suggested the swim, and they'd stopped off at her house, where she'd run in to get them bathing suits. Jess had asked to use the bathroom and Margaret had said there was one at the park. Closed the gate behind her without another word.

"I don't understand why this Ian guy won't invite us in," said Jess. "Because he's home and he doesn't like guests," said Shelly. "Have you ever met him?" said Jess. "No, and I don't think I want to," said Shelly, and she was trying to sound breezy, but then she added, "This is part of why I wanted to visit. I've been worried about her for months. We used to write letters to each other all the time, and now it's just a phone call here, an email there. Something's changed." The front door opened. "Of course, don't say anything, Jess," said Shelly, putting on a smile. "Let's just go to the park and swim."

Margaret returned with a backpack and joined them at the front gate of the house. Wisteria bushes weeping in full bloom on either side. "He's working right now and can't be disturbed but sends his regards," she said. A flat tone. It was hard to read Margaret, Jess would tell Shelly later. "You just have to learn to read between the lines," insisted Shelly. "And when she opens up she shows you everything."

Shelly was the emotive one though, thought Jess. Demonstrative and vocal and physical. As cool as she could be at work, but get her alone, put a drink in her especially, and she'd let everything spill. Shower you with attention. Give you a hug whether you wanted one or not.

Shelly had arrived the night before and was still groggy. The swim was supposed to fix her jet lag. Shelly and Margaret were talking about the last time they saw each other, six years previous. "New Orleans," said Shelly, and Margaret gave a husky, conspiratorial laugh.

"What happened in New Orleans?" said Jess.

"Oh, we just had fun," said Shelly.

Another laugh between them. A dirty little laugh. Had it been that long? Had they been that young?

"Whatever you say, party girls," said Jess.

Shelly thrust her arms around the women, delighted. "I can't believe I get to see the two of you at once," she said. She had come to visit them both in one fell swoop, and then afterward would head to Paris, where her husband would meet her, and where they would shop and see some art and fight, consistently, for days, and then fuck beautifully at night in their extravagant hotel room. Her husband won't understand what's wrong with her, or why she's being such a bitch when she was the one who had suggested the vacation in the first place. Shelly won't understand why she's behaving that way either, why she can't just be happy when she gets what she wants, but she won't tell him that. She will wonder if they are broken, the two of them, or if she is just broken all on her own, and one night she will sob after sex, and then they will both lie there confused, in Paris, beneath gilded bedposts.

But first, she will swim in a pond with her niece in London. And Margaret. Hello again, Margaret. Tall, pale, thin, with her orange hair and enormous eyes and tiny diamond studs and gold hoops running down her ears. Lean Margaret. So full of ideas. How she had missed her.

•

AS THEY WALKED IN THE SUNSHINE, THEY CHATTED EASILY BUT without any real purpose. Jess hadn't had a relaxed day like this in a while. Margaret was pointing out plants and birds occasionally, goldfinches, skylarks, cocking her head at the sounds of the thrushes, and then the conversation would meander on another path, about what Margaret was working on, new sounds, new ideas, new equipment. Margaret spoke for a while about making her album. How many hours she'd spent on it, thousands upon thousands. She had built new computers and written new software to make the sounds she wanted. "I'm still building instruments in Max," she told Shelly. "You're making me miss coding," said Shelly. Margaret talked about her ambitions for it, but also how she was disappointed in herself because she wasn't finished yet. She had released bits of it along the way, but it had been ten years. "I have to concentrate very hard," said Margaret. "Or my mind will ping-pong all over the place." To Jess, she did not sound like she was enjoying making it—if she ever had. She was trying to be a great artist, a great musician, said Margaret. But she couldn't be great all the time though. "I'm hoping it all balances out," she said. "I'm just shooting for OK in the end." "I want us all to be more than OK," said Shelly.

Jess wanted to ask her why she made music in the first place.

How she knew that was what she wanted to do. She was interested in why anyone did anything at all. Doing postgraduate work had made her realize her ambitions were less clear or realistic than those of her classmates.

"I like the idea of being successful, but I'm not sure what my driving force is." She wondered if someone else's purpose could somehow seep into her own. "Your driving force is you're smart and talented," said Shelly confidently. "It doesn't work that way," said Margaret gently. Now Jess was getting the point of Margaret. She was the one who was allowed to disagree with her aunt. She hadn't even known that was possible before.

London had been good for Jess, regardless of her confusion. First thing, she finally shaved off all her hair. Took care of that nonsense almost immediately. Her entire life people had commented on it. She supposed they were compliments. It had felt like attention anyway. It was curly hair with a little wave to it, and she wore it long and it made her feel female, feminine, like a girl. And she was that. She knew how she felt about her body and her insides and the way she wanted to carry herself in the world and the way she felt talking to a man and the way she felt talking to a woman and how she would like to be seen by everyone and where she got her power from and where her weaknesses lay and how that all related to being a woman, a twenty-two-year-old woman, which she now was. But the hair bothered her. It got in her way at the studio and it tangled all around her when she was on her bike, and she didn't like that she twisted it nervously and it was just way too present on her head, in her life. Also, it was a thing her mother liked, a thing her mother admired when she understood so little else about her. She had lived with her mother for a few months before she left for London, and when she cut half her hair off that summer—just to her shoulders!—her mother had freaked out.

But her hair was the most obvious thing about her, thought Jess. It blocked people from seeing anything else. The hair had to go. It went. No one said a thing. Not one of her new art school cohort. She had only been in London a few days when she shaved it all off, so they barely remembered it as it was. Soon enough the hair was forgotten.

Then there were the tattoos, which, if her mother would have hated her shaving her head, she would absolutely murder her for that. But to her, these lines were memories and ideas and a personal history that she would carry around with her, present on her skin, for as long as she was alive. Being away from home, knowing that she wouldn't have to see her mother, emancipated Jess fully. Now she could make decisions in the moment without fear of getting reviewed or criticized for them later. She needed to make them and get used to them on her own without hearing her mother's voice in her head. How far away did she need to go to escape her? This far. How long would it take to turn her physical self into something she actually recognized? Longer than this year. But at least she could start.

She was making a map of something in her work and it was spilling over onto her skin. She was trying to make her way to a kind of complete feeling. Knowing that she would never be done, knowing even then that completion was never attained in life, but there were moments when certain things could be finished. Her art, her projects, these small drawings on her flesh. A tattoo shop on Shoreditch High Street. A man named Georgie with a gray rockabilly pompadour who called her "love," and she felt like maybe he meant it? She had taken a few bar shifts so she could afford the work he was doing on her. She had never minded hard work. Hard work on her art, hard work to pay the bills to make the art. Whatever she needed to do. It didn't hurt that her family always shoved cash in her hand. She had a safety net, she knew it. She would never totally fail. She tried not to think about it. Preferred to pretend that she was the one in charge of her own destiny. She drew the lines, she shaved her head. She was the one who decided she wanted this. She had to at least give it a shot. London would be purgatory for Jess. Putting off reality for another year or two. She did not want to move to New York and be broke for a good long time just to have any real opportunity in her life. Let's see what I can make of this, now, while I'm here, she thought. Let's see who I can become.

•

AT THE POND, THEY CHANGED CLOTHES IN THE SUNSHINE, IN A small clearing shrouded by trees. More wildflowers everywhere. Her aunt glanced at the new lines on her body—Jess caught this—but looked away, said nothing. She hadn't said a word about her hair yet either. They talked instead about Nancy, still working retail on occasion, mostly spending the money Jess's father had given her when their marriage had ended.

"Do you talk to her often?" said Jess.

"Almost never," said Shelly. "Your mother is mad at me." She slipped a bathing suit strap over her shoulder. "I don't know why. Who ever knows why anything is the way it is with your mother?"

That sounded like a lie to Jess. Now Shelly was looking at Margaret as she unfastened her bra, cream-colored, lace. Margaret glancing at her aunt's body, Jess saw that, too. A little pinch of cellulite on her thighs. Everyone was looking at each other. Cool and casual. Margaret snapped on a red bathing cap. They all wore the same suits but in different colors. Jess's was dark green. Now all her tattoos were out in the air. I'm not scared, thought Jess. "You'll be cold in that water," said her aunt, rubbing Jess's bald head, acknowledging it at last.

"We'll all be cold no matter what," said Jess.

"Don't change everything," said her aunt, quietly. "Don't change that face. I like that face."

"I have one, too," said Margaret. "Just a little one." His initial tattooed on her wrist. "It was a birthday present." Jess leaned in closer to examine it. Shelly, ignoring them, bent to smell some flowers instead.

A walkway to the pond, a blond lifeguard with a thick accent of some kind, Eastern European, perhaps. Women swam in pairs in the water, speaking in low voices to each other. It was as quiet a place as Jess had ever been. She realized then she had been throttled by noise since the day she had arrived. The tube, the music from the other studios, the classes, the conversations with strangers, the pubs. A shock to the system, the noise of London.

"You just have to get right in," said Margaret, and she climbed down the ladder. "Don't waste any time or you'll talk yourself out of it," she said. "Once you get moving you'll see it gets better." And then she was off.

Jess dipped into the water. Her chest seized up, but she followed Margaret. The water made her skin sting, fresh and tender. She could feel the cold deeply, and in ripples. Her aunt was left behind. "No, don't leave me," she said. Splashing in the water, sort of laughing. "This is stupid," yelled her aunt. "I won't forgive you for this," she called after them. Jess heard Margaret laugh, too. They both swam easily, steadily, slowly, a breaststroke. Jess caught up to her. "Do you like it?" said Margaret. "Don't make me talk," said Jess. "But yes." Soon enough they were halfway around, and then were nearly back to Shelly, who was still splashing. The lifeguard came over as they passed and told Shelly she had to swim or get out. "Let's go one more round," said Margaret. She was faster than Jess, and Jess told her not to wait. Jess glanced back over her shoulder and could see her aunt was out of the water, huddled, grinning, beneath a towel.

Suddenly the birds were loud. She could hear everything at that moment. She was one with the cold.

Jess swam a few more laps and then got out, to keep her aunt company. She had liked it though. She saw how it was possible to get warm eventually, if you just kept moving. The two of them watched Margaret swim a dozen more laps. "Look at her go," said Shelly, smiling, wide-eyed, admiring.

•

AT DARK, THEY MET FOR DINNER IN THE WEST END. SHELLY WAS wearing leather pants and a white blouse with puffy sleeves and a long camel-haired coat around her shoulders and her hair was blown out and she wore a flattering brown lipstick. "Where is he?" she said. "He's not going to join us," said Margaret. "He's not one for socializing with strangers." "But I came all the way to London—" said Shelly. She stopped talking, wrapped her arm around her friend. "It doesn't matter. We'll have more fun without him. Just us girls." Jess took her other arm, too.

It was a rigorous meal. Shelly wanted to try everything, and so they did. "I'm drinking through this jet lag," she said when she sat down at the table and immediately ordered a martini. An Italian place, two bottles of red wine, and heaps of pasta and fried fish and tiramisu for dessert. They held their bellies, ordered coffee, and now Jess was trying Amaro for the first time, watching the women talk to each other with great intimacy. "Should we have one more?" Shelly waved at the waiter. "I feel like we need one more."

They had two more. Now they were drunk, truly drunk, and they were sweating and full, and then they had left and moved on to a new pub. Jess heard her aunt say something through the noise: "He has no curiosity about your life outside of him." And Margaret didn't hear her—or couldn't understand her through the slur of her words, perhaps—and asked her to repeat it and then Shelly said it twice more, each time louder, so now she was yelling it, yelling about this man she had never met, about his intentions and opinions, and Margaret yelled back, "You don't even know him," and Shelly said, "Well, of course I don't, because he won't even deign to meet me." Now they were quickly settling up, and walking outside, stumbling down the block, and then another, the two women shouting, this one was selfish, so was the other one, the conversation degrading into something even messier, and Jess didn't know how to interrupt them, they were older, they were in charge, they had the money, they paid the bills, they were the real adults here.

Then somehow they were in Piccadilly Circus, among the throngs of other drunk tourists, and this was when the two women lost their shit for real, although maybe Shelly had already lost it earlier, splashing around in that water, when Margaret swam away from her. But in this public square, this was when the both of them got loud and couldn't calm back down again.

There were too many people around. They'd been drinking for a day. It wasn't like it used to be. It couldn't be. They were already hungover. Shelly was still dazed with jet lag. Her niece was different. Margaret was different. Shelly was mad at her niece for being so cool and calm and young. Shelly was mad at her husband. She wanted a divorce, but also a divorce sounded terrible. She didn't want Margaret to be with that man. She didn't know how to articulate any of this out loud. She just felt it. She felt it in her gut. She would be scared to say it out loud. She would take all these feelings to her grave, was the only complete sentence in her head. She would run from these feelings forever, but she would hold them within her, too.

"What about your music, Margaret? What is really happening here?"

"Like you ever cared about it."

"You should have put out three albums by now. You're just sitting here doing nothing. He's slowing you down."

"He's the only one who understands what I'm going through," said Margaret. "You could never."

"I understand you better than you know."

Get a room, you two, thought Jess. She sat down on some stairs that led up to the top of the square. She wondered if she would ever love a woman as much as these two loved each other, with all their glances and touches and screaming and hair blow-dried straight. Cashmere sweaters and criticism. She didn't know what this meant about her aunt but at least she seemed alive, not like she did with her husband. Jess had already had three girlfriends by then—she really could not get enough girlfriends in her life, boy, did she love women; like she actually couldn't get *enough* of women, and sometimes wondered what that was about—and for the first time in her life, felt miles ahead of her aunt.

And then they were arguing about something else.

"You took what you wanted."

"You liked it, don't say that you didn't."

"I was drunk."

"We were both drunk."

This will pass, thought Jess, and she waited for them to stop, but they didn't, they were mad about a million things, slights that they had been sitting on for years.

"I didn't hear from you for months. Not one letter, not one call."

"I was busy with work."

She tuned them out after a while. She was thinking about this Christmas in Arizona when she was young, when her parents had fought, and she had cried, and her mother had screamed in the midst of all of it, "Darling, just remember your daddy was the one who killed Christmas, not me."

When Jess looked up again, there was Shelly, grabbing her hand. "It's time to go," said Shelly, and then they were off. They just parted ways right there in the middle of London. Two angry women storming off in the night. Goodbye, Margaret.

CHAPTER 12
2000

On Robby Beck's last visit to the house on the river, he flew into New Orleans in the morning, taking an early flight from Houston, kissing his second wife, Lorraine, goodbye, in her sleep. Other days he would have stopped first at the gift shop in the airport and gotten a fifth of something or other to take with him to the woods, but he was sober these days, or at least trying to be. Instead, he just grabbed a few magazines, a light distraction. In the front lobby, he passed a jazz band playing that same old song about the saints; they looked like they had been up all night, these musicians, maybe rolled in from a club, but still they were standing, doing their job. He knew what that was like. He tipped them as he exited toward the cab stand, where he caught a beat-up old sedan toward the city. He had a car sitting at his mother-in-law's, but she had no interest in picking him up with it.

He glanced at the magazines in his lap. A new *Time* magazine, with Al Gore and the Jewish guy on the cover. Well, you take what you can get sometimes. Better them than Bush. Too bad Clinton couldn't run again, he liked that guy.

He flipped through some of the pages, sighed. He wished it were a bottle instead of a magazine in his lap. He couldn't stop thinking about it. But there was the matter of his health, which was terrible: he had aged poorly, he knew it. All that time on the road, all that running around, all those drinks with clients where he didn't stop to think about what he was doing, he just went with the flow. He was tall and had always thought he carried his weight well, and maybe he did for a while, but now he just felt fat and unsteady on his feet. There was a grim color to his skin, like it had handed in its resignation papers. Lorraine booked his annual checkups for him and asked him what the doctor said this last time around and she had steadily listened to the response. Then she asked him to stop drinking. She said, "I can't be watching over you every second. It's impossible to do that. But I need to be able to sleep at night. I need to know I trust you—can I trust you to take care of yourself a little better?" And he said that she could.

For her, he would. The other woman, in Columbus, didn't know him well enough to ask him to do anything. His ex-wife in Chicago—he hadn't seen her since 1995—was the one who knew him best of all, even though he had lied to her for years. She would have stopped in her tracks if she saw the way he looked this morning. But he never had to see her again if he didn't want to. He had paid her off for good. He almost thought he'd have to pay her even more, once he let it slip there had been other women. He'd been dying to know if Shelly had ever spilled the beans about seeing him in New Orleans with Lorraine, so he'd flat-out asked her, had presumed Shelly had, and that their marriage was over and done after that moment anyway. But there was a stone-cold silence on the other end of the line. "Maybe she was protecting you," he said. "Maybe she doesn't love me and never did," said Nancy. "Maybe I'm not worth loving." A small sob. He couldn't stand it when they cried. "I loved you," said Robby, and that wasn't a lie. "You were my first and always will be." The next day she signed all the papers. Let her remember him forever when they were young. When his body was still young.

He could try to reclaim his body though. At least a little bit. He could do this for a while, stop drinking for Lorraine until his blood pressure dropped and he could get off these statins, and his skin wouldn't look somehow both pasty and brick red at the same time, and he could get up in the morning without wheezing so much, and his dick, which had been both his greatest ally and biggest trouble-maker all these years, would finally start working again. For all of that, and for her, his most favorite wife, he would stop drinking. He would go to the house on the river and set it up for the season, and while he was there, he would stay dry and clean and healthy. He would do this because he had said that he would.

"Turn up that song," he said to the cabdriver. It was the Rolling Stones, singing about women who were like rainbows.

•

THE CAB TOOK ROBBY TO TREMÉ, WHERE HIS MOTHER-IN-LAW, Olivia, lived, and where he kept a car which she rarely used, except to run errands on occasion. Mostly it just sat under the tin-roofed car cover at the side of her home, a Creole cottage owned by the family for more than a hundred years, saved for, scrapped for, fought for, this house, handed down three generations, and accordingly it was immaculate and beautifully maintained. There had been a time when Olivia would have welcomed Robby into their home, and he would have admired the many portraits of family members on the wall and the gilded mirrors and the heavy floors made of cypress and the walls painted varying shades of soothing reds, and he would have sat on the back porch and drunk beer with her and talked about the news of the day. Olivia worked for the city council, had seen the politicians come and go, had a hundred stories about the corruption of men, and

Robby couldn't get enough of them. Then the two of them, Robby and Lorraine, would have driven up north to Mississippi, to the house he had inherited from his uncle Jack.

But now he was on his own. Banned from the house. Olivia had had enough of him. First there was the matter of why he had missed this holiday or that one with the family, things that had always gone without notice with the other women in his life. Robby was a busy man, and that was just the way it went. If you wanted to be with him, you had to accept he wouldn't always be around. He'd pay the bills, he'd charm you, flatter you, make you feel supported when he was in your presence, so your time together would feel good, you would feel so good about him. But you could only count on him part of the time. He thought he had cracked the code. Then there was no fighting, no squabbling. *I don't get to see you that often. I'm only here for the weekend, can't we just get along?* Even Nancy, who had expected more because they had known each other since they were still kids themselves, eventually gave up on him showing up all the time.

Lorraine had seemed fine with it, too, after he had fully committed to her and their daughter. Lorraine with her upswept hair and tasteful manicures and even-toned manner of speech; she always took care of business but did it with control. Lorraine, who took him to church, which he hadn't known how much he missed. Lorraine had specific, pragmatic needs, and once they were met, Robby felt a kind of freedom, which he almost immediately abused.

Olivia expected more from him though. She had an idea of what was appropriate, demanded everyone for Thanksgiving, everyone for Christmas. He made it for some holidays, but not all of them, and she didn't want to tell her daughter how to live her life (although she really did), but your husband needs to show up for all the damn holidays. However, she kept her counsel. Start the wrong fight and then you lose them forever, she had seen it before. But even though she had no evidence that there was anyone else out there in Robby's life, she could still smell a rat from across the room. Was she shocked or not when she found out about all the women? She knew about the first wife, the Jewish woman in Chicago. Fine. Everyone can have an ex, and an ex with a child, too. Lorraine's father had married twice. But then there was another woman after Lorraine. In New York. With a baby. Lorraine had kept that one secret for so long. And then there was even another one after that. With twins. That was when Lorraine broke. Called her six months ago, sobbing. Said, "Mommy there's only so much I can take." Olivia had let her words fly then. Not someone to curse, Olivia. But that motherfucker. And: you just had to marry a white man. But Lorraine pointed out that Olivia had her own string of cheaters in her past, and they were all kinds of colors.

Lorraine forgave him, of course. She talked about her faith, the forgiveness in her heart. Sure, they were both Christians, fine. But it was more that Lorraine just didn't like change, thought Olivia. Her daughter liked her nice home in the Third Ward, and she liked her community, and she liked the idea of being partnered with someone financially stable, and making alliances with people who would look out for her. Her mother couldn't argue with her about it because these were the values she had instilled in her. To be wise politically.

But he wasn't *her* husband. He was barely clinging onto being a family member at this point, Olivia thought, although somehow he wouldn't let go. Cat's claw in human form. So, for now, he was not allowed in her home. She would keep his cream-colored BMW in her driveway. And she would wave to him from the front porch, as she did today. And she might even offer him a beer someday in the future. When her temper calmed. But she would not pick him up from the airport. No sir, not ever again.

Robby paid the man with a twenty and told him to keep the change, then added a five on top of it. Olivia looked just like Lorraine, thought Robby. Ageless, shapely, lipstick in the morning, eyes the color of seashore sand. They waved, then she clutched her bathrobe tight around her and went inside to get ready for her day.

•

ROBBY THREW HIS LUGGAGE IN THE TRUNK, HUSTLED INSIDE the car, and cranked up the air-conditioning. Late August in New Orleans, and the heat hung inside the car, a presence, a threat. His pulse quickened. He might die right there in that car. The summer might strike him where he sat. He headed out of town, fast. It wouldn't be much better there, but at least he wouldn't be sitting in his mother-in-law's yard. That woman probably wished him dead, he thought.

Two hours north, across the Mississippi state line, he stopped at a Piggly Wiggly. He avoided the beer aisle. He got a porterhouse steak and a sack of russet potatoes and a loaf of frozen garlic bread and two bags of chips, salt and vinegar and barbecue, and a pint of mint chocolate chip ice cream and a gallon of milk and a box of frosted wheats and a watermelon and a two-liter of Coca-Cola, and then, last minute, a pile of fried chicken from the deli, and then he nearly went to the beer aisle after all that but instead swung himself toward the checkout, where a teenage girl rang him up numbly, unaware of his momentary triumph. Someone's daughter, he thought fondly, working her first job. Until someday she would be all grown up.

He drove down the tree-lined back roads and the car cooled, and he relaxed. It felt special to him here. The glimpses of swampland beyond the trees. The dirt road for miles. Sky, air, sky, trees. He thought gently of the summer before with Lorraine and their daughter, Diane, and the lazy days they'd spent floating in inner tubes down the river. Diane's church group was coming to use it after they'd left, so they'd helped set up tents the night before on the acre near the river. Laughing and swatting off mosquitos. He was proud of how normal Diane seemed, at least in comparison to his other girls. She went to college for biology at Dillard, and dated a quiet man who worked as an X-ray technician. She was not argumentative or miserable or stressed-out about her life choices. She simply worked and tried to succeed. He loved his other daughters, too—equally, sure—but there was something about his southern child. He actually enjoyed spending time with her. I'm not being fair, he thought. They all had their quirks, and they all had their appeal. The one from the South, the one from the Midwest, and the one from the East. (And now two more from the Midwest. That woman *claimed*.) It was just that one had turned out easier than the rest.

He parked in front of the main house. A small offshoot of the Bogue Chitto River, higher than usual because of a recent rain, sat a hundred feet away. A half-dozen acres surrounded the house in the other direction, with another two tiny houses in the distance. This land is where his great-grandfather kept his mistresses, like princesses in a faraway castle, as he went through them all, one by one, moving from house to house. The family brothel, it was referred to by his mother. There were surely some distant cousins out there related to him—all that screwing, some babies had to have come out of it—but he would not be seeking them out in this lifetime. He would claim this land for himself and his descendants.

He got giddy whenever he arrived at the house, thinking about the notion of family. He had built something that could be passed down to his children. The house was raised, with a concrete deck beneath it, and three bedrooms atop that. He had torn down the old place, which Uncle Jack hadn't done a lick of work on over the years, worthless and shredding after all this time, and built one brand-new, with central air and heat and new plumbing and floorboards made of pine, so it would last for a hundred more years. A legacy, that was what he thought of this house. Even if it was always changing. Even if it was built on lies.

Ice cream's melting, he thought. He hoisted a few grocery store bags out of the trunk, walked them up the stairs to the house, straight into a thick wave of bugs. They scattered all over his clothes, his hair, his face, his mouth, big, black-winged bugs all over him; he was sloppy with bugs, pairs of bugs connected to each other, fucking. They were lovebugs. Now connected to him. He dropped the grocery-store bags and waved them off, but they clung to him. He gagged. There was a pile of dead bugs outside the front door. He fumbled with the keys, waving off the creatures, making little gasping, horrified noises, and cursing. He got inside, dragged the bags in, and slammed the front door. There was another pile of dead bugs inside at his feet, and he could see the bugs still swarming outside through the window of the door. Must have come up off the river because of all the rain, he thought. They'll clear out by dusk.

●

AFTER LUNCH, HE GOT TO WORK ON THE HOUSE: TAKING DOWN pictures of Lorraine and Diane, a painting of their golden retriever, Clementine, and removing all the religious paraphernalia, various crosses, a small sketch of a baby Jesus, a framed psalm. He placed them all in a cardboard box and carried them downstairs, waving off the bugs yet again, to a set of storage lockers beneath the house.

In these storage lockers, numbered 1, 2, and 3 (the order the girls were born), were the personal items he swapped in and out prior to each daughter's arrival. That these objects were so tantalizingly close to the Ping-Pong table and the outdoor shower and the kayaks they dragged out in the sunshine of the afternoon to take slow rides down the river in search of nothing in particular, just some peace and quiet and fallen tree limbs and birds, felt inherently risky. But then again, was it any riskier than anything else he had done in his life?

He told everyone he locked extra food in there, keeping it safe from the racoons and possum and stray dogs that lived in the woods surrounding the land. No one bothered to question it, and so the lockers remained intact. No one ever questioned him on anything as long as he paid the bills, he thought.

He opened Jess's locker: she would be there in a week. Inside was a blackout curtain (she had trouble sleeping through the morning sunrise); a framed photo of her holding a catfish on a line; a striped set of linen sheets; a coffee mug and T-shirt from her alma mater; a young person's diary, frilly, with a small lock, the key long lost; a sketchbook; some pens; a box of tampons.

A youthful version of Jess was released from this locker in that photo, a once-a-year version of Jess. Happy, quiet, content Jess, when she still had long hair, those big brown gorgeous curls, and big wise eyes, and she could be left alone for hours to play by herself without looking up once, and now, it seemed, could be left alone for months at a time without bothering to pick up the phone. She didn't want anything from him anymore, or need anything, except for the occasional cash infusion. I set it up that way, he thought, as he closed her locker, grabbing what he could hold—the curtain, a picture of Jess, and the box of tampons—for the first trip up the stairs. I turned so many relationships into handout situations. He felt gruff toward himself, and then he felt sorry for himself, dusted a tear away from his eye. All I ever did was try, he thought.

He pulled a step stool from the closet and stood on the top step, too quickly, there was a rush of blood to the head, then he wobbled for a moment, thought certainly he would fall, but then finally caught his balance on the curtain rod. His crumbling arches, his arthritic knee, his high blood pressure, his bad heart, his five daughters, the wives, the girlfriends, all those goddamn women. He swapped out the gauzy white curtains for the gray canvas curtains. Careful, careful, he mumbled, as he stepped back down from the stool. Next he hung the photo of Jess on the wall, replacing a picture of Diane in much the same pose, with her first fish caught, too. For a while, Jess was a vegetarian and wouldn't be caught dead eating fish. Was that still the case? He couldn't keep track. He took the box of tampons to the bathroom; Jess kept them under the sink, usually. He stooped at the cabinet, then found himself sitting down on the floor. There, aside the cleaning supplies, was a handle of Jack Daniel's.

He tried to puzzle it out, how it ended up there, how it was even in the house in the first place. Maybe it was those kids from Diane's church group; they were the last ones to use the house. But they were supposed to be the well-behaved ones! Then, two more thoughts: the pleasure of its company, and the challenge of it looking him right in the face. He'd been sober six days. Not that he was counting. He'd made promises. How easy he had made it seem. If he were being truthful to himself, it had taken everything in him not to order a cocktail on the plane. And now he was alone in the woods with this bottle of bourbon.

Alcohol was one giant feeling to him, like family was. There was no good or bad to the sum of the feeling (although there were certainly good and bad parts to it), it just was one of the pillars of his life, a monolith. Alcohol, work, family, this house. The other houses he owned counted as part of a body of work of investments. He owned a half-dozen rentals, an apartment building, too, but they were objects, they were not home to him. This was the only place where he could see everyone in his life, even if he couldn't see them all at the same time. It was the house that held all the lies in one place.

He took the rest of Diane's possessions back downstairs to her locker, through the wave of lovebugs again thickly screwing each other. We fuck and we die, that's right, he thought. Was there any moment he ever felt sorry for his actions, like he had been a criminal, been inappropriate, been a liar, taken advantage of anyone? Did he feel an ounce of guilt? Too late for guilt, he had thought when Diane was born. Too late to say sorry, he thought when he took his girlfriend in New York City to bed for the first time. Too late for regrets, when Franny was born. Too late to change now.

When he returned upstairs, all he could see was that bottle sitting there.

•

HE COOKED THE STEAK FOR DINNER ON THE GRILL. THE WHOLE steak, just for him. He fried potatoes in one pan, and dumped butter and garlic and cream and frozen spinach into another. Cream cheese, salt, pepper. He took the frozen garlic bread and let it roast in the oven in its foil wrapper. He filled a tumbler with ice and he poured a nice stiff fucking drink for himself. I'm a king, he thought after he finished one drink. This is a meal fit for a king. This is my castle. This was my grandfather's land and it was his kingdom and now it is my kingdom. He put on his favorite CD: OK Computer. Radiohead finally had a new album coming out in six weeks and he couldn't wait. Incredible to him that he'd lived long enough to hear a band this cool. Now he wished he had some weed. To just sit here and get high in the woods and listen to Radiohead all by himself? What a fucking dream. He poured another drink. His heart began to race a little bit, and he knew that drinking was a bad idea, except also it was a great idea. He couldn't seem to stop, he'd never been able to stop taking what he wanted; no one had ever really told him to stop, so why would he?

•

HE HAD WORKED HARD, HE THOUGHT, AFTER THE SIXTH DRINK, laid out on porch, the last gasp of the lovebugs screwing just outside the screen. He was a salesman, flying and driving and training across America. He'd had meetings, he'd shaken hands, he'd made presentations, he'd had dinners and picked up the tab, he'd made jokes, he'd made eye contact, he'd shown up on time and even a few minutes early, he'd invoiced, he'd made deals, he'd sweetened the pot on occasion, he'd done more than the bare minimum and been competent at all times and had never made an error and never been particularly brilliant but had always kept his hand steady on the wheel. He'd never slept with any of his coworkers or clients. He'd never said anything inappropriate, sexual, or racist or in any way insulting, although he had never stopped anyone from doing it themselves. He was professionally honest but never got in the way of dishonesty in others. His concern was primarily the multiple lives he led. He needed to pay for them. So he worked hard just to be able to keep all his secrets to himself.

•

THE BOTTLE NEXT TO HIM ON THE GROUND, NO GETTING UP now. Ten drinks in. All those wives of his had to do was raise those children, he thought. He was the one who had been out there in the world, working, talking, demanding, soothing, assuring, lying, lying, lying. But living his life as much as he could. I did do that, he thought. I am doing that. It's my life, after all.

•

OH, BUT HE LOVED HIS DAUGHTERS, HE DID. WHAT I WOULDN'T do for them. What I did for them.

•

IN THE END, IT'S QUICK, WHEN HE PASSES. HE'S ASLEEP, HE WAKES up, he vomits on the ground next to him, he passes out again, and his heart gives out. Maybe his eyes flutter. He clutches his chest, and then a hand falls. It is a simple, brutal wave of destruction. He is alone in the woods, with no one to save him.

The next afternoon, the lovebugs began to swarm outside the house again, and the afternoon after that, and the afternoon after that. On the fourth day, Olivia drove up to Mississippi, bidden by Lorraine, who swore her husband had promised to be back in Houston in time for another doctor's appointment, more tests on his heart. Olivia had taken a moment to give her the business—"This is what you get with a man like that, running around, disappearing"— and then Lorraine shushed her. "Just do this thing for me," she said. "He's got a bad heart." A bad heart, that sounds about right, thought Olivia, but she acquiesced.

She hated going up there, going into the woods. A Black woman in Mississippi alone in the woods? No thank you. She took her time, took the long way. Stopped for lunch in Slidell. Drove the speed limit. A law-abiding citizen driving to find her cheating-ass son-in-law in the woods. Did I do something wrong here? Did I make a wrong turn in life? But then she thought of Diane, who they all could agree was a good, grown-up, lovely young woman. And that Lorraine was safe and steady in that three-bedroom condo, one room of which was always kept pristine and available for Olivia to visit anytime she liked. He had done a few things right, she guessed. By the time she arrived and found him on the screened-in porch, the half-drained glass of bourbon full of mosquitos on the ground, his body surrounded by the carcasses of bugs, she was ready to fall to her knees and pray for him.

CHAPTER 13

2002

Please don't ruin this place for me, thought Shelly as she took her seat at the restaurant two blocks from their new apartment in Cobble Hill. Please don't fuck up this beautiful little spot, Asher. An ultimatum she had given him, a real risk was being taken: meet me here, at this restaurant we both love, so we can talk about our future together. Where my cell doesn't get service, the thing you perhaps liked most about it because then I had no choice but to look into your eyes the entire time we dined. The one where the manager always remembers our names and where the windows are framed in cast-iron ivy leaf and we always get the last Baked Alaska of the night and there are always squid ink noodles on the menu and we trust the waiter to bring us one martini each and then a delicious bottle of red wine without asking and it is our spot—*our spot!* And where you always took me when you were trying to convince me to come be with you in New York City full-time.

This is an emergency; we are in a state of emergency. Please have dinner with me.

The owner, Ahmet, waved hello and signaled to the bartender to make Shelly her usual. Oh god, she loved this place. When she thought of New York, she only thought of here. Not their home, but here. Neutral territory. A thing they loved to do, dine together. If only they could have met for dinners forever.

A mistake they had made in their relationship. That this would be good for them. That they needed to do this kind of thing to be normal, conventional, safe, sane. He thought it would be easier to explain themselves to the world if they lived in the same place, when actually they only had to explain themselves to themselves and no one else.

In the restaurant she looked helplessly at her phone, no messages forthcoming, no nothing. The light was dimming. It was August, sunset, pleasant weather. The city was still the city then.

End-of-summer light. A waitress moved gracefully around the room lighting small candles on each table, next to petite vases of yellow tea roses, their petals slack after a few days of use. Worn, damp, fading yellow roses. The room smelled delicious. They hadn't even been married a decade. It seemed too soon to fail.

But had they ever even found their footing? They had not so much fought constantly as lived their lives in a state of disagreement. Two successful, smart people who were also deeply idiosyncratic and used to indulging themselves as they pleased. It was generally understood that he liked things one way and she liked them another and their lives together were about finding a way to meet in the middle, find the moments where they could get along and enjoy their time together.

Neither one of them expected much from other people: they were both used to being on their own most of the time, making their own decisions, that to find someone you could get along with, be intimate with even part of the time, had felt like a miracle to them—and when they did, it was spectacular and even comforting. Those tiny moments when they felt less alone in the world seemed like a major triumph. When he had shown up looking for her in Chicago in the first place. Desperate for her, wanting her for his own. He didn't like that she had gotten away from him. Suddenly he knew what she meant to him. That time in their life, those heady first few years, long-distance, every moment they had together felt like they were laying claim to a bigger life.

Things had been better when they lived far apart, she could see that now. Moving into the same apartment, too, not small, mind you, but still smaller than her place in Chicago, which had room after room and a second floor, too. It had forced them into conversations they had always been able to avoid in the past. Sometimes after they fought, she would think about her father and lean into this feeling of guilt that she was still alive and he wasn't. He had never fought with Frieda. He was just happy to be alive. She wondered if this guilt had chased her for her entire life. Every time she complained or was angry, it confused her to assert herself. She was right, but was it wrong? She wished she could talk to anyone about it. But it seemed too deep a cavern to explore. She might get lost in it.

•

SHE WENT OUTSIDE TO CHECK HER PHONE FOR MESSAGES AND the phone rang almost immediately. It was Nancy. They hadn't spoken in a few months. If she called, it was important.

"Sorry to interrupt your life but I'm calling to tell you our mother is moving in with me."

"This seems like a terrible idea," said Shelly. Although Nancy would be better at it than her, she supposed.

"She wants to come back to Chicago. She's sick of hurricane season. I have the room."

"She could stay at my place," said Shelly. "I'm never there."

"She said she wants to stay with me," said Nancy.

I give it a month, thought Shelly. The other line rang. It was her mother. "I gotta take this," said Shelly. "I'll call you back."

"I'm calling to tell you I'm moving back to Chicago," said Frieda. "I'm moving in with Nancy."

"I heard. You know you could just stay at my place."

"She insisted I stay with her, and I don't know how to get out of it."

I don't know why I was worried Asher would ruin this place for me when my family can do it just fine on their own, thought Shelly. The waitress gave a wave from inside the window. Her martini was ready.

•

BUT STILL THE CLOCK WAS TICKING—WHERE WAS ASHER? THEY'D had a big fight a month ago. In their apartment, inspecting the state of renovations. A new kitchen, tile in the bathroom, and they had replaced the windows facing Smith Street with soundproof glass. All nearly complete. They'd both had some travel for work while these renovations were happening. "Hey, I missed you," he said. Touched her face and she smiled and looked away. He pitched that they take a big trip. One month, anywhere out of America she wanted to see. They hadn't traveled together abroad since Paris. "Let's go see the world together," he said. His shirtsleeves rolled up, ready to win this argument, because it would be a good and righteous win.

"I have to work," she said. "I can't take that much time off, you know that." What she couldn't say out loud: she was hesitant to try traveling like that again with him. They had fought so much on that trip. And she was supposed to be fearless. She didn't know how to tell him she was terrified it might end everything for them.

"Work will always be there but what about our youth?" His mother had died recently, immobilized for the past few years before that. Had gone nowhere, seen nothing. He wanted to use his legs while he still could. He was going to be sixty. He had a life he suddenly wanted to live. "What's the point of making all this money if you don't spend it?" he said.

"We spend plenty," she said.

"Closets full of clothes, who cares. I want to travel to, I don't know . . . Bali!" She had never heard him mention Bali before in her life. She said, "What's in Bali?" "Me," he said. "I'm in Bali." She looked at him. She genuinely felt helpless, but there was a smirk on her face anyway. "You're such a bitch," he said, not even trying to be mean. Just being honest.

He stayed in a hotel for one night and stayed and stayed. But tonight, they would be reunited.

She drained her martini and ordered another. If she could have ordered the hangover directly, she would have, just to get it all over with already.

•

SHE WENT OUTSIDE TO CHECK HER PHONE AGAIN. NO MESsages from him. Just an email from Tova.

Tova, out in Seattle, holding down the fort after all this time, losing patience every day with Shelly, who was too distracted to solve this problem—this problem of Monroe—if she even knew how to. Tova, always a few years behind Shelly, forever. Employee 302 instead of employee 35. Same skill set, maybe a little more technical, a little less social. Two kids now versus no kids ever. A husband with a private practice and partners, so no flexibility on cross-country moves. But anyway, Tova didn't want to go anywhere else, she liked where she was. They had a nice house, there was a good Hebrew day school nearby, and the kids were happy and healthy and not fucked-up like her sister's kids in Los Angeles. But that didn't mean she didn't hunger to catch up with Shelly. Although it seemed like she never would. Make your peace with it, said her husband. But Tova was not born of peace. And he knew that.

Subject line: **Monroe**. First sentence: **We need to talk. Again.**

I don't have time for this, thought Shelly. I don't have time to clean up his messes again. I need to take care of my own business. I need to calm down is what I need to do. Go inside, sit down, be quiet, and wait.

Let's table it, messaged Shelly.

All the conversations you have right before your life is about to change you either dismiss from memory forever or never fucking forget.

·

NOW SHE WAS HALFWAY THROUGH THE SECOND MARTINI. SHE tried to think of nothing, clear her mind, and this made her think of Margaret, the great meditator of her life, whom she hadn't spoken to in two years, maybe it was three, although she thought about her every day of her life. They had apologized to each other after that big fight in London but stopped talking on the phone, then stopped emailing, then stopped everything, even birthday cards. But Shelly could not ignore the album, which had come out at last. Jess showed her an interview with Margaret that called her a "reclusive pioneer." Could you imagine being anything as cool as that, thought Shelly. "Your ex-girlfriend's rad," said Jess. "Shut up," said Shelly.

She called and congratulated Margaret on all the good reviews; she had heard one of her songs in a chase scene of a movie, and in the opening credits of a cop show, and a car commercial, and so on. Margaret thought she was making her weird-sounding art, but it turns out all along she was also making perfectly commercial work. Who could have known?

"You're a hit, baby," she said.

"Thanks," said Margaret. "I think I hate it."

"You're being heard," said Shelly.

"Pfft," said Margaret. "I'm background music."

"How does it feel to be background music, then?"

"I'm just happy it's done and out in the world and I never have to think about it again." But it was the most that she could hope for, thought Shelly. For an album about her dead mother. No one would know Margaret's mother, but this music would ensure that she would live on in one small way. And there was money in her pocket, more film work if she wanted it. The way people could make more money so easily if they already had some.

"You could go anywhere you want," said Shelly.

"You know I'm already home," said Margaret. A quiet mouse.

They didn't speak again after that, but a year later Shelly saw Ian's obituary in the *New York Times*. An influential artist, dead after a short illness. Margaret was quoted in it: "It was his generosity toward others in the artistic community that made everyone love him, me most of all." His family money helped him support the arts. Buying whatever he liked, keeping it all for himself, thought Shelly. The obituary referred to her as his wife. His wife! Margaret hadn't even invited her to the wedding. Oh well, Shelly supposed she hadn't invited her to hers either. A lot of good getting married had done either of them. She was probably dining alone tonight, too.

She went outside one more time to check her phone. Through the window Ahmet watched her, this anxious woman, in and out, so many times. He was Turkish, although they served Italian food here. At the time he had opened the restaurant it had been easier to explain that to the neighborhood, and anyway, his wife could cook anything, she just wanted to feed people, and so did he. He had a dignified salt-and-pepper mustache and thick hair the same color, and he wore a gray linen blazer and a white button-down shirt and jeans and comfortable, thick walking shoes. His voice was deep. He drank espresso all night and shook the hand of every man who walked in the door. He and his wife owned and lived in the building, and he had been serving more or less the same menu since 1988, and they would stay open for nearly twenty more years, until the time when people would stop going out to dinner entirely in New York City for a good long while.

The house phone rang. It was her husband. He wouldn't be coming to dinner. Could Ahmet just let her know for him?

Ahmet watched her pace. She was a good tipper, always. Left a little extra when her husband drank too much, but she was always a little fussy herself, too. Nothing was ever quite right, but she had manners at least. It wasn't fair, what he had to do. Do I do it on the street? Do I wait for her to come back inside? Inside, at her table. That would be less embarrassing.

When she had returned and settled herself, he approached her. "Your husband called," he said. "He said he won't be able to make it to dinner after all." He had to look at her face, and see how that made her feel, and now he felt terrible, too.

•

THE FIRST THOUGHT SHE HAD OF HER HUSBAND: YOU COWARD.

And then the second thought: of despair. That she would be dining for one now forever. That she would have to get used to it again, this solo act. Even when she dined alone during their marriage, she had that ring on her finger, which made her feel like she was part of something bigger. A husband in another city, fine. Evidence she was loved, even if she was alone tonight. She would have to recalibrate.

She thought back when she had first met him in Seattle. Dressing like Stevie Nicks, horny and eager on the way to his house. Claiming her sexiness. She had loved that feeling of doing everything just as she pleased, all the time. The sweet satisfaction of independence. How could she get back to it?

What would Stevie do? she thought. Stevie would haunt him.

She looked around the room. At the people who were on their phones. Maybe 10 percent of the crowd, she thought. Busy people in New York City. Looking at their tiny screens. The gentle taps of their thumbs. Or their phones were resting next to them on the table, or in their front pockets. Nearby, easy to reach. In a few years it would be half the people, a few years after that it would be all the people, and no one would notice it for a long time, how they were all on their phones, until it was too late. But for now, Shelly was in the race against her competitors. To get her phones in their hands.

This instinct rustled up inside of her and she wished she could walk around and quiz everyone. She wanted to know how their service was in this restaurant as opposed to the street as opposed to their home. How was the audio quality? What did they use their phones for the most, to text or to talk or to check out on their relationships? How much would they be willing to pay for an upgrade to it if it promised to make their life significantly easier? How much would it take for them to put it away and pay attention to the person sitting across from them? Did they sleep with it in the same room and did it give them comfort or did it freak them out to have it so close to them all the time? What did the phone feel like in their hands? Did it feel good to them, warm to them? Did it feel like love? She wanted it to feel like love. If they had ever lost their phone, how did it make them feel? Had having a phone ever saved their life or solved a significant problem for them? Had it ever made their life significantly worse? Had they ever sat alone in the middle of a restaurant waiting for their husband to call to see if he still loved them anymore? Had they ever had anything riding on the line like that before, and only their phone could provide the solution?

Her life's work: these phones. Her marriage was not that, would never be that.

She asked for the check. "Your husband has covered it," said Ahmet.

At that moment, they dimmed the lights for dinner service, the candles lit at last. At home, around the corner, an empty apartment. A computer screen. She would try then to call him, to find him, to track him down. But he was nowhere to be found. She thought about following him everywhere, leaving him messages on his phone, sending him texts that would ruin him, writing him a mean letter every day for years and years so he would wake up every day missing her again. It was a curse, she thought. I curse you. You will never forget me.

PART V

CONFESSIONS

CHAPTER 14

2003

When was the last time Jess had been back in the suburbs? You couldn't pay her to visit, she'd often said, but here she was, standing at the garage door of an investment property owned by her rich aunt. Shelly, in town from New York, smelling fantastic, expensive, sexy, hair freshly glossed. She wore a long, light, tan trench coat and a red-striped Breton shirt and linen pants. Jess was in ink-stained jeans, a hole in a back pocket. Shelly clicked the garage door opener, an effortless glide. "I've been here maybe twice," she told Jess. It was between renters, but she always kept the car there, paid a neighborhood kid to rev the engine every so often. A pristine vintage Mini Cooper.

A house no one was living in, a car no one was driving.

"This seems like a thing I should not be allowed to have," said Jess. She was scared to touch it; it was so pretty. "Why do you even have this car?"

"I was supposed to look after it," said Shelly tiredly. "I suppose she thought it would give us a reason to see each other again."

"OK, but why do you *still* have it?" said Jess. She could not believe those two women were fighting after all this time.

"Don't look a gift horse in the mouth, Jess," said Shelly. "Just take the car."

Jess's car had been sidelined this winter by a decrepit engine, and she needed a way to get from Pilsen to a job in Lincoln Park that didn't take an hour on the train and the bus. The car was a loan, but with no proscribed date of return. A gift, another gift. To help you succeed in life. There was a disconnect neither one of them was willing to put their finger on. Shelly had been blindly encouraging her for a decade, longer. Here's a car, here's your apartment deposit, here's graduate school, here's your loan payment. The constant exchange of money had numbed them both. Here's some more; no need to talk about it.

"I'll take it for now," said Jess. She needed it to drive to Mississippi, to pick up some things on her dead father's compound. There would be a meeting of the sisters on the land left to them all. Her sister Diane had insisted upon it, said it was time. Jess would never have visited there again if she could have helped it, but she wanted to respect this new person in her life, this sister from another mother. Sometimes she barely thought about her father, but on the other hand she thought about him every single day. How he'd always played Aretha in the morning. That was what she thought about today.

They got in the car. Shelly immediately asked after her gallery. "We parted ways," said Jess. "If they were ever really mine in the first place." "Just keep working hard," said Shelly. "Hard work and talent will pay off. I firmly believe that." After a few years in the art world, Jess had realized that America was not a meritocracy. She hadn't succeeded at much of anything except continuing to work. No point in arguing about it when she was getting a car handed to her though. She was grateful for it but also knew she would never have anything new or special in her life unless it was bought for her by someone else. She was still settling with this feeling though. It had been fine when she was younger. But now she had to decide if she wanted to be this way for the rest of her life. Making art that never sold and working part-time in a tattoo parlor. She was twenty-six. Forever this way? Till she was forty? Sixty? Was this how it was supposed to all turn out in the end? This job in Lincoln Park was really more of an apprenticeship. Learning about herbal medicine. Maybe that would stick.

"Should we go shopping, too? We could go to the mall, that's close," said Shelly.

"It's fine, I've got everything I need," said Jess.

"Look, a new outfit every now and then is not a crime," said her aunt, who loved fashion, went to a different fashion capital once a year by herself—Paris, Milan—to buy entire new wardrobes for herself, which she then had tailored, wore for a season, and then shoved into storage, a cycle she had repeated for years, the earning of money, the spending of it, the shopping, the charging, the squeezing of funds, like it was squeezing her heart tight, and then releasing it with the pleasure of the new object. She was glamorous and impeccable and wasteful, and Jess knew it and admired it and resented it, too.

"I would just get it dirty," said Jess. "I don't need anything new."

"You should dress up for these openings you go to, so people will pay attention to you, see that you can stand out in a crowd. You're an artist. You're special." Her aunt had been saying it for so long. She needed to believe it, Jess thought. That this cycle of spending was not a waste like the rest of them. Maybe, too, Shelly liked the idea of her being something different or special, like she was. Maybe she wanted to support her just so she could feel supportive in general. Why couldn't she just ask her how she felt? So they could both get off this ride.

Jess noticed her aunt was wearing a small delicate gold *chai*. "It's pretty," she said. She touched her aunt's neck. Shift the topic, Jess.

"Your grandfather gave it to me, and one to your mother, too. I just found it when I was digging around in my jewelry box the other day. You like it? I'll leave it to you in the will." Shelly had put it on in hopes of feeling something positive. "Come on, let's go shopping!" she said.

"How about lunch instead?" said Jess.

•

THEY ORDERED FAT EGG ROLLS AND A SALT-AND-PEPPER shrimp dish that made Jess sneeze and Diet Cokes. "What's the latest on the full house downtown? Can you believe they're still living together?" said Shelly. "I did not think they'd make it this long."

"They seem to be getting along OK," said Jess. Shelly wanted some dirt, she could tell. Would those two ever get along again? Jess wasn't spending much time with her mother either, but she still called her every other week, and she liked seeing Frieda on occasion, this brand-new grandmother in her life. "Mom keeps trying to get me to go to one of her work things. I'm resistant. Grandma, too."

"Why don't you want to go?"

"I guess we're afraid she'll try and sell us something."

Shelly laughed. This was what she was looking for. This was the good stuff.

"You won't catch me going anywhere near any of that," said Shelly. "Anyway, I'm just checking up on Frieda."

"As far as I know, it's going fine." Another topic Jess didn't want to tackle. How those two did or didn't get along. What if someday we run out of things we're willing to discuss? Never. Not with Aunt Shelly.

"OK, enough about all that," said her aunt. She licked her fingers. "Please let me take you shopping and buy you a new pair of jeans. I am begging you. Do it for me."

Two hours later: a fresh pair of jeans and two new sweaters for fall and a pair of work boots—and a new car. Quite a day.

Later when Jess decries the notion of "generational wealth" to a tableful of women, some of them working artists, some of them service industry workers, some of them professional caregivers in some form or another, only half of whom have health insurance, they will tell her to fuck off and take the money. They were all fond of Jess—many of them had slept with her—but they all agreed behind her back that the lady doth protest too much.

•

JESS LEFT FOR MISSISSIPPI BEFORE DAWN, TRYING TO BEAT THE rain that was coming up from the South, a storm on the edge of hurricane season. Driving away from a breakup, too, its own kind of inclement weather. The separation had been icy and unpleasant—exceptionally so, she thought. For years, she had watched all her couple friends around her having these breakups where they stayed friends, even sometimes remaining roommates, moving in and out of each other's lives seamlessly, friends, girlfriends, friends, and back again. They made it look so easy, at least in the stories they told to each other over dinner or tea.

But when she and Veronica had parted ways it had been a stone-cold heartbreak. A ruthless dumping, done over email; she could have died. There had been a bad fight one night when Veronica was at her place. An argument about money. Jess was weird about money, said Veronica. She was always splitting the bill down the middle. "There's nothing wrong with that," said Jess. "You never round up," said Veronica. "You round down." "I do not," said Jess, not even knowing if it was true or not or even what was so wrong with that. "You err on the side of cheaper for yourself," said Veronica. "And more expensive for me." "Holy shit, how do you even notice this?" said Jess. "How are you even paying attention so closely to this minute detail? Is it like a fifty-cent difference we're talking about here? Do you want me to get my change jar and you can have it all?" "It's not the money that matters," said Veronica. "It's that you always take a little bit more and I always get a little bit less."

And that translated to their relationship, Veronica insisted. One person (she) was always going to end up giving more than the other person (Jess), and it just wasn't fair. Veronica had jet-black hair with dyed violet stripes and enormous purplish lips and big breasts, implants from the days when she used to dance in the clubs as she put herself through graduate school, an investment at the time in her future, she felt, and she was correct, she was tenure track now at UIC, and she was so hot to Jess she could barely stand it. Could not stand those feelings she had for her at all. "You're hustling me for change," said Jess, unwilling to budge on the initial discussion. "I'm hustling you for emotions," said Veronica. "I'm hustling you for feelings. I'm hustling you for you."

I cannot get far enough away from that, thought Jess.

•

THE DRIVE TO MISSISSIPPI TOOK NINE HOURS. THIS WAS HOW they used to do it as a child, just drive straight through, Jess in the backseat coloring quietly, her mother zoning out, napping in the front seat, rousing herself to sing along to the radio, and her father just focused, driving, getting his family to where they needed to go. This was when he was still around regularly. When did he disappear exactly? What was the age again? Hers, his. When did he become this other person with other families? These sisters of hers she was going to meet in person were younger by six years; one born in Houston and the other in Queens. How had he been so out in the world with so many people when she was just herself, quietly, drawing at home?

It had been three years since his death, and only now was his estate nearly wrapped up. His assistant, Marlene, had been his executor, and she had moved slowly, methodically, and there was much to be unraveled and put back together. She was the only one who had known all his secrets—or thought so. Surprise! Now there were twin girls in Columbus to be dealt with. "Your father," said Marlene, "he got around." Jess wouldn't meet the twins for another decade, and when she did, she would feel a faint connection to them, they were blood, certainly, but she did not have the energy to sustain it or connect with them. When she told Shelly about her new sisters, Shelly said, "Enough already with the secret families." Enough!

Why hadn't they met in person yet? They both had been putting it off. A fear of having to feel something new, thought Jess. Of dealing with the truth. ("Sounds like someone I used to know," said her mother.) Her sister Diane said, "Let's do this, let's push through."

She stopped in Clarksdale for the night, staying in a hotel made of a string of reclaimed shacks, formerly servants' quarters. ("Not slaves," assured the woman who checked her in.) From her porch she watched the sun set across train tracks. A stretch of green grass and then a farmhouse beyond that, and just sky, sky, sky. She felt like she was being held in the hand of the land. Rest, she told herself. Be quiet now. Things hurt, and you must let them be. She cracked a beer and tried to negotiate her feelings, research the source of her pain. She had a notebook. Just lines, she drew lines. It had been a while since she had done that. She missed her ex-girlfriend. Wished she could have her in her life again. Did something dumb. Called and left a message on her answering machine. Did another dumb thing. Called and left another message. She didn't even know what she was saying or how she was feeling. There was an excess of feelings. What she was trying to tell her, she thought, was that all this time she was worried she would turn into her mother she actually should have been worried she would turn into her father. He was the one that loved too many people all at once without ever actually truly showing up and giving himself to anyone. Lies built on lies. Had his love for her been a lie? She didn't think so. Was Jess's love for her ex-girlfriend a lie? No, it was real. She wanted to explain to her that she was just like her dad, that she couldn't sit still with just one person, it was a thing she was realizing now. She wanted to make people feel good but then she had to move on. The first message said, "I miss you." And the second message said, "But I can't give you what you want." (It was strange: in her memory she had talked for ten minutes straight. But, in fact, each message had only been one sentence long, her ex telling her this a few weeks later, adding, "You made your fucking point.")

Later, just before closing time, Jess went to a small bar in town and smiled at the bartender as she wiped down the tables, acknowledged her looks, her energy, how the two combined together to create an *appearance*, as if some magician had waved a wand and there was this forty-two-year-old human woman standing before her. Tired around the eyes, thin lips, but she had a nice body, she fit well in her Wranglers, a bottle opener peeking up from the pocket. A button-down shirt with little flowers on it and pearl-covered snaps. Hair in two braids, which Jess wrapped her hands in as they slow-danced to Linda Ronstadt songs on the jukebox. I'll make you feel good, thought Jess. Just let me try.

SHE MADE EFFICIENT TIME FOR THE REST OF THE TRIP. SHE WAS on the muddy back road leading to her father's land before noon the next day. The pop of the gravel, a flash of swamp in the woods. Someone had built a new house on some of the available acreage. On the land next door to her father's, there was an old camper with some kayaks resting to it, and a water line hookup nearby. Signs of life in the woods.

And then up the driveway, into the cool shade of dozens of trees, a stack of firewood to one side, and she parked next to it. She turned off the engine and wondered: Is this about to be terrible? She walked down to the river, which was low; she kicked off her shoes, took a flight of concrete steps down to its shore, rolled up the cuffs of her pants, and waded into the water, which hit at her calves. It was late September, still warm outside, still warm enough in the water after a brief bite of cold. She looked around for birds, a familiar heron, some random cranes. But surely that heron must be dead by now. She would have been looking for a ghost.

Down came Diane and Franny, her two sisters, and they waved to her from the grass up above. Diane had told her she was biracial, Black on her mother's side, on their first phone call. Diane had already looked her up online, saw pictures of her at an opening. "We don't look a thing alike," she'd said. "Except for his nose." "Better his nose than my mother's," said Jess, but of course that meant nothing to Diane. "It's just more Jewish. That's all." Jess fumbled. Two years ago, Diane had added Jess to her Christmas card list, and Jess had studied the family photos for similarities between them, too. Diane's face was familiar and easy, relaxed, and she had beautifully sculpted eyebrows. Jess was terse, lean, tattooed, and occasionally still shaved her head. And now here they were in person at last, two pictures come to life.

Diane waved hello. She wore low-rise jeans, a hot-pink striped cropped top. They talked on the phone once a month now. Once

Diane had told her she was raised to be "normal" by her mother. "What does that mean?" said Jess. "Do good in school, don't argue, go to church. Go to college. Walk the path." If that was normal, what was Jess? She didn't want to ask; she found herself not revealing too many details about herself beyond talking about work. Work was an easy thing to hide behind. "What were you raised to be?" said Diane. "I don't know," said Jess. "I think I was just raised to be whatever I wanted to be." But that wasn't true either. She hadn't been raised to be the person she was. But she had turned out that way anyway.

Franny wasn't on social media, and though she had sent a picture along Jess wasn't prepared for how cool she was, kind of punk and kicky, spiked hair, a long flowing floral shirt, leather pants, a beautiful, big smile, incredible teeth, a golden coloring to her skin. A young, chic city girl. She laughed easily. She wasn't sullen in the slightest. But she cautiously held a kind of grace to herself; Jess could tell this when she hugged her. Franny gave her just a light pat on the back in greeting. I didn't do anything wrong, Jess wanted to say. Don't blame me.

They were there to meet in person for the first time but also to divide possessions. "Come on inside," said Diane. "I got here early and cleaned up, there were bugs everywhere. The screen on the porch needs fixing." They walked up to the house. "What's the tent for?" said Jess. "I'm roughing it," said Franny. "She doesn't want to sleep in the house," said Diane, lightly. Franny and Diane were both twenty-two years old, born just a few months apart. "I'm not into it," said Franny. "It doesn't feel like home to me." "You don't have to," said Jess. "There are no rules to any of this. But let's have a nice drink on the porch."

Jess dropped off her bag in the living room. The whole house felt different now although it looked the same. White pine floors, an array of lures on one wall, framed maps, a painting of an anonymous golden retriever. Jess stared at the painting. When Jess had asked her father about it once, he had said he had picked it up somewhere in his travels at a vintage store. How sad he'd been that they'd never been able to have a dog of their own, with Jess being allergic. Ah, that must she had always smelled in this house. She had always had sneezing fits when she visited, and had attributed that to being in nature. She felt just fine now. "Was this your dog?" She pointed at the painting. "Yes," said Diane. "She passed a few years ago. My sweet girl." Jess shook her head. "I'll have that drink now," she said.

Diane made them all a Tom Collins, and they sat together and caught the last of the sun.

"Did you ever see the blue heron?" said Diane. "I was looking for him all day yesterday but no luck."

"Yes!" said Jess. "I loved that bird. But I don't think they live that long."

"I never saw it," said Franny.

"He was finicky sometimes," said Diane. "He used to fly right over the river down there, but you never knew when he was coming. He was handsome though." To Jess she said, "You're right—he's probably long gone."

"I've only been here once, so I don't even know about any of that," said Franny. Her mother had been one of Robby's vendors, met him at a sales conference, the affair had lingered, it had even felt like love for a while, and she had wanted a baby, even if Robby wasn't sure. She kept Franny close, didn't want Robby much involved, which was fine by him, he had enough going on, although he called on occasion, sent her checks and gifts, and even though her mother explained to her this was for the best, this didn't make Franny feel any better. The one time she had been here was when she was thirteen—it was blurry now. She had been getting into trouble at school. Franny had thought it was a way for her parents to connect romantically, but it was actually closer to an intervention for her. That weekend all she felt was bitterness, that there was this whole world in this pretty little house on this sweet river, and she had been missing it her entire life. She had snapped at her father as she pleased, and he hadn't snapped back, just looked guilty. Although he did take her down the river in the kayak in the afternoon, but it was silent in that kayak, he was hulking and numb, and she had taken a pill to make her numb, too. Surrounded by nature sounds. "I was high enough that it sounded like an orchestra playing just for me," said Franny. (I'd like one of those pills right now, thought Jess.) It was the last time Franny saw him for more than a quick dinner. How was she supposed to know how to behave after all this time? How was she meant to cope with all of this? She worked as a waitress in a bar while finishing up her degree at Pratt. She was popular and busy. Now she had two sisters. She had her mother's nose though.

Jess started the grill. Diane had brought some hamburger meat and pounded it into patties. Franny kept drinking and followed Jess to the grill, hovered as she flipped the burgers.

"How do you feel about everything? Is it weird to be here?" said Jess.

"I barely know this place," said Franny. "I look around and all I keep thinking is I wish he was here so I could yell at him."

"I'm so hungry I could eat the world," said Jess, now suddenly tired and full of regret. She had driven into a storm after all, she could see that now.

At dinner, Diane said she'd done a survey of the building, gone through every nook and cranny, and she'd put together a few boxes for them to look through. But there was one more thing. The lockers downstairs. "I know those lockers," said Jess. Franny didn't know what they were talking about. Diane thought they corresponded to the three of them. "I never saw him open them," said Diane. "And I never asked him what was in them, but I'm pretty sure there's something in them."

"How can we open them?" said Jess.

"I've got his keys," she said. "I was waiting for y'all to get here. I didn't want to open them without you."

They pulled away from the table, the burgers unfinished. No one felt casual about anything. Downstairs, under the raised house, behind the Ping-Pong table, and next to the ice machine, were three gym lockers. Diane had a giant key ring. Keys to a lot of his properties, she said. Most everything was left to her mother, and Jess had to pretend like she didn't care about this, and really she didn't! (But she did.) But this house was theirs, shared. "Did he think we'd come together here like this?" said Jess. "Is this what he wanted?" "I don't care what he wanted," said Franny. Diane dropped the keys and laughed. "Look, my hands are shaking. I don't know why I'm nervous."

And then they were open. Two full lockers. All manner of objects, books, photos, curtains, toiletries, detritus of childhood. And an empty one, save for a set of pillowcases. Franny looked mortified.

Jess hugged her, but Franny was unmovable. Jess could feel her pain, nearly felt it radiating through her skin. Franny had more immediate needs than Jess did. Her pain felt bigger than Jess's. Then Jess felt her own pain recede as she made room for Franny's. There was nowhere else for it to go, so it began to dissipate, delicately, and in that way Jess could see how she could heal a little bit, get unstuck. She had been feeling bad since he died, and she was tired of it.

"You never came here," said Jess. "You said so yourself."

"I'm just never going to know now what I could or couldn't have gotten from him. You all had time with him, and I had nothing."

"We only had a part of him," said Diane. "It was our mothers that raised us, too." He raised me the most out of all of us, thought Jess, but she kept that to herself.

Franny wandered off down to the river while Diane and Jess looked through their lockers. She smoked a cigarette. This was a quiet moment for them, thought Franny. Let them have it. How quaint for them. How cute. Not for me. But for them.

•

IN THE MORNING, JESS ROSE AND MADE COFFEE, AND HEARD A light disturbance outside, some cursing, too. It was Franny, packing up her tent. Jess wandered down in her bedclothes to help. "You don't need to go," said Jess. "We could fill in some of the blanks for you. Get to know each other. We're sisters, after all."

"I don't need to fill in the blanks. My whole life with him was one huge blank. It was a complete absence. It would take forever to fill in the blanks. He would still have to be alive. I can't think the way you all do. I just have to move on."

"The moving on part, now that's just like him," said Jess. It was a joke.

"Fuck off," said Franny, but then she apologized.

"You get to feel however you want," said Jess. "There are no rules to feelings."

"Aren't you mad at him?"

"Of course I am! Isn't everyone mad at their parents?" said Jess. "I just don't have it in me to stay mad forever."

"I'm not making peace with him today," said Franny. "But I was glad I got to meet you."

Just then, Jess felt like she could be a sister to this woman. Someday.

•

DIANE SLEPT IN, AND WHEN SHE WOKE, JESS WAS MAKING
breakfast, pancakes and eggs and an entire package of bacon crack-
ling in the skillet. Jess told her Franny was gone.

"That's sad," said Diane.

"It's her right to go," said Jess.

They ate everything, a half pound of bacon between them, no regrets, and drank coffee and water and juice, and then they discussed
business matters. Aha, there was something she wanted after all,
thought Jess. Diane made a bid on the house to buy Jess out. Her
church wanted it as a retreat. That was her real work, said Diane,
even though it was not what she studied in school. But, in fact, it
turned out to be. Because someday she would go to divinity school
at Duke, then go on to become a pastor. Jess would fly down to New
Orleans when she was ordained and Diane would gush and throw her
arm around her and say, "Everyone, this is my sister." There would
be a brief pause as the gathered crowd noted Jess's arms and hands,
which were by then covered entirely in tattoos, her fair skin aging
and spotted, her hair gray and spiked, until one of Diane's parishio-
ners would say, "Sure, I see it. Y'all got the same nose."

"We could reinvent this place," said Diane, now, still nascent in
her desires. The faithful have a particular glow, thought Jess, and she
nearly said yes, felt like she just wanted to say yes to her sister, and
her people. Then Jess said gently that she did not think she could
say goodbye to the land forever. That it had been a part of her past,
too, even if there were lies involved. "Use it as you please," she said.
"I just want it sometimes." "We can work it out," said Diane. Only a
little grit to her voice.

"It's still strange to me," said Jess. "To have a sister. After never knowing I had one. Thinking it was just me and my mother and my aunt and that was it, that's all I had in my life."

"I knew about you though," said Diane. "I knew I had this sister out there somewhere, but we were just supposed to ignore it. My mother said it didn't matter, we had each other, more than enough family in Houston and New Orleans." Diane choked up for a second. "But it does matter, it matters to me that I have family, any kind of family at all. And I'm glad you came." Dabbed at a tear. "You got him the most."

"None of us really had him," said Jess.

They left the dishes, dirty, in the sink and took a walk down to the water. To look for the blue heron. Futile. "I keep hoping one of his kin will show up," said Diane. "Every time I come I think that there's got to be another one." Jess thought: It's enough that we had the one.

CHAPTER 15

2004

I t was the year 1998, and we were two divorced ladies, Sylvia and me, just looking for fun. Everyone saw us around town. Footloose and fancy-free. Hair and nails, done. We pinched our cheeks when we walked out the front door, into the great big wide world, and then we gave the world a big hug. We tried it all. We smoked pot. We threw house parties. We kissed men we weren't supposed to. We did all this for a while and then we looked at each other and said, What are we going to do next?

So, we took some classes: meditation, yoga, how to build a business from scratch. Self-help classes, we must have taken fifty of them over the years, and we read plenty of those books, too. Sometimes they gave us the answers, but more often they asked us hard questions about our lives. Once we took a seminar on how to be your best self that lasted for hours where we weren't allowed to get up and use the restroom once. To not be able to pee? How is that being your best self? No thank you. And I just want to say to everyone in this room: you can get up whenever you like.

Still, I loved these classes. When we were done with them, I would still want to keep talking and thinking. I'd have us write down pivotal moments in our lives, and then we'd swap our notes and read them out loud. Then I'd say, "Let's talk about what we want," and even though we couldn't always come up with the answers, it felt good to have tried. But maybe that was OK, to float for a while. We were two best girlfriends. We existed on a plane of togetherness. Two ladies who had experienced the same kind of losses. Do you all know what it's like to have friends like that?

It was all brand-new to me. I had never had a best friend before. I only have a sister, and we have our problems. She's always been an overachiever to the point it's like she wears her success like a mink coat. And she is someone who has problems with honesty. We know each other, and we are blood, but we are not close. I wouldn't call her to go out to dinner. Not if I wanted to enjoy the meal. But Sylvia and I had fun together. Sylvia was someone I could call whenever, go shopping with, encourage me to spoil myself, write me little cards and make me gifts just because. We saw the Steve Miller Band four times together. Fly like an eagle, baby. We were both forty-two years old, and we still looked good in our bikinis. And we lived off alimony quietly; we didn't flaunt it, like some people do.

And Sylvia deserved every penny. Her ex-husband was a well-known skin expert, and she had been his office manager, the brains behind it all. I won't say his name, but he was the Chicagoland area's top dermatologist—but only because Sylvia had the bright idea to call him that in the advertising. She went through a lot with him. Two miscarriages, the divorce, and she was on the other side of it, gathering strength, trying to figure out how to use it. For the both of us, there was the potential to make mistakes. All around us were cliffs we could step off.

One of those cliffs was a man named Max Volstag. A widower, which bestowed a glow on him that he was not necessarily worthy of, but he basked in it anyway. So what, his wife died and he had money? Did that make him so special? We met him at temple, which he joined after his wife Claudette's passing—may her memory be a blessing—he said to connect with God but also to make some new friends. He was rich and handsome. How did he not have any friends? you might wonder. But there he was, sitting by himself at a Jewish singles mixer on a Thursday night. Sylvia and I sprinted over to him like two schoolgirls racing home after class, shoving each other out of the way to win.

Max was part man, part wolf. Hairy chest, hairy arms, and a nice head of hair on top. Men, if they keep their hair, they think they're really special, don't they? He owned three mattress and bedding stores, and two 7-Elevens. He had hustled a lot when he was younger, plus he had some help from his deceased wife's family, at least in terms of business advice and connections, and the fact that he had never had children had freed him up to work long hours. But he was lonely—he told us this the first time we met him at the mixer. Right away he saw me and Sylvia as friends and peers rather than as romantic interests. He put both arms around us at the end of the night and walked us out to the parking lot, and said, "Ladies, I think we're going to be great friends. Finally, some people I can pal around with." We wondered later if we weren't pretty enough or hadn't flirted enough or were in some way awkward around him. But that wasn't the reason, we were soon to learn.

Were we both angling for Max's attention? Maybe. We had each other but still we got lonely sometimes. It had been a few years since my divorce. My daughter, Jessica, was home after college but neither needed or wanted anything from me, and in fact preferred it if I stayed away from her entirely. If I went anywhere near her, made any suggestions about how she might improve herself, particularly in the looks department, because I just wanted her to have a fun summer, maybe spend some time with a nice young man, she rebuffed me. Anything I had to say about her hair. Forgive me for noticing her beautiful hair. She cut half of it off, I near had a heart attack. But I said, Fine, do it your own way, what do I know, and then I called Sylvia and then we would talk about Max for an hour.

Max had a fifty-four-foot miniature yacht, which he took out every weekend on the lake. Every Saturday night, another party on his boat, and we loved to be invited to it. But we noticed almost immediately that the other guests were young. Young enough to be our children? Close. Maybe they thought of us as aunties, the other party guests. We didn't hate it, but it took us a moment to adjust. We knew we had a reason for being there—we had been invited just like everyone else— but what was it? So we just started helping. Serving drinks, putting out the appetizers, cleaning up after everyone. By the time the boat docked, Max could toss a few trash bags over his shoulder and roll out to his Benz, blowing us a kiss goodbye. We were happy to do this every weekend. It gave us something to look forward to all week long. Even if we were the oldest girls at the party.

There was always a new batch of young women every week. Sylvia and I were consistent. They would have a good time, we would gab with them, drink, maybe do a little toot, flirt, be casual and funny, and then they were gone the next weekend. After so many years of the same people, the steadiness of our lives, we found this wild and freeing, although we wondered where they went after their time on the boat. Where did they disappear to? How come they didn't want to stick around? Was there another, better party somewhere else? We weren't really concerned though. We, the divorcées, were the stable ones, on this boat, with the widower at its helm.

These women were not his dates, necessarily, but his accessories. Midtwenties, sure, you've seen the world a little bit. When I was their age I was already married and had had a baby, I told them, and they shuddered. I found myself mothering these women on the boat—no, that's not quite right. Mothering them would have been

tending to them, indulging them. This was something a little different from that. I'd ask them what they really wanted, what they were
looking for from life. What are your goals? What are you dreams?
What have been the most successful moments in your life, when
things have changed for you? Have you ever felt like you failed, and
things switched into a negative direction?

I asked these questions with confidence and authority because I
had taken so many classes in self-actualization by that point, but a little part of me was hoping they'd know something I didn't. The young
will lead the way. And who was I if not a stunted adult? I had somehow
skipped my twenties entirely, with all the moving we did because of
my ex-husband and all his jobs, and then add to that being a mother?
These young ladies were having the time I had not. The time I was now
trying to have.

But then there was one of them that stuck around. Let's call her
Tina. God, she was gorgeous. You know we never really appreciate
what we have when we're young. Everything's firmer and tighter and
we take it for granted like it's going to last forever, or at least longer
than it does. But she had it, youth, in spades. She was a skinny minny
from the West Side of Chicago, this beautiful mutt, just gorgeous
olive-toned skin and huge black curls, a pretty, pretty girl, half Italian,
half Jewish on her mother's side. She hadn't been raised Jewish but
had an interest in understanding it more, which is how she fell in with
us, showing up at the temple, coming out of a storm one night before
Shabbat services, shaking off the rain from her coat, like some sort of
lost puppy who had been trapped outside for too long.

Not that she was a dummy. She was smart. She paid attention to
everyone. But she seemed without direction, and she had a deep,
deep crush on Max. I wanted to take care of her, and I thought by doing that I could take care of myself a bit, too. Things weren't so great
between me and my own daughter, I am ashamed to say this, because

I want to be a model of success and communication. It's good to be able to admit your flaws and mistakes though. How else will we learn from them?

My daughter was—she is—an artist. She has been creative and quiet and special since she was a little girl. Very different from me, sure, but still the same rules of the world apply to everyone. I thought maybe she could get a job, so she could have something to do with her time besides sit in her room all day making her collages and talking to people on her computer, and while I think it is good to communicate, obviously, this did not seem to me to be a positive use of a twenty-one-year-old woman's time. Who was she talking to? Why wasn't she out in the world? What was her long-term plan here? Why was her hair suddenly short when it looked so beautiful long? These were the questions I had for her, but I never got around to asking the right ones. Instead, everything came out sounding like a criticism.

But with Tina I had no problem asking her helpful and probing questions. Isn't it interesting how it's sometimes easier for us to talk to strangers than it is our own family? With Tina everything was free-flowing and easy. Most of these women—"Max's girls," we called them, me and Sylvia—showed up one week and then were gone the next, but Tina kept showing up, and so we began to think of her as one of ours. We were just his friends and we belonged there. We weren't even looking for love necessarily. After all, we'd already been in love once.

My love had been a husband who had practically disappeared into thin air. I had been accustomed to his traveling life—it had been like that nearly since we began our marriage—but one morning I woke up and checked my calendar and I realized he had been gone for months. There was money in the bank account, all the bills had been paid by his secretary, the mortgage, the utilities, my shopping credit card, all of it, taken care of by some faceless person named Marlene I had never met. But no husband. He was a ghost.

That day I called this assistant. I said, "Hello, Marlene, this is Mrs. Beck." And she coughed and said, "Hello, Mrs. Beck," and she paused for so long it was like she was trying to figure something out and then she asked me how the weather was where I was, and I said, "Oh, it's a sunny cool spring day here in Chicago," and she said, "Chicago! Right!" and I said, "Do you know where my husband is?" and she said, "Not in Chicago?" So no one knew where he was or she was covering for him or I don't know what, but I said, "If you speak to him, tell him I'm looking for him."

Five minutes later he called. He was at an airport, he said, although it sounded quiet where he was, like he'd closed a door behind him. He'd been traveling for a month straight. I said, "I don't even care where you are really, but what are we doing here? Do you even live here?" I had known my husband since we were freshmen in college. He was the first person I ever had sex with, and I was the third person he'd ever had sex with, and we knew each other's bodies and bones and we absolutely knew when the other person was lying, so he didn't even try to lie. "I feel like I live nowhere at all," he said. "Are you happy?" I said. I meant in our marriage, but I think he took it to mean about his life. "Am I happy . . . sometimes. I'm actually exhausted a lot of the time," he said. "Do you want something new out of your life?" I said. I was still talking about our marriage. "Yes," he said. "Then let's do it," I said. "Let's move on from each other." I realized at that moment that my marriage was a block in my life that needed to be removed. But also it was a block in *his* life, too. I hadn't thought of it like that before. But then it all felt so simple. I shouldn't be married to this person for a second longer. He offered me a sum, and I accepted.

And then suddenly I had all the free time in the world and no idea what to do with it. I'd always had it, but with a husband or at least the idea of a husband in the background, there was a certain kind of obligation—I imagined this anyway. Now my daughter was gone, too, or would be soon. So it was just me. And Sylvia. And now Tina.

The summer was coming to an end. Soon enough we'd have to bundle up to go out on the lake. Things were going to be less sexy and fun. Jess would go to art school in London and my house would be empty again and I still didn't know what I wanted to do with the rest of my life. I was supposed to be looking for a deeper meaning and purpose for months, years by then, and I had spent the entire summer making appetizers and sweeping decks.

The last time I stepped foot on that boat I brought a seven-layer dip. I say seven layers but really it was eight because I added an extra layer of beans to it. Not a thing people can always tell, if there's an extra layer, but I think they can feel it. I was always trying to do a little bit more for these parties than I did the week before. If I am going to be honest with myself, by the end of the summer Sylvia and I had become competitive with each other. If I made three different dips and a charcuterie plate, she made a chocolate cake and cupcakes and cookies and brought a cheese plate with fresh fruit and maybe a dessert wine, which to this day I will claim was a waste of money when all these people just wanted to drink cans of beer and boxed wine. If instead of sweeping the deck she mopped it, in my opinion needlessly, I shined the brass. Neither of us ever laughed so hard at one man's jokes. Looking back, I could see Max had two full-time chefs, cleaners, deckhands, and hostesses at his service, and he wasn't paying us a dime. And he hadn't even asked us to do any of it, or even really suggested it. Could I blame him? But he hadn't stopped us either. What was his responsibility to us anyway? Do we women ever stop and ask ourselves that question, or are we too busy worrying about how we can be responsible to someone else?

That evening, Tina helped me clean up in the kitchen. It was there that she whispered to me that she thought she might be in love with Max. I said, "No, honey, you aren't." "He's helping me get a job," she said. "Call an employment agency instead," I said. She blushed. They had made love, I thought. And she'd stuck around. Foolish girl. "I think he needs me," she said. "You're never going to win his heart," I told her. None of us are, I thought. I said, "Look at all these other girls coming and going. He's not available." "You never know," said Tina. "For god's sake, the name of the ship is *The Claudette*," I said. I started laughing. We were floating on a boat named after his dead wife. "We're just a distraction," I said to her. Claudette bought all the furniture for this boat, Claudette was the first person to sleep with him on this boat, and there was even a framed picture of her that hung on the quarter deck next to where Max steered us toward the sunset every weekend. "We thought this boat was a midlife crisis, too," I said. "But we have spent enough time here and with Max to realize this boat is a floating tribute to her, and for as long as he keeps it exactly as it is here on Lake Michigan, it doesn't matter how many twenty-five-year-old girls he sleeps with, he's never going to let her go and move on." My voice was too loud, I knew it. "You think you want Max? You don't want Max," I said.

A late summer storm rolled in and caught us off guard. I stopped for a second and looked at the lightning on the horizon against the purple sky and for a moment I wanted to be there, wherever the lightning was, or be the lightning, itself, because it always seemed to know what it wanted, where it wanted to go, where it wanted to land. The boat began to shake and rock and we were only fifteen minutes from shore, but it still felt chaotic. I lost track of people, but also it was that dip, the eighth layer of that dip, that sent my stomach reeling. I spent the rest of the trip in the private toilet. I heard everyone race off the boat above me once we had docked. By the time I was done everyone had left the boat—or at least I thought they had. I heard a little clatter coming from the kitchen, and I thought surely it was Sylvia doing one last round of cleanup. And why should she get to do it alone? I thought. I won't have Sylvia cleaning up after that storm, I thought. I won't have her getting all the credit, being there last.

I entered the kitchen and saw Max's hair-covered ass thrusting in and out, a woman's hands wrapped around his neck, clinging to him like he was a tree. All this slapping and grunting—honestly they sounded like they were having a lot of fun. What's that very crude expression? They were porking. Like animals. I dropped the platter I was carrying in surprise. I had meant to sneak out quietly. Max turned, revealing Sylvia on the counter. I strangely turned very prim. "Well, I never," I said, a phrase that I had never in my entire life uttered besides that moment. "Whore," I said, also not a word I used. And I spun around and left the kitchen. I didn't want to bear witness a moment longer.

But Sylvia followed me. She grabbed me and I turned and I screamed, "This friendship was a waste and a lie." Did we make an agreement not to sleep with him? Not out loud. Did we say casually to each other, I would never? Yes. But we still sought his praise in a competitive way. He was not our ex-husband, but he was some kind of male figure in our lives. An uncle, a father, a brother. OK, maybe an ex-husband, too. He was a presence. Tall men, big men, they have their way with the world, don't they? I was hurt because I felt like she had been dishonest with me. I thought she had been sneaking around behind my back with him—although I was later to learn it was just that one time.

Also, and this was initially painful to admit but helpful to realize down the line: I didn't want Max, but I wanted to be wanted by him. I was hurt because I hadn't had sex in a while, and I was beginning to feel like I would never have sex with anyone again. When Max finally chose one of us, and it was her that he chose, it made me feel unattractive. I say "chose" even though it wasn't like we offered him that choice in any sort of verbal way, but it seemed implied: We were both there for so long, was anything going to happen already? But, of course, we were giving him power. And that was wrong. No one should have any particular power over you, especially sexually, if you can help it. And I gave it to him. I let him make me feel like I was unattractive. But it doesn't matter what he thinks. It only matters what I think. I hadn't processed all that yet though. I couldn't see the moment for what it was.

"This friendship is over," I told Sylvia, lightning all around us, Max probably buckling up his pants somewhere else.

I went home and I didn't know who to talk to, so I talked to my daughter. Jess was sitting in her bedroom with her sketchbook and some fashion magazines, shredding them apart, like she'd been do-ing since she was a teenager. I don't know why she did that kind of thing. I wanted to understand her, you know that, right? Don't we just want to understand the people we love? She listened to me rant for a while about Sylvia and Max and my wasted summer and then I started talking about her wasted summer, too—I was a little drunk, fine—and then she said, "I want to talk about something else," and I said, "I'm not done talking though," and she said, "I need to tell you something, and it's important," and I said, "What I'm saying is important, too," and she said, "You're not listening to me. You're not hearing what I'm saying. I'm telling you something. I'm at a turning point in my life and I need you to pay attention. I'm *pivoting*, Mother." And this worked for me at last. This language worked. This made me pay attention.

Even though she was making fun of me and my studies and also, in a way, my struggles, it was actually the way I could best hear what she was saying. It was helpful language, it had helped us communicate. Did I wish I could hear her on her own terms? Yes. But the real lesson here is having a meeting point, an intersection of how we can talk to each other so we can finally really listen. Today I want to offer you access to that language. And we'll get to that in a moment. After I tell you the end of this story.

I was blind of course. I didn't quite get what it meant to be gay. I didn't have a problem with it, I thought, but I didn't understand it either. I didn't know anyone who was gay or at least I didn't think I knew anyone who was gay. Now I see that there were gay people all around me, but I just wasn't paying attention to it because it didn't concern me. I had an understanding of the AIDS crisis on a basic level, but it was something that seemed to be happening in San Francisco or New York City, not in our small town. It was someone else's disease, not mine. I thought I was liberal, but what does that even mean? I voted Democrat, but didn't even really know why, except that they were the ones who supported women's rights, which, ostensibly, I wanted, although I didn't even know what to do with the ones that I had. My life was so much about pleasing men, seeking their validation in one way or another. I had no idea how to validate myself without it. It could not even occur to me that my daughter already knew how to validate herself without it. I'm not saying she has it all figured out, but she wasn't swabbing anyone's decks for free. And I love her. I love my gay daughter.

A few weeks later, Jess left for London. Now I was all by myself again. I was despondent about Sylvia but I could not bring myself to call her. I needed her to reach out. I thought I would run into her in all our usual spots, but I didn't. Every night for weeks I sat in the Starbucks on Lake Cook Road, waiting for her to walk in the door. I lingered in the self-help section at Barnes & Noble. I hit our regular classes at Curves. I went to Friday-night services, no Sylvia. I learned that getting a mani-pedi is just not as much fun on your own. But I was too stubborn.

It was Sylvia who came to me. She was sitting on my front stoop one day. She looked thinner and paler than ever, but also her eyes were bright with inspiration. What she said to me was, "I miss you, you're important to me, and also I have an idea." I hugged her, I invited her into my home. I said, "Tell me." I opened a bottle of wine in the kitchen and we stood around the island and clinked glasses and I felt so relieved to see her. Like my heart just released. I cried. "OK," I said. "Go."

"You're good at talking to people about their problems," she said. "And I think you can help people." She said that I had helped her throughout our friendship and I had even helped her to be more open about her sexual desires, even though I didn't know I was doing it at the time. I thought the questions I was asking her were about what she wanted to do with her life, meaning how she wanted to spend her time, what she thought her career should be, if she should even have a career, how she wanted to connect with the world in a bigger way, what her needs and goals were. But really what she wanted to do was screw Max. But actually, what it really turned out to be was that she had to screw Max in order to get through this block in her life. Max wasn't the block. But men were the block. Or that kind of man anyway.

And all of this had not been for nothing, Sylvia told me. Our friendship had been neither a waste or a lie, and I had been a part of her becoming the person she needed to be. She said that this was an important moment in her life and she was ready to pivot in a new direction, and that she had learned that from me. All that talk about pivots. All our discussions about turning points. All of it had meant something to her. It meant nothing to Jess, but it meant something to her. And when she told me all that, I realized that it genuinely meant something to me. That helping her gave my life some kind of meaning. And I wanted to do it again.

So I stand here before you offering you my help. It is it a pure act? I can't tell you that. I mean, we're charging you for the service, so it's not a charity here. And to that end, make sure you stop by and sign paperwork with Sylvia as you leave. Yes, she's here. Everyone wave hello to Sylvia. The woman in the stunning pink silk blouse in the rear of the room. Isn't she gorgeous? Give her a round of applause for being such a good sport, letting me talk about her in front of her like that. But she has taught me as much as I have her. Me and Sylvia, here together, for you.

I realized that we would work together in a perfect fashion. Knowing each other's flaws and weaknesses, and strengths, and how they mixed and matched. I, for example, was never going to be the kind of woman to screw any kind of man that would take away my power. And Sylvia had become a person who took what she wanted. So we've started over. Slowly, but surely. Not as divorcées—we're done with that—but as businesswomen. Business partners. Me and Sylvia. People show up in your life for a reason. I see you all nodding your heads again. We're here to help you.

CHAPTER 16

2006

They were stuck in traffic, but at least they had each other. Shelly and Jess hadn't seen each other in a year, but now here they were together, in New York, heading into the city, across the Manhattan Bridge. God, it was good to see her, thought Shelly. Wiry, calm Jess. Not a hair on her head. The way Jess looked was almost starting to make sense to Shelly.

"Will you be happy to see your art school friends?" said Shelly. "I don't know where you're at right now with your work."

"Give me a second to navigate this," said Jess. She hadn't mentioned to her aunt yet that she'd given up her studio space for good, resigned from the collective, locked a few boxes away in storage.

The light finally turned green, and the cars inched forward. They made their way to the other side of the bridge, spilling out into Chinatown.

"I thought this was going to be fun for us, a little adventure," said Shelly. "I'm sorry about the traffic." They had somehow gotten lost and ended up taking the wrong bridge.

"It's all right," said Jess. She had driven from Chicago the day before and picked up her aunt this morning from her apartment on Smith Street. Her aunt shoved a few hundred dollars in her hand for gas money, and then a few hundred dollars more for her time. Jess didn't blink: she just took it.

"It is, it really is!" Chill out, Shell, but she couldn't. Her whole life had changed, she couldn't lose her family, too. "Here we are, together." She patted Jess's arm.

For a while they talked about Jess's tattoos. Not Shelly's favorite topic, but absolutely Jess's favorite topic. Is that what you're doing instead of making paintings? thought Shelly. So determined to support Jess's art. That was her role. She needed a role again.

"And so how is your work going?" said Shelly.

"Don't worry about my work," snapped Jess. "How's *your* work going?"

They'd only just started speaking again. The trial had been unbecoming. Offensive, once the emails had been released. Shelly had been on the stand for only two days, but that was enough. Jess had read about it in the *Chicago Tribune* and then hid her head in her hands, skipped a party that night, prayed it would blow over. For the next few weeks, she dodged phone calls about her capitalist aunt, the great betrayer of women. Then everyone moved on to the next crisis, the next annoyance, as they always did.

She couldn't believe Shelly wouldn't have told her in the first place. "I'm disappointed in you," she told her aunt in one furious phone call, and she marveled afterward at how much she sounded like an adult. When your heroes fail in your eyes, that's when you grow up, thought Jess. "I never want to speak to you again," she said.

But Jess mulled on it for months. She did not feel she could forgive her yet, but she still thought about her constantly. The illusion of her aunt being a supportive person. And how secretive she was. What even *was* their relationship? Finally, she talked to Diane about it. Diane was in Houston, back at home with her mother, still, since the hurricane, hoping to get back soon to New Orleans. She had turned out to be wise counsel even though she was a few years younger.

"What would you do?" said Jess.

"I always lean toward forgiveness if they're asking and it's possible. I always lean toward hope." Diane's mother was suddenly rustling around in the background. "Mommy, I'm making a call here." Jess heard a door shut. "How did I never feel like this was tight quarters growing up and now I'm crawling out of my skin?" she said. "OK, on the other hand, you can actually just stay as mad at her as long as you like. There are no rules here."

But then she went to that speech of her mother's and she was so appalled by it, so angry about what her mother had said about her, her story, her personal life, and how she was using it to make money. She could not have conflict with both her mother and her aunt at the same time; she could be mad at one, or she could be mad at the other, but she could not live without speaking to one of them, and so she chose to forgive Shelly—or at least ignore the facts—and move on.

Jess was still angry, though. And she had a few things left to say.

"I don't understand how you didn't tell me about it for so long," said Jess. "If you had been up front. If you had told me the truth so I didn't have to hear about it on the news. It was mortifying."

"It's complicated," said Shelly. "I signed all this paperwork years ago. Nondisclosure agreements. But I want you to know I regret it. I never meant to hurt anyone." She wiped her face of—what? There were no tears there. The humiliation. "I'm just glad you're here with me today. Thank you for reaching out. I just want you to know it was not me, truly. Not the me you know."

"Listen, this is just a trial—" Jess hit the brakes, and the car jerked them both. A suited man had darted out through traffic. All the cars had stopped again. "Look at this fucking guy," said Jess. She gunned the engine, made eye contact with the man. He carelessly slapped the front hood of her car. "Oh my god, what?" said Jess. "Did he actually just do that?" said Shelly. The two of them started cursing, and Jess honked a few times for good measure.

When the man turned and looked at the source of the noise he could hear nothing they were saying, could only see two dark-eyed women energetically moving their mouths, one woman older, with a glossy, stylish look, and a sheen to her skin, age undetectable, and the other woman, younger, with a shaved head, in a denim jacket, tough, but too small to be a real threat to him. They were both giving him the finger at the same time, and then he was giving them the finger, and then he was through the cars, on the street corner, laughing, because he couldn't hear them, didn't need to know what they had to say to him anyway, and then he was gone, he had somewhere better to be, and they were still there, furious, and stuck in traffic.

•

A HALF HOUR LATER, THEY REACHED THE WEST SIDE HIGHWAY, and things had cooled down. Now they felt better, now they felt bonded again. Joined in anger.

"How's your nana?" said Shelly. She hadn't been to Chicago in months. "Still ailing. I give her acupuncture once a week, and I think it helps." Frieda had been sick for a while. A bad liver, bad lungs. All those years of drinking and smoking. "I like spending time with her," said Jess. "She's led a real life, you know? Her stories are sort of terrible, but also she survived them." We admire the survivors, thought Shelly. "I'm pretty sure she and Mom fight constantly," said Jess.

"I knew that was a bad idea, them living together. But you can't talk either of them out of anything." Shelly's phone rang and she dug it out of her bag. "It's your mother," she said.

"Don't answer it," said Jess.

"I can't not answer it," said Shelly.

"You sure can. I didn't tell her I was coming. I didn't want to deal with it," said Jess.

"I told her you were coming," said Shelly. "She should know where you are."

Shelly just wants Mom to know I'm with *her*, thought Jess.

Forever—the rest of their lives anyway, a few more decades yet—Shelly and Nancy and Jess all took turns being mad at each other, then forgiving each other, and then starting all over again. Not to mention that somewhere along the way Jess and Shelly had become closer than Jess and Nancy or Shelly and Nancy, and it made Nancy furious. Everyone knew it, and they all played it off each other, just taking turns driving each other crazy and making each other feel good or bad, and nobody won, and nobody lost, they were always just in the state of playing this game. This was just how it worked out for these three complicated women in the end.

"I'm twenty-nine years old, it's OK if my mother doesn't know where I am. She frequently has no idea what's going on in my life."

"I'm just going to answer it. I told her we would be in the car together this morning."

"If you pick up that phone, then it's like she's in the car here with us, and then it's different, that's a different experience we're having. And it's not even that it's that bad between us. It's just cold. I know she doesn't really agree with my life or who I am. Or doesn't understand it. And it's tiresome to have to explain it to her. I have to be in the mood to deal with her." Also, thought Jess, did you really tell her what we're doing together?

"I hear you but also she'll know we're ignoring her. So, we either hear about it now or later. She'll just keep calling," said Shelly. "Your mother is the face of persistence."

"Have you seen her face lately? I barely recognize it."

The phone stopped ringing.

"Let me ask you a question, what's the difference between what you do with all those tattoos and what we do with our faces? There's nothing wrong with a little maintenance," said Shelly. "It's rough out there for us old broads." She had more sympathy for her sister than Jess did, but she also knew that everything Jess said was true. When things should have gotten easier between Jess and her mother, when they should have relaxed into just knowing each other and loving each other, really appreciating each other, their relationship was instead fraught and fragile. **How do we recover us**, Nancy had texted Jess on New Year's Day, but Jess hadn't replied.

"She's really blond now, too," said Jess. "It's a little much."

"Well, that I agree with. Platinum blond, I saw that on Facebook. She likes to forget where she came from," said Shelly.

Now they were back in safe territory: making fun of Nancy. Nancy's latest YouTube video streaming from a beach in Costa Rica, Nancy's passive-aggressive newsletters selling all manner of spiritual guidance, naturopathic and alternative medicines, organic clothing, essential oils, vitamins, yoga mats, weekend healing packages. And then there was Nancy's new, weird obsession with vaccinations. "She doesn't even have any kids to vaccinate anymore," said Shelly. "What does she care?"

"I just went to the one speech, and that was enough," said Jess. After years of gathering people in small conference rooms at the Oak Brook Marriott, this past year Nancy had finally begun to fill auditoriums, and hundreds and hundreds of people bought her self-published book each time and online every week, too. Even though she had no medical degree, just framed certificates of workshops she had taken herself. But somehow she had developed a following, and people looked to her for guidance. She was certainly busy. Jess described the crowd to Shelly: all these moon-eyed middle-aged ladies staring up at her mother like she was the second coming of Christ. "These people are obsessed with her," said Jess. And how strange it was to hear her mother talking about Jess herself. The way her mother had used her sexuality in that speech—the way she had used her entire family—as part of the story she told to make money had disgusted her. But she could not deny it had been effective.

"I honestly didn't know she was such a good public speaker," said Jess.

"All those years in retail," said her aunt. "She's just selling them ideas."

She took their money and she gave them a little comfort. There weren't big promises being made here. But still, it felt like a con to both of them. On the other hand, who were they to argue with Nancy making a living?

The phone rang again.

"Please don't. Let it go to voicemail," said Jess.

Shelly's finger hovered above the phone. She didn't know how to ignore her sister. She didn't know how to not pick up the phone. It had been a lifetime of always picking up the phone. Even when they weren't speaking, they still knew what was going on in each other's lives. Even when they were feeling coldest to each other, they still kept a connection.

She picked up the phone.

Jess kept her hands on the steering wheel, and shook her head, pursed the corner of her mouth. These two old bitches, she thought. Love to bitch at each other. Just wait.

"Yes, it's this car we're in now," said Shelly. "I had it for a long time, and then Jess had it for the last year or so? You never saw it? Well, I don't know what you have or haven't seen, Nancy. No, I don't know what she's going to do for a car now. These are questions you can ask her. I'm not giving her one, no. That's not the plan. You'll have to ask her. You'll have to ask her. She's driving. You can't ask her now. Ask her later." She turned to Jess. "Your mother wants to say hello."

"Tell her I'll call her later," said Jess.

"I'm just going to put her on speaker for a second." Jess mouthed, *NO*. "You know what, there's too much traffic. I just want her to concentrate on driving. I know. She'll call you later. I'll see you in a few days. How is she this morning, by the way? Did you talk to her? Uh-huh. She sure sleeps a lot. Maybe that's good though. Keeps her busy." Shelly laughed at the response to that.

Shelly hung up.

"Are you mad? Don't be mad."

"I'm not mad. I just find her exhausting. And now I have to call her."

"Tell you what, call her and I'll buy you a car."

"Not fair. You were already getting me the car," said Jess.

"Just call your mother," said Shelly. And Jess would, later, sitting in Shelly's living room, on speakerphone, Shelly hovering in the background, paying attention to their interactions, making sure Nancy was being kind to her daughter, making sure Jess was giving her a chance to be kind. She knew what it was like to have a mother and to want that mother to show up for you and love you. She knew what it was like to shut your mother out, too. She just wanted everything to be a little easier for the people she loved. There weren't that many of them anymore. So she held them close.

"What's the turnoff?" said Jess. "Forty-Sixth Street," said Shelly. "She's just at Ninth."

"Are you ready for this?" said Jess. "Are you excited to see your old friend?"

"I think so," said Shelly. But still Shelly felt wary. Margaret was one of the few people on the planet who could rile Shelly up. Maybe she was just driving into the fire.

"You had it easier than me, you know," said Shelly.

"You were the one who made it easy for me first," said Jess. "By showing me Grandpa's robes. In the crawl space." The reason why she could never stay mad at Shelly. The reason why she would always forgive her.

"Don't make me cry, it'll mess up my makeup," said Shelly.

Finally, they made their way to Forty-Sixth Street, where they passed an orange-and-silver-haired woman dressed in all black, worn jeans, worn T-shirt, leather jacket, looking happy and slightly mortified to be outside just standing on a street corner. "She doesn't think it's dignified," said Shelly. "Look at her." She laughed. "Poor Margaret hustling on a street corner." "God, you've got such a crush on her," said Jess. Somehow they found a perfect parking spot, as if it had been waiting for them all along.

CHAPTER 17

2007

Two things could be true at the same time: Shelly Cohen could support women in the workplace, but also she could turn the other cheek when it came to her boss's sexual appetites for his underlings. She could start internship programs for women within the company, donate 5 percent of her income a year to a girls-in-STEM nonprofit, seek out female engineers to hire, visit graduate programs, and look directly at the young women looking back at her with beaming, shining eyes. And she could ignore every single complaint about Monroe that came across her desk for the last five years.

She had done it for so long she didn't notice when it was happening anymore. Or she had other things to worry about. But also, she thought: Didn't they know what they were getting into? Hadn't they read the gossip columns? Was there any grand surprise here that Monroe was sleeping with whomever he pleased, and had been for decades? Were they star fuckers, these girls? Maybe, she thought. She couldn't imagine loving him. (Although she did, in her way.) Always this flock of women surrounded him in the office, when she did see him, or on his airplane or at a gala or in an expensive restaurant or off the coast of Malta on a freaking yacht (she had never been on that yacht, not once!), and there were pictures in the paper and on the internet and TV highlights on occasion, although fewer lately because he had only been on the top ten richest men in the world list once in the year 2004, as in one actual day, when all the forces on the global and American markets had aligned, and he was a billionaire that day, many times over, and then the next day, it was done. But it only takes the one time for people to think of you as one of the richest men in the world, thought Shelly, and so she was never surprised, not once, to hear that he was screwing someone new. She only cared when it got in the way of him needing to make an important decision. She only paid attention when he was missing in action or when there was a grumbling of a lawsuit. These women made their choices, she thought. They existed, she knew this problem existed, and then she tuned it out. She was in another office, he traveled around the world. It was too hard to keep track. This is what she told herself.

Only once at a conference in Hong Kong did she see the full physical realization of his behaviors. She saw him with a different woman every night; she ran into two of them in the hotel elevator, two days in a row. Hello, Clara; Hello, Stephanie. They looked nothing like his wife, who was plump and satisfied in Seattle, tended to by helpers, busy with her new horse stables on Whidbey Island, the last of their children newly matriculating at Brown. Another world, these women, who were so beautiful as to seem digitally altered, perfect composites of all the things that were considered attractive in the world. Shelly tried to keep up. Shelly used fillers in her cheeks and took barre classes three times a week and walked fifteen thousand steps a day. Got her roots touched up once a month. But still she had never gotten the work done that these women had, where they had walked into an office and handed a picture to a doctor and said, "Make me look just like this."

Neither had Tova, still in Seattle, fending off offers from Motorola and Apple, using her age and wisdom as a feature rather than a deficit. Tova was strict and physically active and kept an enormous water bottle by her desk and drank from it every hour on the hour throughout the workday until it was gone. Tova took kickboxing classes two days a week and ran 10Ks for fun and wore sheath dresses that showed off her figure but were in no way revealing. Tova had a look and stuck with it. Tova was playing a different game entirely.

Neither game was wrong, thought Shelly. She judged no one for their appearance (and in fact admired them, because who did not like pretty things?) and believed they probably were competent at their jobs, whatever their jobs were within the company. It was simply two paths, two ways of the world, and after many years of trying to help Monroe be a better man, she just didn't pay attention to any of it anymore lately.

Except for that one time, on his private plane, on the sixteen-hour flight back to New York City from the conference, where they would stop for the night for dinner. She had said, "Monroe, as your friend, as your employee number thirty-five, I must ask you, what is going on with all these women? I expect more from a strategic thinker such as yourself." He assured her they all signed agreements, were willing participants, and there was no undue pressure. And then he said, "You know you're the only person I'll let speak to me this way, Cohen," and she laughed, and he said, "Now never do it again," and then she laughed again but he wasn't laughing and then she stopped laughing but then he *did* laugh and he patted her knee and said, "Ah, I'm just fucking with you," he said, but was he? She didn't know.

But when all the bad news came out about him two years ago, that, in fact, some of them had not been willing, that not everyone had signed agreements, and people began to demand he be held accountable for his actions, she wished she had pushed it further, realized almost immediately she had not done enough. Because there was Tova leading the charge against him. Tova had kept records, emails, receipts, when Shelly had shrugged it off. Tova, always two years behind Shelly, finally figured out how to catch up.

But should she have lost her job? When the board removed him so briskly and she was called into court to say what she knew about his behaviors she felt she was on trial herself. All those years, and this is what it amounts to? She was angry at everyone (Monroe! Tova!) but herself, and then a few months later she was fired, falling slowly to earth with the help of that golden parachute. That was the only thing she ever had done with her life, work for them. No going-away party for Shelly. She craved to be remembered. The trails she had blazed! Was any of this fair? But she knew they would just try and forget about her as soon as she was gone. And then, somehow, brutally, just two weeks later, to run into Asher and his young bride pushing a fucking stroller, are you fucking kidding her? Was that fair either?

So when her sister called to tell her their mother was still sick, would be sick for a long time, would, in fact, never get well again, but that she, Nancy, could not regularly, physically, have her in her home any longer, because they were not getting along and it was distracting her from her work, but also she did not have anything left to give to her, that she was now officially tapped out after several years of caring for her, and maybe Shelly could think of someone else besides herself for a minute, Shelly said, "I'm coming home."

•

"I COULDN'T BELIEVE IT," SAID SHELLY, ABOUT SEEING ASHER with a child. "It wasn't even a conversation we'd ever had, not even once, except when we would see children crying in public, and what it did to their mothers, and one of us would say, glad that's not us." Shelly and her mother were playing Scrabble, the board spread out next to Frieda in bed.

"It wasn't that bad when you were babies, it's when you got older and could talk back that was hard," said Frieda. She started coughing and couldn't stop for a while. "Jesus Christ, Mom, you really did a number on yourself," said Shelly, and Frieda said, "Don't make me laugh, it hurts." She was so sick. Shelly began to make a real dent in the stack of old *Time* magazines in the doctor's waiting room. She kept asking him if her mother was dying, and he couldn't really say. "Well, is she living?" she asked once, and he couldn't answer that either.

"Do you need anything?" said Shelly.

"I just need you to be here," said Frieda. "Just tell me what I missed all this time." Shelly told her mother her secrets, not just about Asher but also about her successes, her failures, and it felt good to tell anyone all of those things, and also it felt good to tell her mother. (She left out Margaret; she couldn't say why.) When Frieda asked about her dreams, Shelly said, "If you had asked me a year ago, I could have clearly outlined the next five years of my life. But now I see nothing ahead of me. Not necessarily a bad thing, but also it's terrifying." Her mother promised her it would all work out, and Shelly let herself be assuaged by her words. Why not let herself be soothed by her mother?

Shelly stayed in Chicago another week, and another. She installed Frieda in her town house. It was close to the hospital, and her doctor's appointments, and better grocery stores. One morning she watched Steve Jobs on the internet announcing a new product, the iPhone, and she thought, well, now everything is going to change, now no one will ever feel like they're dining alone again, it's a god-

damn tiny computer you can take with you wherever you go. But
she still could not tap into the drive to make things again. She was
where she was supposed to be. With Frieda. She started to feel like
it was the plan the universe had for her, an idea which made her gag,
because her math brain never left a thing to chance like that, but she
could not argue with the fact that now she was able to take care of
her mother at the exact right time. She never would have come back
if she were still working. That had always been her purpose, to work.

She called Margaret, the third time that week they had spoken.
Margaret, now in New York permanently, leaving behind London,
and his house, which had never quite felt like hers, into the loft, also
his, but at least New York was her city. She invited her cousin, Corrine, now a massage therapist, to live with her, and Corrine used a
spare room for clients, and Margaret liked that, that pain was being
relieved in her home. "Anytime you want to talk about anything,"
said Corrine, and they would go for walks together, down the West
Side Highway, as the sun set over the Hudson, remembering their
mothers, giving each other comfort, making each other feel less
alone in the world.

"How's Frieda?" said Margaret.

"Impossible to say," said Shelly. "No one will actually tell me
how she's doing. Tell me good news from there."

"Slow. Everything is slow."

"You'll get there."

"Slow is fine," said Margaret. "It is just fine, Shelly." She took a
deep breath. "You were always mad at me for taking so long. You
move at lightning speed. I admire that about you. But I'm actually
just trying to fucking function most of the time, Shelly. I am actually just trying to survive." She found herself gasping for air. "I have
been trying to survive my whole life just with living with my brain

and all the things I hear and see. I don't ask anyone to feel sorry for me. I have a lot. I'm just letting you know why things take so long for me. Because I am just trying to survive here."

"I'm sorry," said Shelly.

"Nothing is ever good enough for you," said Margaret, a thing Shelly's ex-husband had said to her, too, and Shelly had never known how to respond to that, because he was right, that's what she had always thought, but she found herself saying to Margaret, "You are," which she knew she was supposed to say, found it easier to say to her, even if she wasn't sure if it was true. Still, it felt good to utter those words out loud. Couldn't she just say the right thing for once in her life?

Margaret asked how long she would stay in Chicago.

"I think for as long as I'm needed," said Shelly.

•

THINGS BEGAN TO SLOW DOWN. THEIR DAYS TOGETHER TOOK on a meditative quality. Shelly had her errands to run, shopping, gym, museums, meetings about her future with various legal advisors. Long lunches with old coworkers. They no longer see me as a threat, she thought. "Am I ruined?" she asked them, and they all told her to maybe consult for a while, and definitely undergo some sensitivity training. But I'm plenty sensitive, she thought. "What if you didn't go back to work yet?" said Margaret. "What do you have to prove?" Everything, she wanted to scream. But she took Margaret's advice. Back to her mother's bedside. They played Scrabble every day and they were fairly matched, still, after all this time. But Shelly took it easy on her mother, let her win a few times. They were softer to each other now, at last.

One morning, there was a friendly text from her ex-husband, bitching about being an old dad: **You were tiring but I was never this kind of tired**. Good, think about me forever, she thought. Let me be the context for the rest of your life.

It was winter, then, and she bought her mother a full-length mink coat, and wrapped it around her in bed.

•

THERE WERE VISITORS. CAROLINA HAD HEARD ABOUT FRIEDA'S illness and came for a week, sat by Frieda's bedside, the two of them roaring with laughter. Eyeing Shelly at first, not trusting her, but then later taking her aside and making some quiet suggestions about how to ease Frieda's pain, a pillow she could purchase, a bed rail that might be helpful, an assessment of how Frieda was using her walker. "You could never have known," she said kindly. "We're professionals after all."

Jess would show up once or twice a week, scrupulously avoiding the times her mother might be there. During her visits, Jess would tell them about work, this small storefront she had opened with a few other women who were also naturopaths. They charged sliding scale fees, so the doors were open to everyone. "It's not a great business model," said Shelly, but Frieda hushed her. She was just happy her granddaughter was done with that tattoo-studio *mishegas*. "I'm sorry. I'm always just doing the math, no matter what. I can't help myself," said Shelly.

"I'm happier than I've ever been," said Jess. "That's my math."

Jess felt comfort in her life. She did not think she could be the best version of her creative self by trying to be an artist. The framework as it existed repelled her. There had to be another way through it all, she thought. Wasn't it enough that she liked to draw her lines? Did she really have to try and sell them, too? She did not feel aggressive in that way. Whatever well of energy she had within her could not be directed toward it.

She was aggressive in her personal life though. Her love life, her sex life. She had developed a language and confidence with women. She had figured out monogamy wasn't for her, although she respected deeply the ability of her friends to partner up so immediately and tightly. But she was better off just giving love freely. Her friendships were her steadiness. Her sisters, her aunt, they steadied her, too. She had a community of women around her that she loved, and she loved them, too.

The best version of her was the one where she touched people with her hands and gave them pleasure and relief. In that release, she freed herself, too. The only thing that held her back, she thought, was her relationship with her mother.

Nancy, barely present in any of their lives. Living high up in the air in her all-white Lakeshore Drive condominium. She consumed only white wine and light-colored food and she had a white Persian cat and her hair was white-blond now and she wore all kinds of beautiful neutral-colored clothes, imported linens and silks and loose pants and caftans. And her face was even blank in its way; she barely wore any makeup at all, although she had facials twice a month, injectables as regularly as her dermatologist would allow it, and her muscles barely moved, except for her forehead, which she left untouched, so people could see she cared when she cared, and meant it when she was trying to make a point.

There was always something new to be learned, she told her students. There was always another level to be achieved. When you stop learning, that's when you start dying, she had told them more than once. No one wanted to die. Everyone wanted to live forever.

She preached all the same things she always had: finding your real strength and power and identifying the most important moments in your life where everything changed at once, and accepting and loving those changes and then climbing them like a tree to its highest rung so you could look out over the earth and see the truth, your truth, your partner's truth, everyone's truth. People loved that part. The tree part. She believed in freedom of speech, limited government intervention, lower taxes, a woman's right to choose what she wanted to do with her body. She was certain the government was watching if not everyone then at the very least her, and people like her—unconventional leaders—every step of the way through phones, internet, and banking, and if it were at all possible they must be stopped. But that last part she said quietly, to herself, for now.

Whether her daughter believed her or not. She had tried desperately to get her daughter to participate in her business, but Jess wouldn't hear of it, she thought her mother was ripping people off. Instead her daughter was busy running her little Communist healing center. It was everything they could do to sit down together at Thanksgiving every year without snapping at each other. What did it matter, she thought. These people she worked with all these years, they were her family. Sylvia with nearly the same ash-blond hair as hers, but a shade or two darker. A wintry ash-blond. She was the backbone of this company. Her best friend for life. It didn't matter what her daughter thought. It didn't.

Nancy would come to visit Frieda only on Sunday afternoons, sometimes driven by an assistant who would wait downstairs, and sometimes accompanied by Sylvia, who spent the whole time tapping on her phone.

"She's unhappy," said Frieda. "Even though she has everything you could ever want."

"I think secretly she wants a husband," said Shelly. "I read her newsletters. So much talk about relationships, even though she hasn't had one for years."

"I suppose that's my fault," said Frieda. "Staying with that old *faygele* like I did. Although he was my old *faygele*."

Frieda rarely spoke of Rudy, and never like that. It made Shelly feel vulnerable, and nervous for Frieda, and she wanted to soothe her. "I don't even know what that means anymore, to be at fault," said Shelly. "What's the point of blaming you when we should all know so much better now?" Shelly was feeling fine without a husband, herself. Humming along with her mother's love.

•

NOW IT HAD BEEN SIX WEEKS, AND CAROLINA HAD COME and gone back to Miami, leaving behind a bright pink lipstick for Frieda and a scented candle for Shelly. "That last little touch," said Frieda. "She was always so thoughtful. She always cared." It was still winter, gray, gray, gray outside, and Frieda didn't leave the house anymore. "Too cold for these old bones," she said. Shelly cranked up the heat in the town house. She hadn't been drinking at all in front of her mother, but one day Frieda said, "If you need something to take the edge off, don't mind me." She was on strong painkillers now, and would be on morphine soon enough, and then on nothing, nothing but air. Shelly poured herself some whiskey, said a quiet prayer—a thing she was doing more lately, asking for peace for her mother—then sat at Frieda's bedside. Nancy was due at any moment.

They talked about what it meant to take care of someone. "It's a gift you give someone else," said Frieda. "I don't have that in me," said Shelly. "Not like you." "And yet here you are," said Frieda. "With me. Like me." Shelly was trying hard not to cry.

Nancy let herself in the front door, breezed in swathed in cashmere. She apologized for being late, but she had been giving a speech, and people had wanted to meet her after. The signing line had been long. "I'm quite popular, it might surprise you to hear," said Nancy, huffy for no reason she could discern, but those were her feelings anyway.

"But I'm not surprised," said Frieda. "You two never saw your father speak, but he was wonderful in front of a crowd. He really opened up his heart to people. I would have followed him anywhere just to hear him tell his story, even though it was a sad one. It's no surprise at all that Nancy knows how to hold a room. That's the Rudy in her."

And there, at last, Nancy's heart warmed for just a moment. A year later, in a new speech she gave to an audience of several thousand people, she would say, "We carry our family with us wherever we go," and the women in the crowd would nod their heads, and then Nancy would add, "Like a curse," and boy did they laugh, and she had them right where she wanted them.

"We're talking about work right now, too," said Shelly. "About how Mommy was a caregiver for all those years."

"It's strange how I never noticed what I was doing that whole time," said Frieda. Her bones as frail as matchsticks. "What my job was, and what it did to me. That I put so much energy into caring for others during the day that of course there were days I didn't have enough left over when I got home. I am sorry I wasn't tender to you as I should have been then, and that in fact I was cruel, but I did not have it in me to be kind; I had nothing left in me. I did not see what the work did to me. It was a job and I had been raised to show up and do whatever work was given to me, that it was my responsibility to do a good job, and parenting was part of that, of course, the main job in many ways, but I was broken down, girls. I am sorry. I could not see how all of it made me feel. I only just lived and worked and tried and failed."

Shelly was crying and holding her mother's hand, but Nancy was cold again, removed, having her own experience away from the two of them. She was rotating images from her childhood in her head. She believed her mother believed what she was saying. She would give her that much. And she certainly was exhausted her whole life, that was true. But she did not feel forgiveness, though she did feel pity.

She thought: Isn't it funny how I ended up being the one to bet on? Life ground her father into the earth, her mother, too. Shelly had lost her man, and that seemed to have ruined her lately, and her job, too. But not Nancy. Nancy was rising. Nancy would have it all. Me. Nancy. I'm on top.

Later, before she left, Frieda asked if she could have all the girls together in one room, and Nancy said, "That's up to Jess, not me," but Shelly knew it wouldn't happen until the funeral, and in fact, two weeks later, that was the case. The mother and daughter sitting on opposite sides of the room.

Shelly stood in front of the gathered crowd: her mother's friends from the synagogue, Carolina making her last trip ever to Chicago in the winter, Nancy arm in arm with her business partner, Sylvia, and, seated with Jess, was Margaret, fresh off a plane. Black pants, black cowboy boots, a white button-down shirt, and a leather jacket. Looking just like hope.

"You go on living after they're done dying," said Shelly, after she had finished speaking some brief kind words about her mother. "Isn't that the craziest goddamn thing of it all? You have to live the rest of your life without them." Unabashed in her mourning; deeply, radically changed. "And we were just starting to get along for the first time in a long time." What do I do now? she thought. We were just getting started again.

ACKNOWLEDGMENTS

This book would not have been possible without the following resources:

Gay Guerrilla: Julius Eastman and His Music, by Renee Levine-Packer, Mary Jane Leach, et al.; *Conversations* by Steve Reich; *Silence: Lectures and Writings* by John Cage; *Quantum Listening* by Pauline Oliveros. *Sisters with Transistors*, written and directed by Lisa Rovner. The music of Julius Eastman and Laurie Spiegel and Mary Jane Leach and Wild Up and Fleetwood Mac. The Flow State newsletter.

John and Rita Ousterhout, who spoke to me about computer science as both an academic pursuit and a career.

Jenny Belardi of Carnegie Mellon University and archivists and oral historians Katherine Barbera, Kathleen Donahoe, and David Bernabo of Carnegie Mellon University Libraries, who shared their Oral History Program research on women who studied or worked in computing in the 1980s.

And thank you to:

My early readers: Claire Cameron. Kristen Arnett. Laura Van den Berg. Priyanka Mattoo. Megan Giddings. Lauren Groff. Courtney Sullivan. Ladee Hubbard. Patricia Lockwood.

My beloved agent, Katherine Fausset, who always goes above and beyond, and the supportive team at Curtis Brown.

My talented and compassionate editor, Helen Atsma (who, incredibly, still believes in me after all this time), and all of the wonderful people who work at Ecco.

Anderson Stockdale for sharing her life as a desert baby with me.

Ajai Combelic for his generous insights on musicians and composition.

Jerome White for explaining the nuances behind high school math team competitions.

Lizzy Stewart for taking me on a walk and a swim in Hampstead Heath.

Maris Kreizman, Jason Diamond, Isaac Fitzgerald, Emily Goldsher-Diamond, and Josh Gondelman. Sonya Cheuse. Alison Fensterstock. Katy Simpson Smith and Rien Fertel. Caro Clark. Chrissie Roux. Jason Kim. Jacques Pierre François. Sara Novic. Bobby Finger. Amanda Bullock. Deesha Philyaw. Stefan Block. Kayla Kumari Upadhyaya. Jasmine Guillory. Anne Gisleson and Brad Benischek. Ryan Walsh. John Supko. Kiese Laymon. My 1000 Words community.

With love, as always, to my family.

ABOUT THE AUTHOR

JAMI ATTENBERG is a *New York Times* bestselling author of seven books of fiction, including *The Middlesteins* and *All Grown Up*; a memoir, *I Came All This Way to Meet You*; and, most recently, the *USA Today* bestselling *1000 Words: A Writer's Guide to Staying Creative, Focused, and Productive All Year Round*. She is the founder of the annual #1000WordsofSummer project and maintains the popular Craft Talk newsletter year-round. Her work has been published in sixteen languages. She lives in New Orleans.